SAM CRESCENT

EVERNIGHT PUBLISHING ®

www.evernightpublishing.com

Copyright© 2019

Sam Crescent

Editor: Karyn White

Proofreader: Laurie White

Cover Art: Jay Aheer

ISBN: 978-1-77339-932-4

SAM CRESCENT

Sam Crescent

Copyright © 2019

Chapter One

"You're not supposed to be here," Nico Garofalo said.

Ugly Beast tensed up at the insult. Here they stood in the fucking mansion of the Italian mafia, after standing by their side in a war that was created by the Mafiosi over a slight of one guy wanting a girl. Personally, he never saw a good reason to allow pussy to get in the way of business. Women were good for one thing and one thing only: fucking. It's why he never got involved with problem pussy.

He didn't understand the guys from all over the club, chapter to chapter, why the fuck they'd want to settle down with an old lady. Now, he didn't mind a couple of the women that cooked. They were all right and didn't make waves. They knew the lifestyle, and even if they hated it, kept their mouths shut. It was better that way.

Hell's Bastards MC didn't like a whole lot of

things. First, they didn't like any motherfucker who believed they could use them and discard them like trash the way this piece of shit was doing right now.

Nico had some dealings with the Americans, and rather than risk his own ranks, he'd reached out to them, the MC. Now, Smokey, the club president, was more than happy to help for a price.

They'd lived rather happily side by side. Nico's men didn't interfere with club business, and they stayed out of anything owned by the boss. Anything touched by Garofalo, they ignored. The city was big enough for all of them, and he didn't see a reason to poach on their land.

Besides, most of the associates Garofalo and his mafia mob did business with, wouldn't give their club the time of day anyway.

It always made Ugly Beast laugh that the wealthy were happy to rub hands with men that had a lot more blood on them than the MC, also a lot stricter rules as well. They were a little backward in their thinking as far as he was concerned.

"So, tonight's celebrations do not include the very men who put you back on top?" Smokey asked.

Ugly Beast kept watch on the men in the room. He was aware of the soldiers who held their guns. No wonder they were having so many problems. They all looked like they couldn't piss in a freezing cold wind, let alone fight them.

He wasn't worried, but he had already assessed the dangers.

Returning his attention back to Garofalo, he made sure to make eye contact with his Capos as well. There were five here that he counted. He had heard their American friends had taken out three of them before the Hell's Bastards took over.

"Tonight is a feast. A reuniting if you will."

"It's a damn soiree where you all pat each other on the fucking back for a job well done." Smokey sat down on the edge of the desk, showing to the men in the room he wasn't afraid of their boss. Their king.

To be honest, Nico Garofalo put fear into most men and women. The only difference was, the MC had seen far worse in their life than this man, and that was saying a lot.

Smokey whistled. "Check out that piece of ass." He lifted a picture from the desk before tossing it out to his men. Hunter caught it first before handing it over to him. Ugly Beast glanced at the woman, passing it around, seeing the tic in Garofalo's face. He didn't like the disrespect. He'd already noticed the signal he'd given his men to stand down.

In both of his hands, Ugly Beast had the knives, waiting and ready to strike out. He didn't do politics. That was Smokey's job.

For him, all he did was make sure they got out alive. The scars on his back and face were a testament to that.

He'd gladly look death in the face and laugh. Until then, he was going to make sure each and every single person stayed out of the club's way. Simple as. It's why he was the Sergeant at Arms.

"She your wife? Your mistress? I bet a horny fucker like you would have a whole stash of sluts stashed around the country, huh? I bet he does."

"It'll be easy to find out," Rock said.

"Hell, yeah, give them all a real good initiation with the club. We love ourselves some pussy, and we don't have a preference, ugly, fat, nice, evil. We'll take them all."

"Please, leave us," Nico said, finally speaking up,

and looking at his men. Ugly Beast would bet money Nico had never begged or even asked someone to leave nicely. Most of the time, he guessed men and women who were not welcome left here in body bags. For the Hell's Bastards, Nico had no control. He wasn't the one in charge here; Smokey was.

They didn't hesitate and were out of there.

Smokey clicked his fingers, and some of his men left as well. There were five Capos at Nico's back, along with his Consigliere. Smokey had kept six men. The difference between them and the mafia was they really didn't give a fuck if they came out alive. Nico and his men always had to have one man standing otherwise another crew would take his turf.

"That's more like it. So, tell me, Nico, why weren't we invited?"

"You're aware our association cannot go noticed. We must remain quiet."

"Oh, I know. What I want to know is why I wasn't given a fucking invitation. This doesn't have your politicians, your businessmen, or your associates. This is family, made men, and a celebration. Now, last time I checked, we were the ones that handed you the American mob's head; Black, I recall his name was."

Nico raised his head, clearly not liking the truth that he'd failed whereas they'd succeeded.

"Now, forgive me if I'm wrong, but that makes this our celebration."

"Then go ahead, join us," Nico said, standing up.

"You want to disrespect me and my boys, give it a try. You think you succeed in this city by your muscle that don't look old enough to stroke their own dicks, let alone handle a gun, give it a try. By the end of the week, you'd be out of business, on the streets, or behind bars. I know the deals you've got going down all up and down this country, and I can end it with the snap of my fingers."

Doing business with Garofalo was not something they'd entered into lightly. With this man, the streets would run red with blood and had been before they intervened.

Smokey had his reasons—Ugly Beast wasn't sure what they were—but he never questioned his president's actions. It was up to him what he wanted to have done. If it was ever life-changing to the club, they would all meet at church to discuss. They had debated Garofalo for over six hours before they agreed to help him. Some of the brothers weren't happy with forming an alliance, a true one, while others figured it was inevitable.

For him, he couldn't give a shit. Whatever the club decided he'd live by and had been doing that for a long time now.

"What is it you want?" Garofalo asked.

"You came to me for help. You promised me this would benefit me, and the first moment you could prove that, we're not even invited. You don't want to *associate* with us, don't ask for our help and expect consequences when you do."

The picture was thrown back to Smokey, who placed it very gently on the desk.

"We don't have any way of forming an alliance," Garofalo said. "We also agreed that we didn't want our union to be recognized outside of our main members."

"That is true. However, your main members are here, and I realize your word means shit. Next time you got someone knocking on your door, find another MC." Smokey stood up. "Any other cut besides the Hell's Bastards steps foot on this turf, I'll take that as a message for war."

In another token of disrespect, Smokey presented

the men his back. They really didn't care what the men were about. In this room, the MCs were the ones that ruled on top.

He heard them muttering.

"Wait," Nico said.

They all stopped at the door, just as Smokey knew they would.

Tonight's meeting was about getting reassurances from their newfound friends that they were not going to get fucked over at the first opportunity.

"What?" Smokey asked.

"Forgive my … rudeness. In our world, a way we agree to an alliance and make arrangements is through marriage."

"You sell your daughters for peace and power."

"I don't believe you'd be quite so willing to make such an agreement. Your way of life is very different from ours."

"Oh, you mean we treat women like human beings and you treat them like cattle," Smokey said.

He watched carefully, seeing the insult spread across each Capo. They clearly didn't enjoy having their truths thrown at them.

Interesting.

"That's how we form a peace treaty and an alliance. Marriage. If you're willing to consider it, then please, show me a member who'd be happy to have a bride. Vigo has a daughter. She's nineteen, and he's been trying to find a husband for her."

"Does she look like a dog?" Hunter asked.

"If you are agreeable with her, then we can negotiate."

Smokey was silent. "She here?"

"Yes."

"Go and get her."

Now this did surprise Ugly Beast. Marriage wasn't what they wanted. He didn't show their enemies he was shocked though. No, he waited to see how this would play out.

The Capo now known to them as Vigo left the room.

"Isn't this all exciting?" Smokey said.

Ugly Beast chanced a look with Hunter, who was also holding his shit together.

Who was getting married today?

"So, your men are agreeable with the prospect of marriage?" Nico asked.

"Yes. I'm their president. They know I put the safety of the club above all else."

This was a ploy, it had to be, or Smokey wanted to see how far he was willing to go for their help.

Seconds passed.

No one said a word.

Ugly Beast didn't mind silence. He was always prepared for the worst though. Silence was always the setup for pain. It was during these moments, he'd prepare himself, be ready in time for the torture yet to come.

Their peace was interrupted by the sound of the door behind being knocked on, and in walked Vigo, holding the arm of a girl.

Ugly Beast didn't get a good look at her as she passed. Her floral scent filled the air. It was sweet, pure, how he imagined most girls of the mafia families were.

"Ah, Abriana, it is a pleasure to see you again," Nico said.

"Get your head down, girl. Show some fucking respect." Vigo pushed her head down, and she did.

Ugly Beast admired her from the back. He'd seen several of the wives as he entered the house, and this Abriana wasn't like a lot of them. She wasn't slender.

The dress she wore, which fell to her knees, molded to every single curve, and she had a nice ass. The dress was so tight it showed the outline of her panties.

"How old are you, Abriana?" Nico said.

"Nineteen."

"The perfect age for marriage, and look at those child-bearing hips. You remind me of my mother," Nico said. "Well, Smokey, come and have a look at her."

Ugly Beast watched his president walk over to the girl. He lifted up her chin, grabbed her face, turning her this way and that.

"She's a bitch with a pussy. I don't know what I'm looking at," Smokey said. "She got any diseases?"

"My daughter is clean. She is pure. Never touched."

"Is that right?" Smokey asked. "Your pussy never known a cock, Abriana?"

He noticed her hands were clenched at her sides. She didn't like this, but rather than lash out at them, she remained silent, her lips pressed firmly together.

"No."

Her voice was so soft, gentle. She stood out in a room full of men who would likely chew her up and spit her back out.

Smokey turned her to the group.

She had long brown hair, and it was glossy and thick. There was minimal makeup on her face, but he saw her large brown eyes were wide. She was afraid and struggling with being manhandled.

No one said a word to each other as they all looked at her.

Finally, Smokey looked at him. "What do you think, Ugly? You like her?"

He nodded his head, seeing no reason to dispute it. She wasn't the most stunning woman in the world, or the ugliest. Some would consider her plain, but again, her eyes. He stared into them, and there was something there that struck him hard. There was an instant tug inside him to help her.

"She's all right," he said.

Smokey burst out laughing. "This the reason you're having trouble selling the girl. No one fucking wants her. Wow, in our world, put a virgin amongst the wolves and that bitch would be a slut begging for dick within a few hours."

Abriana's face was so red, and she stared at the floor.

Clearly, she wasn't happy being here in this room. For Ugly Beast, he was pissed off that her father didn't stick up for her. The men looked bored.

"I'll take her," Ugly Beast said, speaking up.

This made her look up.

"Good, because it was going to be you that I picked," Smokey said. He shoved the girl toward him, and Ugly Beast made sure to hold her. "What do you guys say? We get down to the nitty-gritty basics, seeing as we're now family."

Abriana didn't fight against him. The moment she was steady, he removed his hands from her shoulders and watched the men in the room.

"Is this what you want?" Ugly Beast asked. "Marriage to me?"

"She'll do as she's told. She's a good girl. You don't have to worry about that. She knows to keep her mouth shut and to be loyal or to face the consequences. All of the women know what to do. You can leave, Abriana," Nico said.

Abriana nodded her head, but Ugly Beast wasn't happy. He grabbed her wrist, stopping her escape.

"Did I fucking ask you?" he said, glaring at Nico.

He didn't like the mafia. In fact, he'd rather shoot them all dead right here, right now. Smokey laughed.

"Do you want to get married?"

Abriana stared at him with startled eyes. She wasn't going to tell him the truth.

She nodded her head. "Yes, I serve for the family." She bowed her head like a good little servant, and seeing it set his teeth on edge. He still wasn't happy.

Nodding his head, he watched her leave. She was so silent, the door barely making a sound as it closed.

He wondered what she was thinking in that moment.

He didn't want a wife. The last thing he expected coming here was for him to become eligible as a husband.

"So, now that we're all going to be one big, happy family. Let's talk real now. Money, guns, drugs, pussy, and power. That's all I'm interested in."

Smokey finally took a seat, ready to make a deal.

It was the first time for Ugly Beast that he wanted to put a bullet in his president's head, with all the love in the world, of course.

****

Abriana tried not to smooth out her hair for the hundredth time. All of them were laughing at her. It was her engagement party, and so many people across the family and the associates had come to see' the laughingstock of what was to be her life.

She was being married off to an MC.

Bargained off like every other woman, only her match was considered less.

"I heard he's a monster. His face makes mirrors break."

"I hear he takes women and rapes them. That's his deal."

"That's all men. They are pigs and don't know when to keep it in their pants. They all need to be castrated."

She tried not to think or show what their words were doing to her. Glancing at the time, she saw her betrothed was already an hour late. The whole MC was late, and she knew her father was getting angrier by the second.

The past three years, she'd been a real disappointment to him and to her family. She was the oldest of five. She had two brothers that were older than she was and already made men. She was the oldest girl. Her sister Chantel was the beauty of the family, but she was only fifteen and already had men wanting to take her to a dark room and fuck. Where Chantel would make a glowing bride, Abriana was the ugly duckling in the story; only she'd stayed ugly.

For three years now, she'd been put on strict diets, forced into exercise, and been advised over plastic surgery.

She was worthless.

Her father had spent many nights pointing it out, and when they didn't have guests, he liked to randomly hit her, hoping to smack the ugly right out of her. If he couldn't use his hands and fists on her face, he liked to kick.

From what she heard, the MC wasn't much better.

She stayed in the corner of the room, praying for this man to arrive. Even if it meant she'd die sooner rather than later, she'd take it. She didn't know how much more she could handle of her father's abuse. There was no one to turn to.

He was Capo.

She also knew Nico adored her father and their

family. If she went to him with a complaint, she'd be the one punished. No one else.

Locking her fingers together in front of her, she tried to hide her curves that she'd been told time and again were ugly.

Her mother often dressed her in black to hide her body. She knew her mother tried, but it was no use.

"Are you okay, honey?" her mother, Carina, asked.

"Yes, I'm fine."

"He'll turn up."

"And if he doesn't?"

"Then, stay in your room." Her mother patted her hands as if it was the most natural advice a mother was to give to a daughter.

Abriana kept her mask in place when the truth was, she was screaming, petrified, and wanting to do nothing more than run out the front door.

After the first beating, Carina taught her how to pretend. How to lie and to make it look convincing. Whenever her father started to hit her, she simply floated away and imagined herself elsewhere.

It was a hell of a lot easier than suffering.

She took a deep breath as she watched her father and Nico talking. They kept looking toward her, and she knew they weren't happy.

Her father made his way toward her, and she couldn't think of a single way to escape. Frozen into place, she waited for his cruelty. He wouldn't hit her in front of their guests, but his words were just as bad as any hit.

She tensed up, hoping someone distracted him.

As if appearing out of nowhere Ugly and Smokey slammed open the front doors, letting all know they had arrived.

"Where is the bride to be?"

She didn't think it was possible for an MC to be her savior or for her to be grateful for it.

Abriana stayed in her corner as bikers began to appear. They hadn't changed for the event. They were still in their leather jackets, complete with their insignia. Jeans, shirts, leather cuts, and hard boots, stood out against the suit-wearing family she was used to.

She rather liked the contrast.

The one with the label of President noticed her and came over to her. He pulled her into his arms, hugging her tightly.

This, again, was inappropriate.

"Excited for the big day?"

She forced a smile to her lips.

Lying didn't come natural to her. She often found a smile, a tilt of the head, or even a nod, helped to evade her having to answer truthfully.

When her husband to be, fiancé, came forward, his men were clapping him on the back. He didn't look any happier about being the center of attention, and she rather liked that he was … unhappy about it.

She hoped he didn't call it off. She wouldn't get in his way at all.

What would life be like for her after their wedding?

She'd only known women within their circle marry made men and soldiers. Rarely were they allowed to marry associates. For them, it was against all protocol.

From the few snippets of information she'd accidentally heard, she knew the MC had been vital to a recent conflict.

There were times she hated being a woman more than anything. In her world, men had the power. Women were commodities to be sold on or passed around for their use.

She knew her father had mistresses, and her own mother didn't seem to mind either, apart from when he brought them home.

Abriana had seen them, and she hated it.

"Abriana," her fiancé said.

She forced a smile to her lips.

He held out his hand, and she stepped toward him. He took her hand, placing a kiss to her knuckles before letting her go.

There was a round of applause at his actions.

She chanced a look around the room and saw a mixture of disdain, disgust, terror, and humor.

Some of them thought it was funny.

Soon, the MC took over, and the music was changed, and there was dancing.

Abriana found her corner again, and when no one looked in her direction, she made her escape to the garden.

It was a warm night, and she took a deep breath. She knew guards were posted all around the grounds, and she always tried her hardest to ignore them.

She didn't have to think about them while she was staring out into space.

Staring up at the night sky, she saw it was a crescent moon. The noise from the party filtered out into the night, and she closed her eyes.

It's going to be okay.

Women and children died in their line of work. She had been to so many funerals. The first one had terrified her, as the casket was open, death so clear to see. So cold. So alone.

"You shouldn't be out here by yourself."

She turned to see her fiancé watching her. Usually, she was so aware of her surroundings, no one was able to sneak up on her.

Gritting her teeth, she nodded her head. "I'm sorry."

"Are you okay?" he asked.

"Yes, of course, I'm fine. I just needed some air."

He tilted his head to the side, watching her.

"We don't have an audience now. Tell me the truth, do you want this?" he asked.

"There's always someone watching here," she said. "Yes." She made sure to look past his shoulder so she wasn't staring him in the eye.

The truth was, she didn't want to marry anyone. She didn't want to be Vigo's daughter. Whenever she went out shopping, which was the only activity she was allowed to do, with armed guards, she found herself envying women, outsiders, for their freedom. They could come and go; they were not forced into a life they didn't want.

Whereas she had no future. Her life was purely at the mercy of her father.

Tucking some hair behind her ears, she forced a smile to her lips. "Do you want this marriage?"

"No."

She tensed up but didn't say a word.

"Oh. Are you going to cancel?"

"You're afraid," he said.

"I … I would hate for you to have to do something you didn't want to do." *Irony!*

"This wedding will go ahead at all costs, Abriana. You won't be harmed by the club. You'll be my old lady."

"I won't be staying here?" she asked, pointing at her home.

"No. You'll be living with me. I have a place. I'm not sure it's what you're used to—"

"I'm sure it'll be fine." Whatever happened, she had to get out of this house. She wondered if he was the kind of husband that demanded his rights.

Unlike some of the women she knew, she knew what was required of her in the bedroom.

One of her father's many mistresses had taken the time to sit down with her and have the female talk. She later learned the mistress had stolen drugs and money and was raped, beaten, and killed, her body dumped in a lake.

She'd never asked about the woman, only heard men talking about her.

Still, the woman had been surprisingly nice, and had told her it was only rare for some men to be complete assholes. That sex, with the right guy, was wonderful.

Staring at this man, her fiancé, whose name she didn't know, she wasn't sure if she ever wanted to commit to allowing a man inside her body, giving him even a smidgen of herself.

"What's your name?" she asked.

He smirked, and it made the scars on his face stand out more. Her heart raced as he took a step closer to her. She didn't know what to do or say. It was against the rules to even be out here with him, but seeing as he was supposed to be her husband in a matter of days, she didn't know why it would be a problem.

"My club name is Ugly Beast," he said.

"Ugly Beast?"

"It's what I'm known as."

"I don't want to call you that."

"It's all you're going to be able to call me. Now, let's go inside. I don't like how these sons of bitches are looking at us."

He placed a hand at her back and moved her back

into the house. The kitchen was bare, and as they made their way back toward the party, she stopped, placing a hand on his shoulder, stopping him.

"Just a moment. I don't want to go in just yet."

With each step they took into her old family home, the feeling of being trapped flooded her.

"It's fine."

He moved them out of sight, into a dark corner where there was no light. She enjoyed the dark so much.

The door to their right opened, and she saw three women leaving the bathroom.

"Did you see his face?" the woman asked.

Abriana didn't recognize them.

"I know. He's a monster, but then, she's so plain as well. They're going to make really ugly babies."

They started to laugh, and Abriana glanced up at Ugly Beast.

She was used to having people say bad stuff about her looks. She was plain and had known that for a long time. Even her mother refused to sugarcoat it for her and had told her at a young age to accept any guy that found her desirable.

What kind of person did that?

When she had children, she'd tell them every single day how much she loved them. How much she cared. It would be a complete contrast to her own childhood.

"I'm sorry," she said.

"What for?"

"For what they said."

"Do you want me to slit their throats?"

"You're offering to kill them?" she asked.

"They disrespected you in your home. When you're mine, any bitch that tries that will get killed. Simple as."

"You can't kill them. They're wives and daughters. They're protected."

He leaned down. His lips brushing against her ear. "In case you haven't noticed, sweet cheeks, your men don't give a fuck about women. One pussy is just as good as another."

"Isn't that the same with all men?" she asked.

"Yeah, it is, but we've got standards. You're loyal to the club, we're loyal to you. Fuck us over, you're gone."

He was so close, and she saw how blue his eyes really were. Most of the time he was glaring, like he was now, but there was something different. Ugly Beast was a strange man, one she wasn't entirely sure she liked, but even still, he gave her a semblance of hope, which was more than anyone had ever given her.

"It's time for us to join the party."

Whatever spell had fallen over them, was gone. He grabbed her arm, and before she could protest, they were heading back to the main throng of the party.

She recognized the women from the bathroom, who gathered around.

"It's time for the ring," Smokey said, coming toward them.

She saw the disapproval in her father's eyes, and tried to ignore it.

"You guys good for me reaching into my pocket?" Ugly Beast asked.

There was a round of snickers as he opened up his jacket, and she waited as he pulled out a small velvet box.

This was it.

The moment that would engage her to this man. Her mother and father were doing everything to organize the wedding, and soon she'd belong to this man. All of

her life, she'd been told her life would be forever bound to a man. This would be her future.

Her hand shook as she held it out, hoping no one saw.

Weakness wasn't something they liked to see in their world.

She was surprised by the ring, a single silver band with a tiny diamond. It was, in fact, incredibly beautiful.

Staring up at him, she realized he was watching her reaction.

"It's beautiful."

He gave her a nod, and that was it. His men took him away, and she watched as they drank with revelry, without a care in the world. All the social gatherings she'd been part of had always been reserved, filled with tension.

She'd seen people die in front of her.

Blood.

Death.

She'd even been forced to step over brain matter.

All of this and still, she found the courage to keep on going.

She watched Ugly Beast and his MC. They were … amazing. The other women felt sorry for her, for the life she was about to have as an old lady. Nineteen years old, bound to a man whom she knew nothing about, and yet, in that moment, she felt a little wave of excitement about what it could all mean for her. This was a new chapter in her life, one she couldn't wait for, and yet she was equally scared.

Chapter Two

The feel of bones crunching beneath his fist filled Ugly Beast with satisfaction. This piece of shit, John, had been trying to steal from the club. He'd been hanging around their necks, pretending to be a prospect, and now was the time to end him.

From the moment he entered the clubhouse Ugly Beast hadn't liked him. There had been something about him that completely irritated and annoyed the fuck out of him.

He'd seen right through him.

The only thing this bastard wanted was money. From the track marks on his arms, he also wanted dope as well. The club had plenty of the shit, but for prospects, that stuff had to be earned.

Screams filled the basement, but no one came running. In fact, Smokey was sitting on the stairs, watching, waiting.

It was Ugly Beast's wedding day.

Nothing like a bit of torture before having his balls twisted in a vise.

"You got anything to say, fucker?" Smokey asked.

"Please, I didn't do anything."

"We've got you on camera and the evidence stashed away in your room."

"I still didn't do it." The guy started to sob. "I want to be part of your club. Please, I'll make it up to you. Please. I'll do anything. Anything."

Raising his brow, Ugly Beast turned to his president. The kid denied it and then accepted it. He wasn't confused.

John was clearly a junkie, and they'd been so consumed with this Garofalo bullshit, they'd not caught it.

This was something Ugly Beast often saw. It was part of his job to weed out the fakers from the genuine men who wanted to join the club. Being a Hell's Bastard wasn't easy. They underwent years of hell as a prospect. It was the right of each man to earn the patch on their jacket.

Smokey sighed. "This what you want?" He held up a syringe.

The love in John's eyes disgusted Ugly Beast. In all of his years, he'd never caved to the drugs on offer. Most of the guys didn't. The drugs were the dope they sold and distributed.

He moved toward the sink and began to wash his hands. His pristine white shirt was covered in blood.

Staring at the marks, he thought about changing for his wedding. He didn't have another shirt, and he wasn't going to be late today. Something about Gable Vigo rubbed him up the wrong way.

He wanted to hurt the son of a bitch, and laugh in his face as he did. He also didn't like the fear Abriana tried to hide. She shouldn't be afraid of her father, and yet it was right there, lying beneath the surface. He'd seen the way she tensed whenever he was near.

Being a man that doled out punishments, he knew what it all meant, and he didn't like it.

Abriana was used to getting hit.

That would change.

She looked like she needed taking care of, not being hit.

The white sink was tainted with the blood on his hands for a few seconds before running clear.

He grabbed the towel, washing them. He'd split his inked knuckles, and the cuts were irritating. The pain would help him to focus. It was what he needed today.

Being around Garofalo and his men, it always set him on edge and made him want to reach for his trusty little blade.

"Please, Smokey, I'll do anything. I'll suck your cock, or you can fuck my ass. I don't care."

Smokey burst out laughing. "Why the fuck would I want to do that?"

"I'm good. I will fuck every single member of the club."

"Can you believe this fucker?"

"His addiction has taken over." He shrugged. "You done here?"

"He's no fun to toy with."

In Smokey's other hand was a syringe. He lifted it up, and in the next second, he plunged it into the man's neck.

The overdose of pure heroin took him over, and Ugly Beast waited for the man to die.

"We need to be more careful. He was nearly pulled over, and this dope is ours."

"Next time, we need to not put whatever Garofalo wants first. That was our first mistake." Ugly Beast stared at his president, seeing the anger in Smokey. "You going to tell me what today was all about?"

"You don't think for a single second the mafia are happy about needing an MC on their back, do you?"

"I don't know. You tell me."

Smokey laughed. "Garofalo has been trying to get rid of us for years. It still pisses them off that they had to come to us for help. You've seen how we look. We stick out with them. They like their pristine suits and fucked-up bitches. I'm not someone's dog to be called upon with my pack because they couldn't handle it. They think they can pass us off with a couple of hundred grand, that's fine. Insulting us, however, that won't play in my book."

"You're toying with them."

"I'm seeing how far they're willing to go. Giving us one of their girls, it makes me curious."

"She's not coming here willingly," Ugly Beast said.

"Didn't you see the look on her face?" Smokey asked. "The engagement party, even with all those pretentious fuckers with their noses in the air, looking down on us, she was happy we turned up. You're not the least bit curious about that?"

"They don't like her." He'd heard that in the women. They were spiteful bitches, and he'd had about enough of them.

Abriana … he couldn't even have a solid thought when it came to her.

She was always so calm, so collected, and yet, the mask she wore was false. She was afraid.

"You know they're going to demand you fuck her tonight," Smokey said.

"What?"

"Got a call from Vigo. The brothers are staying at his home tonight. All of us. You have to fuck her, prove her virginity, and show the bloody sheets for all the family to see."

Ugly Beast clenched his jaw.

"And people think we're fucking disgusting."

"Why me?" Ugly Beast asked.

"Huh?"

"You heard me. Why me?"

"It could have been anyone, Ugly. You offered yourself first." Smokey folded his arms, watching him.

"And I know you, Prez. When you want something, you make sure you get it. Regardless of me putting myself forward like that, if it's not what you wanted, you'd move me aside, and use a brother you want. You had every intention of getting a marriage deal out of Garofalo. I want to know why?"

Smokey smiled. "I got to tell you all my reasons."

"As your Sergeant at Arms, I need to be prepared for everything. To protect you and the club, I need to make sure I'm ready for whatever you think is going to happen."

"This is why I picked you, Ugly."

"My dashing good looks."

"No. You really are fucking ugly. I feel for Abriana, but then she's as plain as they come. I figured a chick like that would be grateful to have any husband. What I want is for you to find out all of their secrets. They've got them, and you need to find them."

"Abriana won't tell me their secrets, Smokey. She has to become loyal to our club and rid herself of nineteen years of training to keep her mouth shut."

"Ugly, I didn't say this is going to be overnight." Smokey slapped a hand down on his shoulder with a smile. "You've got to charm her."

"I don't charm women."

"You will this one. You see, while Garofalo thinks I'm pissing in the wind and not taking this serious, I learn a lot by being in his territory. Seeing how he works. The women, they are nothing but pawns to them. Get the right girl, dangle the right kind of life in front of her, and you're in."

"You think Abriana is the right kind of woman?"

"I think she's exactly who we need to find out their secrets. You also get to have a good fuck out of it. I don't see where the problem is."

"She's a virgin," Ugly said. He didn't even know why he was arguing this point. He didn't want to get married, and yet, he'd been the one to step forward when he saw her.

"She's a blank canvas to make her crave your touch. I trust you, Ugly. You've got to do this or I'll give her to Kinky."

Ugly Beast tensed up. Kinky was not someone a virgin should ever have to deal with.

"Fine."

"You got this for us. I know you do."

"I never planned to marry," he said.

"Which is why this is going to work. For the club, for the brothers, Abriana will help us."

"Are you after Garofalo territory?" Ugly Beast asked. He knew Smokey wouldn't tell him the complete plans or what he truly wanted, not until he knew for sure what they were all dealing with.

"I'm after a show of respect from their slight. I don't allow that kind of shit. Remember that. I demand respect for my men." Smokey gripped his shoulder tightly. "Let's ride, brother."

They left the basement.

Ugly Beast grabbed his leather cut he'd placed on his chair. No one had touched it, which was exactly what he'd demanded. He didn't have time to change shirts.

Smokey organized everyone. The few prospects and club brothers would stay behind to dig a nice big grave out in the back for John, while the rest of them rode toward his wedding.

He made his way outside, heading toward his bike.

One look at his baby, and he gritted his teeth. White streamers with beer cans attached to them were on the back of his bike.

"Who touched my fucking bike?" he asked, staring at a few of the brothers who were all laughing.

"We were going to drip blood on them, but decided that was too scary, even for your wife." Hunter was laughing as he came toward him.

He slammed his fist into Hunter's face, and the other brother took the pain and still continued to laugh.

This was why he stayed away from the brothers with all their pranks. His bike was his baby. His pride and joy, and now they'd messed with it. It was going to take him some time to get the damn glue off, and they'd tied pink ribbons to his handlebars as well.

Shaking his head, he climbed on the damn thing and revved it up. The purr of the engine helped to calm him. The club didn't need to arrive at his wedding bloody. Even though it would certainly send a good sign to their enemy.

He had a feeling Abriana would be a laughingstock.

When it came to her, he didn't even know why he cared about her so much. He was never going to have feelings for her.

One, she was too young, and he was thirty-five years old. For another, he didn't do relationships, or care about what women wanted.

Having a wife was never on his list of things to do. He rarely knew how to talk to a woman, let alone anything else.

When a whore was in his bed, he used her for his own satisfaction. With his messed-up face, he knew no one wanted him, or even cared to be with him. They only saw his face, and often, women were more interested in making sure they didn't have to see him when they fucked him.

He'd become quite partial to a nice piece of ass.

They presented their ass to him, and he spread the cheeks wide, and often fucked their anus rather than their pussy.

Besides, most of the club brothers had already

used most of the sluts that hung around them.

Smokey came out, climbed on his bike, and they all rounded up in their places. Hunter took his position next to Smokey, while he took the other side, being sure to stay close.

Even though they were heading toward a wedding, it didn't mean they wouldn't encounter trouble. The club had many enemies, some justified, some not. For the most part, they ended their enemies. They were not a club to give second chances.

If people fucked with them, they died. Simple as that. Their club was fucking law, and even the cops knew to step aside for them.

Riding out of the clubhouse, Ugly Beast followed Smokey, with the brothers at his back. The children they passed on the street waved at them. A few of their mothers rushed out, covering their eyes as if trying to stop them from seeing sin and hoping they wouldn't grow up the same.

Assholes.

Most of the time, their daughters were hanging out at the club to see what all the danger was about.

He didn't mind. It was when their boyfriends or dads thought it was their place to intervene.

Gunning his engine, he picked up speed to keep pace with Smokey. The open road was calling to him, begging for him to ride it.

He fucking loved to ride.

It was the one time he actually felt free. No one here was king. They were all victims to the drug of freedom.

The fire that lit them up from the inside was begging to be unleashed.

He basked in that shit.

At any point they could be killed.

Taken out.

Destroyed.

Ruined.

It was his job to keep them together, to be the one to make sure they were standing. The scars on his face and body each told a story. There were not many scars he held from a single incident.

There was a time he was considered the sexiest member in the MC. Perfect, flawless face, pretty-boy looks. His blue eyes calling to the bitches.

They would seek him out on a Friday night to fuck. He used to have a harem of women, ready and willing.

That had all changed with his face. He saw the true women now, not the faces they liked to pretend to the world.

When Smokey slowed down, part of Ugly Beast wanted to keep on going, to keep on feeling the wind on his face, the freedom spreading through him. Instead, he turned into the driveway of one of the biggest country houses he'd ever seen.

At first, he thought Smokey had gotten the address wrong, but he recognized a few of the guards.

Also, Garofalo was waiting for them on the doorsteps. He'd demanded a meeting before heading to the church.

Church.

The brothers were each going to be forced to sit inside a church for a fucking sermon and wedding.

It pissed him off, but he had a feeling Smokey wanted this.

Either way, his loyalty to his president and the club meant he'd play whatever dance Smokey wanted.

****

"You've got to just lay there and let him have his

way," Carina said.

Abriana sat in the bride's rooms at the church, listening to nonstop sex talk. Only, this wasn't the kind of sex talk her father's ex-mistress had told her about.

This was brutal.

"They all want one thing, and that's what's between your legs. You've got to learn to spread your legs and think about something else. It's what a lot of women have been doing for a lot of years. You can do it as well." This came from her Aunt Hilda.

They wouldn't stop.

"The pain will stay with you for a few days, so long as he only has you the one time. I don't think that will be a problem. I hear their club is filled with women, sluts, who want to give them everything. I bet even if the women don't want to, they still do it."

Abriana clenched her hands into fists. They were now talking about rape; only in their world it wasn't rape.

Whatever a man wanted, he got. There was no force or rape in their world. Men wanted you, they had a right to you, especially your husband.

It was a man's right to have his wife. She couldn't say no. She was merely a possession for him to use for his pleasure.

Abriana didn't know how much she could stand.

"I need some air," she said, standing up.

She left the room before any of her family could protest. There was a small balcony overlooking the church grounds. Her room had the perfect view of the graveyard. How … odd?

Was it giving her a message?

She'd end up dead soon.

The door opened and shut silently behind her. Abriana glanced back to see her sister, Chantel.

"Hey," she said.

"Did you hear everything they were saying?" Abriana asked. "Like it's okay."

"To them it is okay." Her young sister came to her, putting a hand on her back. "It's going to be okay, Abriana."

"I don't know if I can do this."

"You've got to."

"Does it really matter if I follow through with this wedding? They all laugh and mock me anyway. I'm a laughingstock."

"Shh, it's okay. You don't have to worry about a thing. None of those bitches would ever marry him."

"This is not helping." Abriana gripped the balcony, taking several deep breaths.

"I don't know if your biker will be kind and gentle, but sex doesn't have to be brutal. It can be … nice."

This made Abriana turn to her sister.

"You're not old enough."

Chantel shrugged. "I know what I'm talking about. It can be a wonderful feeling. Especially if your guy knows what he's doing."

"You've had sex?"

"Don't act so surprised."

"I … what about Dad?"

Chantel's nose wrinkled. "I don't care what he thinks. He's not the boss of me."

"I hate to disappoint you. You do realize we're at my wedding. We don't have control, and if he ever finds out the truth…"

"You're the older sister, Abriana. You're the one that is tied to this. You're the one being used as a pawn. I'll be free to live my own life. I can do whatever I want."

Abriana stared at her sister and felt sadness.

Chantel really believed she could do and say whatever she wanted and there would be no consequences. If their parents ever found out the truth of her lack of innocence, she'd be made an example of.

Abriana had seen them make examples of women before, and it wasn't good. Some of those women, even daughters, were never seen again. The rumors though, they were the worst. Some of them believed they were sold to the highest bidder into sexual slavery. Others believed they were killed. Or another, they had to work at the whorehouses.

Tears filled her eyes, but she didn't let them fall.

"Who is the lucky man?" Abriana asked.

"That I can't say. I just … he makes me feel amazing. You know, and I don't want that feeling to ever stop."

"I hope you know what you're doing."

"I do." Chantel hugged her.

The door to the balcony opened. Their mother smiled. "It's time. They've arrived."

This was what she'd been dreading.

Actually, she'd been worried that Ugly Beast— she was never going to get used to his name being that— would realize he didn't want her, and not turn up.

Chantel left, offering her another quick, comforting hug before leaving.

She took a deep breath and followed her mother into the room.

"Your father is just outside. You look stunning, Abriana. Better than even I thought you could look." Her mother kissed her cheek. "He is lucky to have a stunning bride, that is for sure."

No other words were spoken. Her mother left, and then her father entered the room.

Gable didn't look happy, but then, he never did. He stared up and down at her. "You're going to have to do."

She didn't expect anything less.

You're too ugly.

Fat.

We're never going to be able to use you.

She was used to the insults, the slights. His disappointment was no different than any other day.

Only now, she couldn't exactly do anything about it, or then, in fact.

It was the pain of his blows that she hated and feared even more so.

Stepping in front of him, she waited for the strike. He couldn't mark her face, but her body, would he risk it, considering the wedding night?

There were still some bruises left over from the last beating he'd given her.

"You will hold your head high. You're a Vigo and belong to Garofalo. I want you to remember that. You are ours, no one else's. You will serve your husband, but you will also serve us." He gripped her shoulders tightly, and she simply nodded. "Good. You will learn to do as you're told. Do not make waves. You will be the perfect bride."

"Yes."

"Good."

He presented his arm. If she could, she'd have smacked him in the face.

She took his arm and ignored that deep yearning to strike out at him. To hurt him so he knew what it felt like.

Had anyone ever hurt her father?

She wondered if it made her a sick person that she wanted to see it.

The wedding song was already playing, and she worried they'd taken too long. The last of the bridesmaids her mother picked out was still leading down the aisle.

Like all weddings she'd attended, the church was full.

When she was a little girl, she'd loved weddings. They had always seemed like great, luxury affairs. As she got older, and became more aware of the reasons for them, the fear of the bride, she'd hated them.

She would often find herself looking at the bride, waiting to see if she was happy about being married, or terrified.

For herself, she was scared shitless.

Her options were completely limited though. She either married this man who was tall, heavily inked, scarred, and completely the opposite of every single fiancé she'd ever seen standing there, or she risked being a failure to her father, and getting a beating for it.

Her life was screwed either way.

With her family, she knew she'd suffer through pain. With this man, she didn't know what the consequences were, and right now, he seemed like the better option.

Her father's words worried her though.

Did he expect her to talk about her husband's activities? To spy on him and the club? That wasn't a great start to any union, and to think, she still had to sleep with him.

It's okay, Abriana.
Wear your mask.
It'll be fine.
Take it one step at a time.

Her father lifted her veil, pressed a kiss to her cheek, and then handed her over to Ugly Beast.

I can do this.

She stared at Ugly Beast's hands. His knuckles were split, and it looked like scabs were already starting to form.

She wanted to touch them, to see if they hurt. The same kind of cuts had been on her father's knuckles many times. He'd even bloodied her clothing from the few punches he'd given her.

Ugly Beast had been fighting before their wedding.

Did they have to drag him to the wedding?

Was she really that detestable he had to be forced to marry her?

It was strange. After all the insults she'd had thrown at her, she really didn't think she could ever be affected by such anger and hatred again. Only, that wasn't the case. She felt raw, emotional, hurt. All because the thought of Ugly Beast not wanting to marry her filled her with regret.

The priest stopped talking as Ugly Beasty reached across, placing a finger beneath her chin.

"You okay?" Ugly Beast asked.

There was a gasp from the crowd. No one had ever stopped the priest from talking just to ask the bride if she was okay.

This couldn't be happening.

She nodded her head. "Yes, yes, I'm fine. Please, continue."

Ugly Beast kept hold of her chin. The priest didn't start right away, and looked toward her future husband.

Her words were not worth anything to anyone. Even the priest sought out the answer from her soon to be husband.

She wanted to scream at the unfairness of it all.

Like so many women before her, she remained silent.

Ugly Beast didn't let her go even as the priest resumed speaking. For the rest of the wedding, he held her chin, staring into her eyes. She didn't like how he kept looking at her, assessing her, watching her.

Gritting her teeth, she tried not to think, not to feel. It was hard to do so, especially with him forcing her to look at him, and seeing the glare in his eyes. If he didn't want her, why didn't he call it off?

They skipped past the vows. She hadn't been required to think of any and neither did Ugly Beast say anything. The priest had clearly been updated on what was required of him.

Once the time came for the pronouncement of husband and wife, she was suddenly pulled against Ugly Beast, and his lips were on hers.

She heard the MC.

It had to be them.

Her family merely clapped at the kiss whereas his club was roaring, whooping, cheering, and hearing them was quite infectious. She liked the feeling as it flooded her veins.

Ugly Beast kept on kissing her.

No one stopped him.

Only when someone slapped him on the back did he let her go. His arms were still wrapped around her, but his lips had released her.

Staring into his blue eyes, she licked her lips. They were numb, and a warmth had spread through her body from his touch. It was … strange.

"That's how we do it. Welcome to the family."

The club president pulled her into his arms. One by one, she was hugged by the MC, becoming part of their own.

They were all so happy.

Their cheers and happiness, and the way they drew her in, she didn't want that feeling to stop. Each one made her feel comforted, which was a new experience for her.

"It's time for the pictures." Her father's voice disrupted the moment, and she knew she'd never be free from her family, from her obligation.

Nodding her head, she felt a little sick.

Ugly Beast took her hand, and with the MC at their back, they were led outside to where pictures were already being taken.

"Do you want me to kill him for you?" Ugly Beast asked, his lips near her ear.

"Who?"

"Your father. He looks like he could use a bullet."

She couldn't help the laugh that erupted from her lips. It was insane to think of anyone threatening her father.

"He's Capo," she said.

"He's an asshole that could do with a bullet. Say the word, and consider it a gift."

It wouldn't be that easy though. Killing her father wouldn't change her fate, it would seal it. War would ensue. She knew her father was close with Garofalo. If something happened to him, there would be blood.

She hated her father.

This life.

The unfairness of it all, but she didn't want innocents to die because of her hatred.

"I'm fine."

"You're going to have to learn to grow a backbone, Abriana. If someone offered the same to your father, no one would be able to stop him. You're nothing more than a piece in a puzzle. He doesn't care about

you."

"It doesn't mean I have to be the same. I know you don't understand, but I know what it means for war."

"I ended one of your family's precious wars. I get it."

She expected him to storm off at their disagreement.

He didn't.

Ugly Beast held her hand and didn't let go. She liked this, enjoyed having him by her side, even though she was now more nervous than ever before.

"Why are you shaking?" Ugly Beast asked her.

He whispered this.

"I'm sorry for upsetting you," she said.

"I'm not upset."

"You're not?"

"No. It's going to take a lot more than you disagreeing with me to upset me. I'm a grown-ass man, not a child. I can take it." He let go of her hand, and she missed his touch instantly.

Ugly Beast didn't let her go though. He wrapped an arm around her waist, keeping her close.

"I'm sorry."

"You're going to be saying that a lot while we're married, aren't you?" he asked.

"I don't mean to."

He kept staring at her.

For a few precious seconds, the world seemed to fall away, and the only two people that mattered were the two of them. She didn't have to worry about her sister, her father, responsibility, duty, nothing.

All she had to focus on was Ugly Beast.

She had heard some women describe him as the most horrible thing to look at, but she didn't see it. Sure, he had scars, but did they really matter?

"In the club, you can't apologize for everything. It'll be a weakness."

"Your clubhouse?"

"It's the Hell's Bastards' clubhouse."

"Will I get to go inside?" she asked.

He stared at her. "You don't do a lot here, do you?"

The spell was broken, and she had no choice but to glance around. No one was paying them any attention. "I don't know how to answer that."

"No, you don't." He sighed.

"I'm sorry."

He glared. "I wonder if I should put a punishment in place whenever you say that."

She gasped, not liking the thought of being hurt. She knew what real pain felt like, and the thought of being hit repeatedly made her feel sick. "I'll be good."

Ugly Beast kept on staring at her. "Wow, fucking wow. I'm not going to hurt you, Abriana. We're going to have to talk, but not here, not in front of your family."

Chapter Three

Ugly Beast finished his beer and stared across the room. His new wife was doing the rounds, which was what he'd been told he had to do. He wasn't rubbing shoulders with pieces of shit. He had a feeling Abriana was hurt in some way, and knowing that pissed him off. What he also hated was the fact he had to go and fuck her in her father's house, and then present the sheets to them tomorrow.

This wasn't him.

"You okay there?" Smokey asked. "You look like you want to kill someone."

"I want to spill someone's blood." Two someones, actually. Garofalo and Vigo; he wanted to kill them both. Only, he wanted to take his time to make them wish they'd never been born before he got his hands on them.

It would feel so good to watch them bleed out. He liked blood and had gotten used to it during his time as a Hell's Bastard.

"You will. You're going to pop a cute little cherry. She's going to be so fucking tight."

"Don't," he said.

Smokey raised a brow.

"She doesn't deserve that, and she doesn't deserve this."

"You don't even know the girl."

"I know enough to know this isn't right." Ugly Bastard finished off his beer and got to his feet.

Smokey did the same. "Do not screw this up."

"You think I'm going to leave her here with those assholes? You can fucking forget it. There's no chance of that ever happening. You got to do what you got to do, but she has to remain out of it."

"For all you know, this bitch could be a spy and already you're willing to roll over because she what? Has a virgin cunt?"

He stepped up close to his president. It was the first time he'd wanted to silence the words coming out of Smokey's mouth. This girl didn't deserve his compassion or his concern, and yet it was there. He felt responsible for her, and he wanted to take care of her.

"Don't."

"Be careful, Ugly Beast. There's a reason why I picked you for this. I get that she's young. Remember she's still a Vigo, and that makes her a liability."

"If she's so liable, why did you even bother doing this bullshit marriage?"

"I told you. I've got my reasons, and when I need to explain them to you, I will. Until then, play the happily married man."

"You need to tell me what game you're playing."

"Not playing any game yet. The moment I do, you'll be one of the first to know." Smokey nodded at him, and Ugly Beast gritted his teeth. This wasn't what he wanted to hear.

Glancing over at Abriana, he saw her father was gripping her arm a little too tightly for his liking.

As he pushed his way through the crowd, several stepped out of his way. The fear on their faces was pleasing him. He liked their fear and knew he could get anything he wanted.

"I want this dance." He took hold of Abriana's hand, feeling her tremble, and shot a glance toward her father.

Vigo looked like he wanted to say something, but Ugly Beast tugged her. The dutiful little wife came with him, exactly how he knew she should.

He pulled her into his arms in the center of the

dance floor for all to see. He had nothing to hide in his need for this woman. She smelled incredible, something floral and sweet. Unlike the women he usually fucked, she was untainted, unspoiled, brand-new.

Abriana was every man's dream in being a virgin.

"You're tense."

"Sorry."

He hated it whenever she used the word "sorry." There was nothing to be sorry about, and yet it spilled from her lips like a broken record. He really needed to change that.

"What was that about?" he asked.

"Nothing."

This time, he tensed up. "Don't even for a second think you can protect him."

"He's my father."

"He's a piece of shit, Abriana. The moment I put that ring on your finger, you became club property. You need to understand that you haven't got the time to shake your loyalty now, sweet thing. You've got to devote your life to us, to me. If you step out on the club, Vigo property or not, you'll be fucking dead."

She flinched as he called her Vigo property. He saw the tears in her eyes.

"Will you be the one to kill me?"

"If it's what's demanded of me. We're a club. We're brothers, and now you're my wife. What did Vigo want?"

She looked toward her father.

Ugly Beast knew he was prowling around the edge of the dance floor, watching their every move. He had a sudden urge to drop his pants, and show him his ass. Once Abriana was with them, there would be no reason for this bullshit show.

"He was telling me how to please you. How I

should … conduct myself this evening."

"I thought your mother was supposed to guide you in that."

"She has."

"And?"

"My dad felt it was necessary to remind me that I've got a responsibility to them as well as to you. I'm just a pawn to be used, and it's up to you how you use me. He reminded me that the blood between my legs is only worth one time."

Ugly Beast tensed up.

"After that, I'm worthless."

"And they think they've wasted that precious cunt blood on me."

She went pale, and her gaze dropped to his chest. "I don't know what they think."

He noticed she never said his name.

"You have an idea?"

"No. I don't know what they think. I never have."

He nodded. It was honest, and he could handle honesty.

"It's time for us to head on up. I'm sick of all the bullshit."

This time, Abriana looked even more afraid.

"You think I'm going to hurt you?" he asked.

"I don't know what you want to do with me."

"Simple, we're going to do what your tradition states, and then we're leaving in the morning. I can't stand these pompous assholes for another minute." If he did, he really was going to stab a bunch of people, and that would ruin their nice and neat diplomatic crap Smokey had going on.

His boys gathered around, whooping, sending out suggestions on what he should be doing to her. He ignored them all. Abriana's mother was there as well.

She was no longer pale but clearly so embarrassed.

The way to their bedroom had been lined with a red carpet. Back at the clubhouse, the carpet leading to the bedrooms was stained with blood, sweat, and probably a whole lot of alcohol and spunk.

Abriana was in for a rude awakening when they got back home. His home was clean but modest. He didn't have any of the fancy mansion shit that they all seemed to like.

Once inside their room, he closed the door and flicked the lock into place. They were alone.

When he glanced around the room, the huge four-poster bed dominated the entire space, and he shook his head at the extravagance of it. He also noted the white sheets. They looked brand new and so white.

Moving past a shaking Abriana, he opened another door and saw it was the bathroom.

"I'm taking a bath. When you're done fucking shaking, thinking I'm going to rape you, come in."

He left her alone, heading into the room.

He placed his cut on the back of the door, removing the robe, and dropping that piece of shit to the floor.

He removed the rest of his clothes, glad to be out of the penguin suit. It had fit a little too tightly, and he truly felt like he was being strangled.

Once he was naked, he started the bath. He was tempted to look out at Abriana. He wondered if she still standing there, staring into space.

Could she even think for herself?

The women in the mafia were always being told what to do. He didn't want to have to constantly tell her what to do every single step of the day. That would be exhausting, and he didn't get off on telling a woman how to live her life twenty-four seven. He liked giving out orders when it involved his cock, but anything else though, and it pissed him off.

Running a hand down his face, he added some bubble bath and waited for the large tub to fill up.

Moving across the room, he stood in front of the large mirror fitted against the wall. The frame seemed to be made of gold. Everything was always so fucking expensive-looking.

He even picked up a gold-handled hairbrush. So much fucking gold.

Putting it down on the counter, he stared at his reflection. His scars seemed to be more pronounced today than ever before. The ink on his body also looked out of place in the bathroom. Tribal ink, images of death, the imprint of his club, all of them stood out. He was the Sergeant at Arms, and he wore it like a badge of honor. He had no intention of ever fucking up, of ever not wearing this badge. This was who he was, and no one would be taking that away from him.

His cock was rock-hard and his balls tight.

Stepping away from the mirror, he turned off the water, checked the temperature, and climbed in.

Still, no sign of Abriana.

He slid beneath the water, wetting all of his body. The moment he broke the surface, he tensed up. Abriana stood in the bathroom.

"Erm, can I sit with you?"

"Sure."

He ran his fingers over his face. "You can join me if you'd like."

"In the bath?"

"You've never shared a bath before?"

"No. Never."

"You ever had a guy touch your pussy?"

"I'm pure…" She nibbled her lip, and still she

didn't say his name. Not even a whisper of it.

"You're not going to say my name?"

She shook her head.

"Do you even know what it is?" he asked.

"Yes."

"Then say it."

"Why?"

"I want to hear you say."

She hesitated, and he waited.

Grabbing the soap, he lathered it across his body, wiping away the day. He didn't wear a wedding band like he'd given her.

"Ugly Beast." Her voice was so small he only just heard it. "Why do you like being called that?" she asked.

"It's my name, baby. You got to get used to calling me that."

"You have a real name."

"I do, but it's not important. The only one that is important is Ugly Beast. None of the brothers would like you for disrespecting me. Sit down." He pointed toward the toilet.

She lowered herself down.

"You want to join me?"

"I'll wait."

"I'm not going to fuck you in the tub if that's what you're afraid of."

"I don't mind."

"Come here," he said. She needed to learn to get over this fucked-up fear of being near him. It was starting to piss him off, and he hated being pissed off.

She was shaking even as she approached him.

"Turn around."

She did as he asked without even questioning him. He didn't like her submission. Women who were subservient were not of use to the club. They needed to be constantly told what to do, and he didn't have the energy for that.

Standing up, not caring to cover his nakedness, he walked over to his jacket.

Pulling out the knife, he saw her panic.

"I'm not going to cut you. Unless you really fuck up and step out on the club, you're safe, Abriana. I'm many things, but I don't abuse women, unless they ask me to."

"Women ask you to hurt them?"

"Some. They like the pain, but again, I've got standards when it comes to that kind of thing, and so I like to make my own rules." He slid the knife between the fabric, being careful not to press the tip right next to her skin.

The buttons dropped to the floor from where he sliced, and he was more than satisfied as it fell to the floor.

"Good."

He stepped back into the bath, closing his knife and watching.

"You want me to just get naked?" she asked.

"Unless you have any other bright ideas on how to bathe. This room can fit six, probably even more."

She laughed. "Water would be everywhere."

"I may exaggerate, but still it'll fit a lot of people." He winked at her.

"Could you close your eyes?"

"Will that make you comfortable?"

"Yes."

"Done."

He closed his eyes long enough to hear the rustling of fabric, and then he opened them. He wasn't going to have her nervous about being naked in front of him. One look at her body, and he wanted to commit fucking murder.

"Who the fuck did this to you?" he asked.

She held the dress against her. "You said you wouldn't look."

"It was your dad, wasn't it? That's why he was around you like flies on shit. He wanted to make sure you keep your mouth shut."

"I don't know what you're talking—"

He wrapped his fingers around her neck, silencing the lie that was about to fall from her lips. "I'd be really fucking careful about what you're about to say to me, Abriana. I'll take a lot, but you lie to me, and I'll consider it a bad start to our marriage."

Tears were in her eyes. Her shaking had gotten worse.

He couldn't give a fuck. He wanted her to know the kind of man she was dealing with. Wife or not, he would fucking end her if she even tried to put the club in danger or risk it in any way.

He wasn't joking either, not about this. She had to learn her place.

"Yes."

"It was your father?"

"Yes."

"How long?"

"I'm not good enough, and so I have to be punished."

"What the fuck?"

Her tears were falling thick and fast now.

"I'm ugly. I'm fat. I'm a waste of air. He doesn't want me around."

"Has he touched you in any other way?"

"No."

"You're still a virgin in all things?" he asked.

"Yes."

He gritted his teeth. Slowly, releasing her neck, she took a step back, or at least tried to. He wouldn't let her.

"No, you don't walk away. You don't fucking stop. Get in," he said.

He let her go and waited as she removed her underwear, exposing her body to him. The bruises across her stomach and back, they were what came from a beating.

Vigo had beaten the shit out of his daughter, and right now, Ugly Beast wanted to show him in kind exactly what he'd done.

****

Climbing into the tub, Abriana had never felt more afraid in her life. This was the first time she'd been naked in front of a man, and it scared her. Really fucking scared her. Ugly Beast looked ready to kill someone, and with how he'd held her neck, she knew it wouldn't have been hard for him to snap her neck.

This man was just as much of a monster as her father was.

Sitting at the opposite end of the bath, she was thankful the bubbles were high so it covered most of her body.

"Does Garofalo know what you do?"

"No."

"Of course. Everything you guys do is in fucking secret. You being a woman, well, that doesn't matter to them either."

"Does it matter to you?" she asked.

"You're my wife. No one touches my property. Do you understand me?" He snapped out each word.

She nodded her head, wanting nothing more than to run. To run and to hide.

Still, like so many times, she sat with him,

waiting for him to be done. To move on, and to let her be.

This is your wedding night.
He wants something more.

"Come here," he said.

She lifted up her head, hating that he watched her. If she denied him, he could make her life even more miserable than it already was. Her father had already given her a warning to be everything her husband wanted. To not make waves. To make sure he was well looked after.

She didn't know what she was doing, so she moved toward him, staying low in the bath.

He grabbed her arm, spinning her around so that her back was to his chest. She let out a little whimper and hated how weak she sounded, even to her own ears.

"You've got to learn to stop being afraid."

"I'm not afraid."

"You're shaking."

"I'm in the bath with a naked man, of course I am."

This time, he chuckled. "Relax."

That wasn't going to happen.

Her heart pounded as he traced a finger down the curve of her neck. He didn't stop there. That finger moved down, over her breast.

She gasped as he cupped her tit, both of his hands holding her.

"I like a woman with a good pair of tits, Abriana." He let her go and fingered her nipples. "I love your tits." He'd lifted her out of the water, holding them as he looked over her shoulder. "And I'm going to be seeing a lot of these."

He teased her breasts, holding her, kneading the flesh, until he finally let them go, but his explorations didn't stop there. He moved his fingers between her thighs, stroking her flesh. She cried out at the sudden pleasure as he fingered her. He cupped her pussy, and one of his fingers glided between her slit, touching her.

"You're dry."

"We're in water."

"Still, you're dry, and I'm not going to fuck you like this. You're not wet enough, and it's going to hurt."

His fingers left her body, and then he was pushing her into the water. She didn't know what he was doing, until he dunked her under, wetting her hair. Much to Abriana's shock, he started to wash her body, lathering her hair and using the shampoo to soap her body at the same time.

When he put her beneath the water, her face didn't go under, and she could breathe. He washed her clean and then handed her the shampoo to do the same.

For a few seconds, she looked at the soap, and didn't have a clue what to do with it. What did he want?

"You wash me."

"Oh."

With shaking hands, she put the soap to his skin.

Ugly Beast let out a chuckle, and his hand covered hers. "You need to do it properly. I won't bite, and none of these scars hurt anymore. You're safe to explore."

She did as he asked, rubbing the soap into his body, rather mesmerized at his ink and the scars. Each one, to her, wasn't ugly. They made him strong.

This man, her husband, was a fighter. His loyalty to his club screamed from his skin as his club position was inked across his heart.

That's what Ugly Beast was devoted to, the Hell's Bastards.

She'd never had anyone devoted to her.

Once she was finished with the soap, she lathered up his hair in the same way he'd done for her. When it was time for him to rinse it, she moved away and watched as he went beneath the water.

Clearing the shampoo from his hair, he sat up, wiping the excess water from his eyes.

She waited for him to finish, but he climbed out of the bathtub, extending his hand to her.

She took it.

Her hand was still shaking a bit, but she also didn't hesitate.

Ugly Beast hadn't hurt her yet, and he'd looked more angry at the bruises on her body and knowing the cause was her father. Technically, she didn't break any of her father's rules. She didn't say a word of who it was. Ugly Beast had already guessed.

Biting her lip, she followed him as he made his way to the bed. She didn't fight him even as her body grew even tenser. She knew what he wanted, but she wasn't ready.

He dried her down with a towel and then worked on his own body. They were both naked, and while he was preoccupied, she couldn't help but stare at his dick. He was hard. The length of him stood out.

When he dropped the towel, she looked away, hating that he could have caught her.

"Don't look so panicked."

"I'm not panicked."

"Yes, you are, beautiful. No need to be." He took her hand and led her to the bed, helping her into the center. "Lie down, spread your legs."

She was starting to get even more nervous, but arguing was out of the question. She lay down in the center of the soft bed and opened her thighs.

Ugly Beast had moved to the bottom of the bed,

and he climbed on top. His gaze was on hers, but not for long as he stared down at her.

Her hands were on her stomach.

"Lift your hands up. Put them against the bed. Keep them there."

She felt tears fill her eyes. Should she watch what he was about to do? Could she even handle it?

Closing her eyes, she waited.

When his lips touched her chest, she gasped.

Opening her eyes, she stared down at his head, seeing him kissing down her body. His lips were so soft, not what she expected.

Unable to look away, she watched as he cupped one of her breasts, his hands holding her in place as he flicked his tongue across the pointed tip.

Her body tensed up, but she felt this swirling ache deep inside. When he bit down, she gave a cry at the sudden burst of pain, but it felt really good as he tongued her tit. He spent so long on one breast, driving her crazy. He moved his tongue down the valley of her breasts, moving to her next and giving that tit the same pleasure.

She wriggled beneath him, needing the pressure to be released. Something was happening to her body. She'd never felt this way before, and it was … amazing.

Arching up against him, she wanted something between her thighs.

When he let her breasts go, she let out a whimper.

He chuckled. "All in good time, Abriana."

He kissed down her body, his lips creating a fire, and when he moved between her thighs, she had no idea what he was going to do. He held her open. His fingers held her sex, and then his tongue slid between and she cried out. The sounds erupting from her shocked her.

He sucked her clit, his tongue repeatedly flicking back and forth. The pleasure, and that was exactly what it was, pleasure, flooded her body and made her ache in all the right places.

Ugly Beast controlled her body, using it against her for his own needs.

She felt the moisture between her thighs, and knew she was close to orgasm, close to that mystery thing that her father's dead mistress had told her about. The orgasm that they said drove women wild when men got it right. That it wasn't to be afraid of. To find it, to take it because there were few men in the world who even gave a fuck that a woman was having a good time.

Something was building inside her body.

It was amazing.

She cried out as her entire body peaked, thrust over the edge, and fell into orgasm. It was unlike anything she'd ever experienced, not that she'd gotten the chance to experience a lot.

Her entire body felt on edge and at the same time, like molten lava. She was wet.

Ugly Beast moaned his approval against her pussy. He didn't linger there long. His fingers ran through her slit, and he nodded.

"Now, you're ready."

"Ready?"

Her voice didn't sound like her own.

"You look so fucking beautiful when you come."

Ugly Beast moved between her thighs. She didn't know how it was possible for her to feel so small against him. He was big, and so was his cock that brushed her thigh.

In the bathroom, it hadn't looked so scary, whereas now, well, it felt terrifying. He held himself above her, but she didn't dare look at him, or his … length.

He stared into her eyes, but his hand moved

between them. The tip of him glided between her slit, bumping her clit.

She gasped out at the sudden burst of pleasure. It was scary, even with the fear of what he was about to do.

"This is going to hurt," he said.

She nodded.

"Your blood has to be on the sheets."

"I know."

"You're wet. It won't hurt for long."

"Is that why you…"

"Licked your pussy?" he asked. She nodded. "Yes. I don't lick a woman's cunt."

"Why not?" She wanted to cover her face, but her hands were still above her head, waiting for the next instruction.

"Most women have ridden a guy bareback. I've no interest in tasting another man's cum."

Her face heated. She knew what he was talking about. Was that double standards? From what the dead ex-mistress told her, men liked to fuck a woman's throat. She really needed to stop thinking about this.

She cried out. Moving her hands from above her, she grabbed his chest at the sudden burst of pain.

The fire between her thighs scared her, terrified her.

Ugly Beast didn't let her go. He grabbed her hands, which she'd started to hit him, trying to get him off. To stop him from coming anywhere near her. He held her to the bed, and tears blurred her vision. He'd pushed inside her while she was distracted, only he wasn't finished. He thrust in further, and she screamed. The pain was completely different from the beatings she'd taken at the hands of her father.

She'd never felt anything like this inside her. It hurt but in a different way from her flesh being kicked and hurt.

"I'm nearly in," he said, whispering the words against her ear.

She wanted this to be over.

He slammed inside her, and she couldn't help it.

"Please, stop." She sobbed out each word.

He held himself still within her. It didn't matter now as he held her close to him, but his cock was pulsing inside her.

Ugly Beast pulled up, and she looked at him, hating that he'd given her pleasure and turned it into pain.

This was what women had to go through. Even the dead ex-mistress had told her a woman's first time was painful. None of them had been wrong.

Swallowing past the fear and pain, she waited.

Ugly Beast didn't move.

She couldn't say anything either.

This was her duty.

Being a Vigo daughter, a mafia daughter, this was her job. To lie down, spread her legs, and let her husband take her. The precious virginity they were all so ready to sell off now soiled the sheets. She didn't even know if there was blood. Again, the dead ex-mistress had told her some women didn't bleed. It was just another thing that made her afraid, that she worried about.

If she didn't bleed, they'd think she'd given her virginity to someone else, which wasn't the truth.

She was a virgin. Unlike her sister, she'd not even kissed a guy.

No kisses.

No touches.

Just pain delivered by her father's hand.

Now, Ugly Beast.

"I'm sorry, princess," he said.

He slowly pulled out of her, and she tensed up as he began to rock inside her. There was pain but something else.

She didn't know what it was, and she stayed perfectly still, letting him do the work. He knew what he wanted.

He held her hands beside her head, holding her down, keeping in control. In this moment, she was just a body, something for him to use for his own pleasure. She didn't matter, not now, not ever.

He began to fuck her harder, going deeper as he slid inside. Each thrust seemed to go easier inside her.

She watched him, not really paying attention. Any arousal she had had died in those few seconds.

Ugly Beast groaned as his body slammed into hers. Each thrust was harder than the last. He pounded inside, and then with a groan, he filled her one last time and she felt the spill of his cum as he filled her.

With each pulse, he moaned.

Tears spilled down her cheeks, but she didn't let out a noise.

This was why their mothers rarely told them anything of the night of their wedding. She was prepared more than most thanks to the dead ex-mistress. Even with her words, Abriana had hope, but now, she hoped Ugly Beast found his release with other women. There was no way she could go through that again.

Her body was hurting a little, but her emotions hurt in more ways than the beating her father had given her, and she felt so humiliated that she couldn't just do something right.

Ugly Beast pulled out of her, and she kept her eyes closed, only for them to jerk open as he picked her up.

She was tempted to fight him, only she knew how

useless that was. He could do whatever he wanted. Her father had told her to be the perfect lady, to take what was coming to her as she was a Vigo.

Ugly Beast made her stand up, and she was a little confused but then saw what he was doing. The sheets had her blood on them. He stripped them off, as well as the sheet beneath it. Her blood had soaked through. He pulled back the rest of the covers, and with a gasp, he lifted her up, laying her back down.

Neither of them spoke as he disappeared back into the bathroom.

When he returned seconds later with a cloth, she tensed up as he opened her thighs and cleaned her off.

Words were not needed, and in truth, she didn't welcome any kind of conversation with him.

Chapter Four

The following morning, Ugly Beast left Abriana to sleep in. He arranged for some food to be taken up to his new wife, and with the sheets in his hands, he made his way down to the men who he'd been told were waiting for him.

This tradition was bullshit. What was more, he had a problem with Vigo, and he wasn't leaving here until that bastard knew at the first opportunity he was as good as dead.

Smokey met him at the bottom of the stairs, smoking a cigarette, even as a woman glared at him for clearly violating house rules.

"Well, how was it?"

"I've got the sheets, don't I?"

Smokey burst out laughing only for it to die down at the look on his face.

Ugly Beast wasn't laughing. He didn't find anything of last night funny. He hadn't even gotten any sleep last night.

The sound of her scream and the sob for him to stop kept on playing inside his head. She hadn't asked him to do it again, but he'd not stopped. He'd continued until he came. He figured the rush of his cum inside would help spill out any more blood if there wasn't enough. He didn't have a fucking clue how this tradition worked. Abriana was his first and only virgin. There was no fucking way he'd ever do this again. No fucking way.

Running a hand down his face, he stared at his president.

"I want to kill Vigo."

"Why?"

"He put his hands on her."

"She wasn't a virgin?" Smokey asked.

"She was. She was also covered in bruises. Not by me but by her fucking father. He put his hands on her."

Smokey kept on staring at him.

"What?"

"I'm just…"

"Don't give me fucking shit, Smokey. She belongs to us. He had no right to touch her, and as far as I'm concerned, he hurt what belongs to us, to the club."

"You want payback."

It wasn't a question.

"I want him to know that when he touches what belongs to us, he needs to know, Vigo or not, there's a price."

Smokey nodded. "Where is your wife?"

"Sleeping."

Ugly Beast held onto the sheets and stormed into the room where the men were already drinking. It wasn't eight in the morning, but the scent of scotch filled the air. The dark liquid was easy to see in their clear glasses.

Vigo was right next to Garofalo.

Storming up to them, he threw the sheets down at his feet. "I'd like a word." His gaze was on Vigo.

It was subtle, but he saw the way the guy tensed up.

"It's not necessary. As you can see, she was pure. Now she belongs to you. I see our matters are settled."

"You seem to think I'm asking." Ugly Beast didn't break eye contact. "Now."

He watched and waited as Vigo put his glass down.

Garofalo also followed, but Ugly Beast didn't have a problem with that.

They entered his office, and the maid that had been cleaning it scuttled out. *Good.*

He waited for the door to close. Smokey was with him. His president allowed him to take the floor with this one.

"What is the meaning of this?" Garofalo asked.

Without waiting for another word, Ugly Beast grabbed Vigo by the jacket and threw him across the room. Smokey held onto Garofalo as he tried to intervene.

With his hands still in the jacket, he slammed Vigo up against the bookshelves. Drawing his arm across his neck, he watched the fleeting panic in the other man's eyes as he cut off the air circulation.

"What's the matter? You can only fight little girls?"

Vigo's eyes went wide.

"You think I wouldn't give a fuck? You think I wouldn't see those bruises you wanted her to hide? Is that it? You think I'd fuck her with the light off or maybe from behind?"

"Get off me," Vigo said.

"Not happening. You, piece of shit, disrespected me. The moment you gave her to us, she became Hell's Bastards' property."

"She's my daughter. She needed to be taught respect."

Drawing his arm back, he punched him in the stomach, relishing the man as he bent forward, catching his breath. Not giving him the chance to recover, he clocked him under the chin, smiling as he fell to the floor.

He placed his foot on Vigo's dick and began to put pressure, almost as if he was going to stand up.

"Then I think it's time I taught you a little about respect. Abriana belongs to me. She's my wife. That cum on those sheets is all mine. Her body is mine. You try to

touch her again, and I will fuck you up. You even try to use her to get to us, and I'll do more than fuck you up. I'll fuck your entire family and every single person you need. Try me, Vigo. You think you know what you're doing here, but don't for a second think you're the boss of her." He drew his leg up and slammed it back down.

Ugly Beast was never one to fight dirty. Even as he wanted to kick him again, the bastard was down, and he had a lot more respect for himself than most.

Standing up, he looked toward Garofalo.

Smokey finally let him go.

He stepped up to the boss, the big man in charge.

"You can't even keep your Capos in line."

"It's time for you to leave," Garofalo said.

"I'll leave when my wife wants to. Until then, you will treat her with respect."

With that, he walked out of the office. The door closed behind the two of them.

"Feeling any better?"

"Nope," Ugly Beast said. "Tell me I can go back in there and kill them."

"I wish I could, brother. Not going to happen. Not today."

"When the day comes, I want Vigo."

"When the day comes, I'll be the one to watch that masterpiece."

Hunter picked that moment to make an appearance. "What's up?" he asked. "Why do I feel like I just missed a party?"

"You did, but don't worry about it. There's going to be more than enough time to party when we're home. Get the bikes ready. It's time for us to get this shit show on the road."

Ugly Beast left the boys to get ready. He made his way back up to his room toward his wife. The door was partially open, and he stayed outside listening in.

"How was it?" Chantel, her sister, asked.

"It was fine."

"You hated it?"

"I really don't want to talk about it."

"He looks like the kind of guy that would be selfish. Did he even make you come?"

"Chantel, this is not appropriate."

"Right, always playing the obedient girl, right? Dad just sold you to make a peace treaty with the MC. They have power that the family wants."

"You keep running your mouth like that it's going to get you killed."

"Only if the wrong people hear. I bet your guy has got a big dick, or is it small?" Chantel chuckled. "From the look in your eye I'm going to say he's a big boy. Well, sis, you're going to need to learn how to service that cock, otherwise he's going to find a slut to use. He'll probably give you some disease or something."

"Did you come to say goodbye or do you just want to make me feel like crap?" Abriana asked.

"If Dad does decide to marry me off, he'll save me for a guy that matters. You're not the prettiest girl, and so your ass was passed to one of the ugliest MC—"

He'd heard enough.

Opening the door, he didn't look toward Abriana, but to Chantel. She went a little pale even as her gaze shot fire at him.

"You know, little sluts like you are a dime a dozen. I'd be careful who you run your mouth to. I may be ugly, but I can tell you one thing, one word to your dad, and you'd be sold to a fucking rancid dog with an infected cock. You think you've got value because you're pretty. I can already tell you're not pure." He smiled. "You may have a lot of guys fooled, but not me. I hear you disrespecting my wife again, I'll fuck you up, kid or not. A whore with a mouth like that deserves what she gets. Get the fuck out."

He watched her go before turning his gaze to his wife.

"You shouldn't talk to her like that."

"As my wife, you don't have no bitch disrespect you. It's time you learn to take care of yourself. You start to believe the vile shit she spews, we're going to have a problem."

"She was just upset because Dad wouldn't give her what she wanted."

"Your daddy can suck my dick, Abriana. Sister or not, she don't get to talk to you like that. I won't allow it. Where we're going to go, there are going to be bitches who'll hurt you. Who'll stab you in the back."

"Then leave me here."

"Not happening. I spunked inside you last night. I need to make sure no spawn is going to come of it. It's time to go."

He picked up her suitcase.

He was impressed with her choice of jeans and a large shirt. He pulled a sweater out of his bag and handed it to her. "It's going to get cold. Put this on."

She took it from him and quickly pulled it over her head.

The clothes she wore were much too large, and he didn't get a good look at her body, even though he wanted to.

Shaking his head to clear the fog that had entered his mind, he turned his back and started to walk away. He heard her following him.

Her steps were fast as she rushed to keep up.

"Do I have to go and say goodbye?" she asked.

"Anyone wanting to say goodbye will be outside waiting. We don't have time for this. It's time to go home." He was done with all the bullshit. If he stayed here another minute, he was putting a bullet in Vigo and Garofalo's head.

It had been his idea to do that at the start. As far as he was concerned, you could never trust a made man or a capo, or anyone to do with the mafia. They always had their own agenda, and it never included outsiders, not when those outsiders were more powerful.

The Hell's Bastards had proved that time and again by defending Garofalo. In doing so, as far as he was concerned, he'd shown the mafia how powerful they all were. That was his fault. He shouldn't have done it, but he had. There was no getting away from that.

Once outside, he noticed no one had come to say bye to her. Not a single person. Not even her mother.

Glancing toward the house as he grabbed his bike, he saw no signs of anyone. Securing her back to his bike, he tossed her a helmet, waiting for her to drag it over her head. Her long brown hair disappeared inside the helmet. He wanted to do a great deal of things to her body, to feel her against him. There would be time for that soon enough, he had no doubt.

He climbed on his bike and waited for her. She gripped his jacket as he straddled his bike.

"Hold onto me," he said.

She did so, but not tight enough.

He jerked the bike forward so she had no choice but to hold onto him. He was getting sick and tired of the bullshit with chicks. They were either too grabby or not enough.

His wife was going to make him work for it.

Smokey was the first to leave the parking lot, and he revved his engine, taking his turn, leaving the house behind. He didn't look back, not once. He had a feeling this wasn't going to be the last time he saw this place. Garofalo would need them again and soon, he could guarantee it.

As he drove down the long dirty road, he tried to ignore the woman at his back. Her arms were tight around him now, but it wasn't her grip that was exciting him. It was the feel of her body pressed against his back, and the fresh memory of her silken, tight pussy wrapped around his length.

Taking her virginity had been a disaster, but she'd been wet. He worked her clit, getting her ready to take his cock, and she'd felt like a dream as he slid inside. She was the first virgin he'd ever been with, and he could guarantee, she'd be his last. However, he'd been with a lot of chicks. The bitches that sniffed around the club were more than happy to service MC cock, even his.

He took them, fucked them, forgot about them. They were not even worth a second or third thought. The problem was, Abriana was his wife. She belonged to him, and since being inside her, he couldn't get her out of his head.

It hadn't even been twenty-four hours, and he wanted her again. Once he was sated, no other woman mattered to him. They were always a means to an end.

He couldn't figure out what it was about Abriana. Maybe her virginity was messing with his head. She was no different from all the other women. When he got back to the clubhouse, it would all return to normal and he wouldn't have to give a fuck about anyone or anything.

Gunning down the road, he smiled. The open road always freed him. There was nothing to hide here, or to avoid. He fucking relished every single second of freedom. The life they led, they always knew there was a risk of jail time and death.

He'd been locked up for a couple of years when he was a punk-ass kid who didn't know how to handle himself. He'd paid the price, and it made him grow up.

That was all in the past. He now had a wife to deal with and also a father-in-law, he wanted to kill more than anything else.

Surely this was normal for a lot of husbands. He would just have to deal with it.

****

The Hell's Bastards clubhouse was huge, bigger than her father's house. That was Abriana's first thought as they entered the large parking lot. The other club members aligned their bikes, including Ugly Beast. It was a perfect line of bikes parked.

Within a matter of seconds, the engines were off, and she heard the door slam open. Men, women, and kids fell out of the door, all of them rushing toward the men.

After she climbed off the bike, with Ugly Beast's help, he took the helmet from her, grabbing her bag.

She stayed close to his side and tensed up as two women ran toward him.

They looked a little older than Abriana. One threw herself into his arms and the other went around his back.

She stepped back, wondering what to do.

They were hugging her husband. The blonde with her legs around his waist kissed his face. "I want to suck your dick. I bet you've got blue balls. I can take care of that."

Ugly Beast laughed, letting the woman go.

What was she to do? This woman had just blatantly said she was going to suck his dick. His very married dick.

You're nothing to him.
You're just a peace treaty.

You mean nothing.

"Before you ladies get crazy, let Ugly Beast get his wife settled," Smokey said.

All gazes turned to her.

She hated being the center of attention and would have gladly disappeared.

"Wow, you really went through with it," the blonde said.

"Don't be a jealous bitch." Ugly Beast slapped her ass. "Come on, Abriana. We're staying in my room tonight."

Abriana, like the good little slave, followed behind him. She didn't want to be here. Why couldn't he have left her at home where she knew what to expect?

She noticed several gazes were on her. They also didn't even attempt to whisper either.

"She's fucking plain. Poor Ugly, I bet they thought he'd be grateful."

"He's fucking ugly but good in the sack. I doubt she'll satisfy him. He'll be back to us in no time."

"He could always put a bag over her head."

She was very much aware of her plainness. According to her family, it was her worst trait. She had tried to be a good girl, always doing as she was told, but no matter what she did, she would always be ugly.

They moved to the back of the clubhouse, and she didn't even bother to lift her head. She wasn't going to be staying here all that long. He said he had a house. She wondered if that was where she'd spend most of her life? At his home.

After walking up three flights of steps, Ugly Beast turned left, then right, before coming to the third door on the left.

"When we're here, this is where we'll be staying. A lot of boys stop by from other chapters and sleep wherever they crash. When they're here, you stay in this room."

He opened the door, and she saw it was a decent size, not like her old room. There was a large bed that dominated the room.

"We share a shower on this floor. Make sure to lock the door. We don't have any fancy gold shit. It's all standard stuff."

She wanted to tell him she wasn't the one in charge of decorating at home, but figured it was useless.

Putting her bag on the edge of the bed, she turned to look at him. He was rubbing the back of his head, looking a little out of it.

"I can handle this."

"You sure? I want a beer, and I'll bring you up some food when it arrives."

"Okay."

It wasn't okay. He brought her here, and now he was going to leave her.

"Good." He left the room without another word, closing it behind him. She stared at the door, a little shocked.

He just left her.

Staring around the room, she went to the window that overlooked the back of the house.

It was such a large backyard, and she saw trees at the edge of the dirt path. She saw off to the left, there was a large shed with a single chain on the doors. It looked ready to fall down if someone gave it a single push.

She watched in amazement as one of the brothers she didn't recognize pushed a woman up against the shed.

The woman wasn't fighting. The man pawed at her body, and then he shoved her down in the dirt so she was on her knees.

Right there, in front of anyone to see, his dick was in her mouth.

"Men love to think we can swallow dick. It can be done, but you need to take time to learn."

Stepping away from the window, she covered her face. This was not like anything back home. The most she had seen was torture and death. Men and women had died in front of her.

It was their life.

She stood at the base of the bed and opened up the bag. The few clothes she'd brought with her seemed to mock her. They were all outfits designed to cover up as much of her body as possible.

Zipping up the bag, she put it on the floor.

Spinning around the room, she saw he didn't even own a television, nor were there any books.

She stepped up to his chest of drawers and stared at the photographs that were there. Not too many. Most of them were of his bike or club. Not enough to give her any insight into the club.

Once she had stared at all the things in his room that didn't mean she snooped, she sat on the edge of the bed again.

Boredom flooded her.

She was used to being sent to her room. It was always random, but she had books to keep her company. This was boring.

Rubbing her hands together, she folded her legs, and then waited. There was no clock in the room, so she didn't know what time it was or how long she'd been there.

Heavy music was playing downstairs. The house seemed to vibrate with it.

She started to pace the room, trying to calm

herself, but that didn't work. Sitting down on the floor, she folded her legs again, put her hands on her knees, and tried to meditate.

It was something she often did after she'd been at the mercy of her father. The bruises still hurt, but she was able to focus.

Breathing in.

Breathing out.

When that didn't work, she grabbed his pillow from the bed and placed it on the floor, lying down to stare up at the ceiling.

Did he say she couldn't leave his room?

Was she banished here until he remembered her?

She was starving.

She hadn't had the time for breakfast before Chantel came in and ate it. While her sister threw accusations her way while eating, she'd gotten changed and packed.

Rubbing at her temples, she felt a little wave of sickness.

Would it be so bad to leave the sanctuary of the room? She sat up, picked up the pillow, brushed it off, and placed it back on the bed. She walked to the door, breathed in, and began to open the door, only to close it.

What was she doing? She had to wait.

She sat on the edge of the bed again. Tears filled her eyes at being left alone. Was this the kind of life she was going to have?

Just get up and go downstairs.

It can't be that bad.

Other women are here.

Standing up, she squared her shoulders and waited. Opening the door, she waited to see if someone entered to yell at her. When no one did that, she peeked her head out, chancing a look down the long corridor. No one was around, and the noise was louder. Stepping out into the hallway, feeling so stupid for the way she was behaving, she shut the door. Her stomach chose that moment to make a noise.

Folding her arms around herself, she slowly made her way down the stairs. Each time she got closer, the music got louder.

She'd never been to a party like this. The parties her family had were always quiet, social events. There was no room for loud music, or dancing. There was always the chance of a threat. The men that gathered together often hated each other.

On the ground floor, she paused when she saw a woman having sex with one of the club members. His jacket was on, and she noticed all the men wore them. Each one declared their membership to the Hell's Bastards.

"That's right, fuck me. I need it. I need it so badly."

Cheeks heating at the need in the woman's voice, Abriana moved toward the door. Glancing inside, she saw the men were all partying.

She opened the door slightly and stepped inside. The noise was so intense.

"Our boy is married. Come on, ladies, show him a good time."

Several women were naked, dancing on tables. Abriana saw a stage was set up with a stripper pole.

No one had noticed her entering.

It was probably a good thing. No kids were in sight anymore, and there was just so much alcohol and naked women.

A moan to her left drew her attention, and she saw one of the men with his fingers in a woman's hair as he bucked against her. He tugged on her hair.

"Show me."

He watched the woman open her mouth, showing a load of his cum.

"Good girl, swallow it."

Averting her gaze at the display, trying to stay out of sight, to find the kitchen, she paused when she caught sight of Ugly Beast.

He was sitting in a chair as a woman ground on him. She was completely naked, and Ugly Beast was clothed.

Seeing the smile on his lips tore at her. She barely knew this man, and yet he was looking at the woman as if she was someone special.

"You're the new girl, aren't you?"

She turned to a raven-haired, pretty woman. She wore a leather cut and a lot more clothes than any of the other women were wearing.

"Erm, new girl?"

"You're Ugly Beast's old lady?"

"Huh?"

"Wife."

"Oh, yes."

"One thing you got to learn about the club, sweetheart, these men are not taken. You can be upset and hate the sluts, but the men will do whatever the fuck they want."

"Are you a wife?"

The raven-haired woman snorted. "Not a chance. I wouldn't have any of these fuckers even if they begged me."

"You wear a leather cut."

"I'm one of them, sweetheart." She turned, and Abriana read the words, "Only Female Member."

"Oh."

"I earned my patch. Are you here to cause shit?"

"I just want some food. He was supposed to … bring me some food."

"The name's Raven," the woman said. "We girls got to stick together. None of the old ladies are here. They knew the boys were going to throw your boy a party. There's going to be a lot of pussy on offer tonight, and well, the boys don't take kindly to them interfering. Come on, I'll make you a sandwich. The pizza was eaten an hour ago."

So food had come and gone.

One last look at Ugly Beast, Abriana knew she would never rely on him, nor would she want anything to do with him.

Following Raven into the kitchen, she stared at her. The other woman looked so sure, so confident and happy as she hummed to herself.

"Take a seat, sweetness. Are you allergic to anything?"

"No."

"Ah, peanut butter sandwich it is. We usually have shitloads of food here. Looks like we're going to have to go shopping."

She slammed the door closed on the fridge.

"So, you're a mafia brat."

"Mafia brat?"

"Yes. What's it like being in the mafia?" Raven asked, spreading the peanut butter thickly.

"It's not a lot of fun."

"You see a lot of death, or do you get put away on a shelf until the men need you?" Raven asked.

"I've seen men die. At some of the parties they have, there is always some death."

"Your men have parties?"

"Not like this. They're always tense affairs. It's mostly to make deals, talk about betrayers and stuff like that. Women are there for … I think for them to look at. I don't know."

"Is it true you're not allowed to do anything but make babies?" Raven put the plate down in front of her.

Abriana took a bite. "Thank you. Yes. I was homeschooled, but there are schools for girls where they are kept, trained, and ready for marriage. It's what we're supposed to do. We're allowed to shop. We're not allowed to know business."

"What can you do?" Raven asked.

"Not a lot. We can read. Listen to music. Whatever we do cannot cause a distraction or make waves."

"Fuck. That sounds so fucking boring. Girl, you are in for a real eye-opening experience. Here, you got to learn to speak up for yourself. To take a stand."

"What would you do if it was your man getting a lap dance?" she asked.

Raven laughed. "Bitch, my man wouldn't even have the balls to look at another woman. I'd be riding his dick, and he'd know it would be cut off."

"Oh." She took another bite. "I'm not like that, and he doesn't have to like me or anything. He's taking me back to his home."

"Girl, you are a disaster waiting to happen, you know that?"

"I'm good."

"You know what, I'll help you out. I know you're going to need my help."

"I … do you have a book?"

"A book?"

"I'm a little bored in his room."

Raven rolled her eyes. "You know what, I thought Ugly Beast was different. Piece of shit drops his wife off and just fucking leaves." Raven slams the chair back as she gets to her feet.

"No, no, it's fine. I don't want to make waves, I promise. It's fine. I can go to sleep."

The other woman cursed. "Fucking useless. You got to grow a set to handle those men."

Abriana finished her food off and rushed toward the sink to clean up her dishes. Raven was already gone, and nerves hit her square in the stomach. This wasn't what she wanted. She had only been there a day, and already she felt like she'd done something wrong.

She walked to the door and looked out. Raven pulled the woman off Ugly Beast. She gasped, covering her mouth as the woman landed on the floor. Raven didn't stop there, and she slapped the woman around the face.

This was bad. In the next second, Raven was yelling and pointing toward the door.

Everyone turned to the door, and Abriana ducked down so no one saw her. Her heart pounded. Glancing around the room, she saw there was nowhere to make an escape. The door in the far corner opened up, and in stepped the man and woman she caught earlier by the shed. They were laughing.

Seeing an opportunity, she rushed out of the door. She didn't know where she was going, but she kept on running.

There was a chill in the air, but the fresh air felt so good. She wondered if she could keep on running and finally be free.

Chapter Five

"What the fuck, Raven?" Ugly Beast got to his feet, but Raven had a hold of him, dropping him back into his chair.

"So that's all it takes, huh, for you to be a piece of shit. The right smile from a blonde slut and you forget to feed your wife!"

The music was turned down, and now all the boys were watching them. Raven was the club's only female member. She was a first-class bitch, loyal as fuck, strong, and most of the boys wanted to fuck her.

He wasn't one of them. He could bet this woman would kill a cock rather than suck one or ride it.

Abriana.

He was supposed to take her up some food. The pizza was all gone, and the boys kept him in his chair to give him a party.

"Now you start to think," Raven said. Her foot landed on the chair between his thighs, so close to his dick.

Glaring at her, he looked toward the kitchen.

"Don't worry, asshole, I fed her. She saw your little display. You think these whores would want your ugly ass any other day? They're being paid to want you, Ugly Beast, but I guess virgin pussy has gotten to your head." Raven let her foot go. "You're all fucking pricks." With that, Raven stormed off.

The girl who had been grinding on his lap had bloody hands. Raven had broken her nose.

Any fun he had was long gone now. Getting to his feet, he headed to the kitchen. He shouldn't have forgotten his wife. Raven was wrong. It wasn't about the blonde bitches showing him attention. He didn't need to be told they were being paid for the pleasure of riding his cock.

He was just having some fun with his boys, and while there was free pussy on offer, none of them would question him about his time with Abriana.

"Where's my wife?" he asked, looking toward Brick as he had a club-whore pinned to the fridge.

"Is that the new piece of ass that just rushed out of here?" Brick asked.

"Yes." He gritted his teeth.

"She's outside. That's all I know."

"You didn't think to stop her?"

"I didn't know we were keeping chicks prisoner here. I figure she needed some air." Brick shrugged.

He wasn't trying to keep her prisoner. She needed to be protected and kept safe.

Ignoring the other brother's inquisitive stare, he left the kitchen, heading straight out into the night.

He spotted her on the ground, not too far from where they'd buried a body. Yeah, when she was here, he was going to have to start laying some ground rules down.

When he got near her, he didn't pull her into his lap or force her to sit with him. He sat down on the hard ground and chanced a glance toward her.

She wasn't crying. He figured that was a plus. The last thing Ugly Beast felt he could handle right now was tears.

"I was hungry," she said.

"I know. I forgot to bring you some food."

She turned toward him. "Were those women your girlfriends?"

"No. They service every single man in the club. They're just good at riding cock."

"And your men still like them?"

He turned toward her, seeing the curiosity in her

gaze.

"You can't be servicing any of the brothers. You're mine, Abriana."

"I wasn't thinking of having sex. It's just, in my world, she wouldn't be well respected."

Ugly Beast laughed. "She'd be fucking loved all right, but only for as much cock as she can suck. She'd be the entertainment. It's the wives that would hate her fucking guts. They don't like any bitch stealing their men."

She shook her head. "I doubt that's it. Most of us don't want their men to touch them. Besides, they're not ours. We always belong to them, but they are never ours."

"Is that what you feel like with me? You don't want me to touch you?"

He waited as he expected her hesitation. Running his fingers through his hair, his dick had long lost any of its hardness.

"No, I don't want you to touch me." She looked at him. "You can sleep with those women. I don't care." She got to her feet, brushing her clothes down. "Sorry if you felt you had to come and see me. I just want to go back to your room now."

"You don't have to go to our room. You can stay." He noticed how she didn't call it "*our* room." He didn't like that.

Abriana needed to learn she wasn't under Garofalo's rule anymore. She was part of the club, and she could sit around, party with the brothers. They all knew not to touch her.

"Raven will be back to party soon," he said, trying to coax her.

She smiled. "I liked Raven."

"I bet meeting her was a bit of a shock." He

laughed.

"How do you mean?"

"You're used to women abiding by the rules. Raven has always done and will always do her own thing. She'll take care of you though. No doubt about that. She is fucking loyal." He got to his feet. Moving to her side, he wanted to touch her, but he held himself back, recalling the previous night's tears. "You ready to head inside?"

She nodded.

Walking side by side, he didn't like the distance she'd created between them. It pissed him off, and he wanted to fill the gap.

Instead, he stayed as close as he could without touching her, which was a lot harder than he thought it would be.

They entered the kitchen. Brick was fucking the woman now. He grabbed Abriana's arm and moved her past the vision of Brick's naked, spotty ass. It was a sight he always wanted burned off his retinas.

"Is it always like this here?" she asked.

"It is. You don't have to stay."

They entered the main clubhouse, and the women were still stripping down. More women were here, which meant only one thing, their strip club, Tits, had closed for the night. The girls always liked to unwind here. Some of the brothers brought them along for some fun. Most of the time, the women were up for anything, especially after a night of having guys hard for them. Some of the women went home to their families as they were only working there for the money.

He spotted Raven sat at a table. She had a couple of green bills, and she was whooping to the crowd for the girls to keep on taking their clothes off. He didn't get that woman. One moment she was yelling and shouting at him. Then, the next minute, she was wanting chicks to get their clothes off. None of them knew if Raven was gay or not, or bi. He was sure some of the guys had a bet on for them to find out, but as yet, none of them had fucked her to find out.

"Abriana, come here, girl."

All eyes turned toward her, and he waited.

"If you're waiting for an order, it's not going to happen. You're free here. I told you that."

She tucked some of her brown hair behind her ear. Even dressed in jeans and a shirt, she stood out. She was not one of them, but that didn't mean in time she wouldn't be.

"I'd like to stay."

"Then go and take a seat."

He knew Raven would make her feel like home. The female of the club was always helping others, and he'd seen her helping out around the city, and the nearest town where they always made a stop to fill up with gas before making it home.

They were not too far from the town, and their clubhouse was stationed between the town and the city. No one fucked with them for that very reason. He even had a deal with the local sheriff, that he would make sure no one hurt their town, and that there were no gang wars, and in return they would turn a blind eye to some of the goings on in town, which included some of the women working in one of the empty warehouses on porn.

The club had business everywhere, and they made sure to be more than comfortable when it came to money. She hesitated for only a second, waiting for him to clearly take her decision out of her hands. He did no such thing, and waited for her to go to Raven.

Ugly Beast watched her as she approached Raven's table. The woman was sitting on her own, and he saw the faint smile on Abriana's lips.

She was a mafia woman.

Soft.

Gentle.

Poised.

No, she wasn't a beauty, at least not at first glance. It took a guy a couple of minutes to see the kind of beauty she held.

"You sure that shit should be allowed?" Smokey asked, coming to stand beside him.

"I don't know, but it beats her staying in her room. With Raven around her, she'll know how to take care of herself." He needed her to be able to take care of herself. She wasn't back home. He didn't want men guarding her at every turn.

One of the boys placed two beers on the table, and he sat down, taking some whiskey for himself to watch her.

"You don't want to head back into the fun?"

"Nah, I've got other things I could do right now."

One of the strippers approached Raven's table.

Abriana covered her face, laughing as Raven began to put bills in the woman's pants. Her tits were all out, and clearly from Raven's demands, she held her arms out, and began to shake them.

Then, for the entire club to see, Raven touched them.

"Those babies are real," she said.

All three women were laughing. He waited as Raven and the stripper pointed for Abriana to touch.

Sipping at his whiskey, he saw her hand tremble as she reached out, touching the other woman's tit. His dick was back to fucking attention, watching her. She didn't seem frightened.

The family she came from, half of the women

looked terrified of even breathing, let alone speaking, or touching.

He didn't get the mafia. As far as he was concerned, women were to be enjoyed, but keeping them under lock and key, never really experiencing the world, well, that shit just didn't sit well with him.

Running his fingers through his hair, he caught the blonde smiling over at him. Her gaze wandered down his body, and she nibbled her lip, very clear what she wanted from him.

He was used to his body being admired. Even though his face was scarred as shit, he had a great body and kept himself in good shape. He worked out to stay on top. Protecting the club was his main priority, and he took that shit seriously.

Downing his beer, he returned his attention to Abriana.

She stuck out at the club, but none of the boys were laughing at her. Raven had pulled her from her seat, and with the help of the stripper, they were all dancing.

He smiled, seeing her laugh. It was when she laughed, that it really showed her beauty. Her eyes sparkled, and her face just drew you in.

The blonde came to his table, cutting off his view of his wife. She didn't wait for an invitation as she sat down in his lap.

"Is that your wife?" she asked.

"She is none of your business."

"The girls have been telling me how long your cock is. How your wife is a virgin and couldn't take a man like you."

He stared at her. "And you think you can."

"I can take anything." She leaned in close, her lips near his ear as her hand moved to his dick. "I love it in my mouth, my pussy, and my ass. No part of me would ever be off limits to you."

Ugly Beast smiled.

Wrapping his fingers around her neck, he jerked her back. "If you think I'd be interested in your used-up self, try again. Next time you want a free ride to your shit, wipe your nose of the debris." He shoved her off him. "Get out of my sight."

He'd not become the club's Sergeant at Arms for nothing. He had lost his pretty-boy looks for this club, and he'd head into battle at any opportunity. This club was his family, his life, and he fucking loved it. Every single ugly piece of shit that wore the badge.

Abriana didn't stay down for too long before making her excuses to head on upstairs.

Raven didn't leave him waiting long either to head over to his chair.

"So, I like your wife. You should keep her around."

"I intend to."

"Good." Raven left again, and he smiled. Finishing off his beer, it was his time to head on up.

"You really leaving now?" Smokey asked with a woman on his dick as he moved to pass.

"It has been a long couple of days."

"And you've got a nice piece of ass to keep you warm. Got it."

Ugly Beast didn't see the point in arguing. Smokey could do and say what he wanted. Leaving the main clubroom where all the fucking and partying was going on, he went straight for his bedroom.

He hesitated outside, wondering if he should give her more time to go to sleep.

Seeing as it was his fucking room and she was his wife, Abriana still needed to learn her place.

Entering the room, he saw her passed out on the

bed. The jeans were gone, and he spotted them neatly folded on his chair. She wore a shirt, which covered her ass and went to mid-thigh.

She looked tempting.

Closing the door quietly, he looked for any signs that she was awake.

He didn't get any.

She was completely out of it. Stripping out of his clothes, he put his leather cut up on the door where the knob stuck out for him to do so.

Climbing onto the bed, he was so quiet as he did it. She didn't even wake up. She had to be sleeping deeply.

Putting a hand on her hip, he drew her back against him, and yet, she didn't wake up either. He closed his eyes, feeling her softness against him, and loving her being there. She smelled amazing, and even as his dick hardened, he ignored it.

All he wanted to do was sleep.

****

"This is where you live?" Abriana asked, climbing off Ugly Beast's bike. None of the club seemed to own a car.

Her thighs were sore from the riding yesterday and now today.

Looking at the house, she saw it was modest. The neighborhood looked nice, and she wondered how they felt about having a biker for a neighbor.

"Yes, it's not a mansion like your folks', but it's good. The people know not to mess with shit while they're here. You'll be safe."

"You don't have any guards in place?" she asked.

"None. I told you, Abriana, you're not going to be expected to play a role. Not the one you've been playing." He walked up the steps.

There was a small lawn out front, and it looked like it had been mowed recently.

She liked his house, more than liked it. Whenever she had to go out shopping and their driver took them down long country roads, and she saw estates like this, she always wished she was one of the kids out having fun. They always seemed to be having fun, and she wasn't used to that kind of feeling.

Ugly Beast stepped over the threshold, and she fell in love with the place. It wasn't like her parents' house in the terms of size, but it looked … homey.

He held her case and closed the door behind her. "A quick tour. Living room, dining room, kitchen, storage room, out back is the garden. It's not much, but I've got a pool. It's small and not like one of those sports ones."

"Okay."

"Follow me."

They walked upstairs to three bedrooms and a bathroom.

"I never shared a bathroom back at home."

"Yeah, well, you'll be sharing this one with me. Not negotiable. I didn't have time to decorate your room, but we can handle that shit later on. I've got to head back to the clubhouse. You think you can handle being here for a couple of hours on your own?"

"Yes." She had never been left on her own before, but she wasn't going to tell him that.

"Great. Do what you want with the place, apart from burn it down."

With that, he turned on his heel and left her. She flinched as he slammed the door shut behind him.

She was alone inside his home.

She moved to the bag he'd dropped on the bed. Opening it up, she set to work putting her clothes away.

She hadn't taken a whole lot, but she didn't know what he'd be able to take as he rode his bike, and well, she was used to driving in a car. Not that she'd ever driven herself. She wasn't allowed to have a license. Anything she ever needed would either be catered to by a driver, or her husband would deal with it.

When she glanced around the room, it was small, but she liked it. She left the room and moved across the hall to the other spare bedroom. There was no bed in this one. In fact, the room was empty.

She left the door and checked out the bathroom. There was a shower and a bath, along with a toilet and a sink.

The space was so small in comparison to what she was used to, but she didn't mind it. She adored the room as it was how she imagined her own home like this.

She moved on to Ugly Beast's room.

She hesitated outside of his door, but she wanted to get an insight to the man she'd married. Pushing the door open, she waited for him to come breathing down her neck, hurting her.

So far, he'd proven to be nothing like her father. It was only in recent years that she had been on the end of his fist though, and she'd gotten to see a whole other side to him.

Ugly Beast's room was exactly like her own. The bed was made, and not a wrinkle in sight. He had three chests of drawers along each wall, and a closet door was open.

She left his room, not wanting to invade his privacy. She knew what it was like to have men randomly come in and trash her bedroom.

Her father had often made his men do searches of the house, which included trashing the place. Some of the maids had tried to rat on them, and she'd never seen them again.

She walked downstairs and went straight to the garden. Stepping out onto the back porch, she saw a small barbeque to her left, and across the garden, his pool.

It looked amazing.

She inhaled deeply, feeling that sense of freedom that had never been hers.

Even to inhale air, someone had been watching, assessing, reporting back to her father as if she was some kind of child.

Hands clenched at her side, she took a step into the garden, then another. She walked toward the pool in the back. A few leaves had fallen from the surrounding trees.

She sat down at the edge of the pool, putting her hand into the water as she felt the cool liquid as she ran her fingers up down.

Kicking off her sneakers, she removed her jeans and folded them up, placing them beside her. She lowered her feet into the water, and watched. There was nowhere for her to be. No fear of someone spotting her.

She was alone and free. Smiling, she kicked her feet out, and then lowered them back in.

Being married to Ugly Beast wouldn't be so bad.

"Here you are."

She jumped and quickly stood when she caught sight of Raven.

"Wow, chick, don't look so panicked. I was knocking on the door for a lifetime."

"Don't you have a meeting with the club?" she asked. Her hands were shaking and she was trying to calm down her nerves, but nothing was happening.

"That shit ended a short time ago. Don't look at me like I'm going to shoot you. I wanted to hang out.

Ugly Beast has some errands to run. I'm bored, and I figured you'd enjoy my lovely company."

"I would."

"Go back to putting your feet in the water. I'll join you."

Right there in front of her, without even trying to be modest, Raven shoved down her jeans, showing off her smooth legs and the thong that sat between her ass cheeks.

Abriana averted her gaze and slowly sat back down on the edge of the pool. She gripped the ledge tightly, trying to find her composure once more but failing. She hated being this weak and allowing people to see it.

Raven let out a sigh, putting her feet into the water. "This reminds me of a time at the beach. We were all on a club run, and we needed to make a stop for the night at the beach. It was so fucking busy during the day. Not a drop of sand could be seen because of all the bodies. Anyway, I rolled up my jeans, removed my boots and socks, and ah, the pleasure."

"I've never been to the beach."

"Really?"

"Yes, it's the truth. My family didn't see a point in a vacation. I was used to staying at home."

"Is it true you were homeschooled?"

"Yes." She nibbled her lip. "Our purity was important to our fathers."

"I hate fuckers like that. It's just a piece of flesh." Raven shook her head. "I think every woman should have a voice in how their first time should go."

"Are you a virgin?"

Raven burst out laughing. "Me? Hell, no. I lost mine back when I was sixteen, in the back of a truck."

"How old are you now?"

"Twenty-five. You?"

"I'm nineteen."

"Holy shit. I had no idea you were so young."

"Does my age bother you?"

"Nah, it just makes me sad that for a teenage girl, you don't know how to have fun. When's your birthday?"

She gave her the date.

"Six months from now." She watched as Raven flicked her legs back and forth. "You know, I think I should make it my personal mission to help you have a normal teenage experience."

"Normal?"

"Yes. Staying out late. Going to the movies. Getting drunk. We should totally have a girls' night."

"I don't think that would be allowed."

"Has Ugly Beast told you that you can't do something?"

"No."

"Tell you what, let me handle this." Raven pulled out her cell phone.

Abriana looked over the woman's shoulder as she tapped Ugly Beast's name on the screen.

"Hey, big guy. You're going to have to stay at the clubhouse. I'm going to show your wife how to have a good time, you cradle-snatcher you."

She didn't hear what Ugly Beast had to say, and with Raven's smile, she didn't know if it was good or bad. With the cackle she unleashed, she was going to say bad.

"Yeah, yeah, you'll thank me some day." Raven hung up. "Come on, it's time for us to party."

Abriana was pulled into the house. She had snatched up her jeans before she left them outside.

Raven grabbed a leaflet off the fridge. "What do

you like on pizza?"

"I don't know."

The other woman looked at her. "You're going to tell me you didn't have pizza?"

"Our cook didn't agree to make pizza. She hated the street food."

"Your cook needs to have my boot rammed up her ass. Don't cook fucking pizza. Pieces of shit. Hey, yeah, I'm going to need one of every single pizza you make. To deliver and put this on Ugly Beast's tab. He knows." Raven hung up. "So, I'll be back in a few. I don't live that far from here, and I've got a few things I want to play with. Have a quick shower, and I'll meet you back here."

Abriana watched the other woman leave, and she didn't have a clue what to do. Glancing around the room, she stared down at herself. She still wasn't wearing the jeans.

Would it be so wrong to have one day where she wasn't afraid of her own shadow or what she was doing?

If Ugly Beast had a problem with her having fun, he'd tell her, right? She didn't have to worry about being with Raven. She was a club member, and she wasn't doing anything wrong.

She walked upstairs to the shared bathroom. Stripping out of her clothes, she stepped beneath the hot water and breathed out a sigh.

This, she could handle.

It was easy.

Spending time with another woman.

Not that she had much in the way of experience. The women back home didn't like her. They only ever had time for the women who they felt were going places because of their looks. Being pretty in their world meant a rich husband, or someone of prestige.

Shaking her head, she pushed those memories aside and washed her hair.

She finished washing her body and hair, and climbing out of the shower, she went to her bedroom, wrapping her hair up in a second towel.

"I'm back," Raven said.

Abriana didn't have time to change, so she quickly pulled on a robe and headed out to see her new friend.

Raven was carrying a large case, and three bags.

"I've got everything we need for a party. Get your ass down here, baby."

She was gone as the doorbell rang.

Abriana was still walking down the steps when a guy entered, carrying a huge pile of pizzas.

"Enjoy, ladies."

"There is so much food here," she said.

"Don't care. Cold pizza is the bomb. Believe me, Ugly Beast will thank me for it. I promise you." She opened up one of the cardboard boxes and took out a slice. "Fuck, that is good. Have a slice."

Abriana stepped forward and picked up a slice of pizza. She took a bite. It had pepperoni on it.

"See, this is as close to a food orgasm as a woman can get." Raven finished a slice before Abriana had even gotten to a second.

"I bought some clothes. Now, you're bigger than me, and I yoyo with my weight like crazy." Raven went to her bag. "We need to give you a whole new look. The school mom is working for you, and it's sexy as hell, but you need to have a whole other look if you want to fit into the club."

Within seconds the entire living room was covered in clothes.

"I may have a weakness for clothes shopping."

Raven laughed.

The curtains were closed, and Raven held up a pair of jeans.

"I wear jeans."

"I know, but these ones will do wonders for that figure. Come on. We've got a lot to get through. Take your robe off. Come on. Come on."

Removing her robe, she stood before Raven completely naked.

"Piece of shit! Did Ugly Beast do that to you?"

Abriana looked down at the bruises and shook her head. "No. Of course not."

"Who the fuck thought they could put their hands on you?"

"It's nothing."

"Did I fucking ask if it was nothing? I want to know who did this shit to you." Raven put her fingers on the bruised flesh.

"I made my dad angry."

"Why?"

"I'm ugly and useless and he can't use me, so he hurt me." She stared at Raven. "It's not hurting much anymore."

"If I ever see this piece of shit, I'm going to hurt him."

"You can't. He's a Capo, and to hurt him in any way will incite a war. I don't want to cause trouble."

"Oh, honey, you won't be the one causing trouble. It'll be me." Raven winked at her. "Try on the jeans."

Abriana took the jeans from her, and sure enough, they fit her body like a second skin. Raven cheered and let out a squeal. "Those whores will not know what hit them when I take you back to the clubhouse."

"I don't think I should be going back to the

clubhouse. It's not my place."

"Because you're Ugly Beast's woman? Sweetie, you have a right to be there more than those bitches. Now, with all good jeans, we need a sexy as fuck shirt. Those tits need something to hold them and ah-ah. I've got just the thing." She held up a really tight-looking white shirt, and Abriana shook her head. "Girl, trust me."

So, for the next couple of hours, Abriana ate pizza and changed into all different outfits that Raven loved. She didn't like most of them, but she didn't say anything to her new friend. She didn't even know if she could call the other woman a friend.

All of her life she'd been on her own, and she knew she couldn't trust anyone, not with her family's secrets or with her life. In her world, you trusted no one, not even your fellow women.

Chapter Six

Ugly Beast was nursing a bad fucking headache. It was so bad he held a bag of peas to his head. After doing the meetup last night with Ortiz, he'd come back to the clubhouse and just drunk himself into oblivion. He had no choice but to drink until he passed out. Thinking about his wife and Raven together was enough to make any man's dick shrivel up. Not Abriana, of course. Raven, though, that girl was a law unto herself. Some of the guys didn't even know how she became a member of the club in the first place. They only knew they initiated her into the club.

He knew.

His memory wasn't so short.

Raven was a fucking fighter and loyal to the club. She had earned her patch long and hard, taking shit from the brothers at every single turn when she was a prospect.

"There a reason you defrosting my peas?" Smokey asked.

Ugly Beast pulled a few dollars out of his jeans. "Now they're my peas."

Smokey laughed. "I got a call last night from one of our guys."

He stared at his president, waiting.

"They said Garofalo has eyes on the club. They don't know who or what, but they're watching."

"You think it's Abriana?" Ugly Beast asked.

"I don't know who it is, but I want you to get every single person here checked. I want to know who they are, where they came from."

The club was known for their parties, and like all parties, there were always a few hangers-on. It wouldn't take him long to identify the newbies and get all the intel on them.

"It can't be your wife, Ugly," Smokey said.

"Why not? She's new here."

"Exactly, I don't see her around the club, and if Raven had any reason to doubt her, she'd be all over her. We can count on Raven to sniff out the pieces of shit."

He couldn't argue with the man, but still, if Garofalo was to try to get information on them, why not use his wife? She was Vigo's daughter, and like he knew, they were close fucking buddies.

As if mentioning Raven had conjured her out of thin air, she walked through the clubhouse door. She looked like fucking fire and ice. He saw she was looking for someone. Whoever it was, he felt sorry for them. She was famous for kicking ass, and the look on her face told him she was out to start a fire.

Her gaze locked on his, and now he wished he'd stayed in his fucking room. She stormed up to him, and several of the guys looked really fucking happy about that.

"You going to kill her fucking father?" Raven asked, slamming her hands on the table.

"You spend one night with her and already you want to kill someone?" Smokey asked.

The president should have kept his mouth shut.

"You saw the bruises on her?"

"No."

"Then you don't get a say. President or not, she's one of ours, and if you saw them, you'd be pissed."

"I already gave the fucker a warning," Ugly Beast said. This conversation was not helping his headache in any way. Raven was only reminding him of how much he wanted to kill her father.

"Really? A warning. Wow, let's everyone call the cops here. He got a fucking warning."

"Raven, enough," he said.

"You know what, if that had been me, he wouldn't have his dick. Just saying."

Smokey grabbed her arm, and right in front of the brothers, he dragged her into his office. Ugly Beast didn't want to follow. His day was already going to shit, and right now, he didn't want to have to deal with a screaming bitch.

Still, he got up out of his seat and made his way over to Smokey's office.

"Get the fuck off me," Raven said.

Smokey tossed her onto the nearest sofa; one that probably had so much bodily fluid Ugly Beast opted to stand.

"You want to go screaming your mouth off about the unfairness of shit, you can leave my club."

"Abriana is club property," Raven argued right back.

"She's *my* property," Ugly Beast said. "She's my wife."

"You will keep your fucking mouth shut because that is what we need."

"I don't like this."

"Boo-fucking-hoo. I don't give a shit what you like or don't like, Raven. This is club business. Abriana is club business. Her family has connections. She's our tie to them, and through them we deal with business."

Raven stared from one man to the other. "Shit's going down?"

Smokey laughed. "When is shit not going down?"

"This is different. I thought it was strange when you told us Ugly here was getting married. Abriana, she's a pawn."

"For now. We know Vigo's going to reach out to her."

"We want her loyal to the club," Ugly Beast said.

"We need to know what they're planning and when."

"What you're going to ask her to do is fucking dangerous."

"No different from what we've all faced ourselves," Smokey said. "Don't get comfortable with her. She may be a bad seed, and you know how we deal with them."

Raven sat forward, elbows on her knees. "Your couch stinks. I don't like this."

"You're not the boss."

"This is not what the club is aware of."

"We don't want the club to treat Abriana any differently," Smokey said.

"Vigo will make his move soon enough, and then we'll know how to deal with her. Once that happens, we'll handle her."

Ugly Beast clenched his hands into fists, watching the play of emotions across Raven's face.

"I don't like it."

"Stay out of the fucking way," Smokey said.

"Abriana is just a girl."

"She's a married woman," Ugly Beast said.

Raven shook her head. "You're wrong about her."

"Don't let your crush get in the way of logic."

Raven stood up, getting into Smokey's face. "Who the fuck—"

She was cut off as Smokey grabbed her throat and pressed her to the floor. "I'm your fucking president. Don't you ever talk to me like that again. I can toss you out of this club so fast you wouldn't even know what hit you. Show some fucking respect. Abriana is not club property. She belongs to Ugly Beast, and until I say otherwise, she's an outsider. By all means, be nice to her, but don't for a second think she's your friend. She's still our enemy." He squeezed her throat tight, and Ugly Beast waited.

Raven submitted.

Once Smokey let go of her throat, Raven coughed, drawing air back into her lungs.

"We won't be having this conversation again."

Raven nodded.

"I'll give you a few minutes to compose yourself, and then leave." Smokey was out of the door in the next second, gone.

Ugly Beast leaned against the desk, watching Raven.

"You know he puts the club first before anything else."

"What about you?"

"The club will always come first. Wife or not. Don't meddle with this."

"You don't want me to be around her."

"You can. I don't want her to think we're watching her or waiting. You play this game Smokey's way. He's never steered us wrong before."

"Abriana is not like some club-whore, only after dick. She has … feelings."

He chuckled. "I've no doubt."

Raven got to her feet. There were red marks around her neck, and he watched as she pulled down her hair and styled it in such a way it covered the marks, or at least, didn't show them off.

"Why are you so protective of her?" Ugly Beast asked.

"She's innocent. She's been thrown into this world, and she doesn't have a clue what she's doing."

"You handled it."

"I wanted this life, Ugly. Just like you did. You and I, we know what the world wants from us. Abriana's too afraid to have any kind of fun. She's always looking over her shoulder, and if you try and get close to her, she flinches. She's used to being hurt. I got a problem when big, tough men think they can hurt young women. You know that."

When they'd been on runs together, stopping off in bars, witnessing men pawing at women, Raven was always in the thick of it. He knew there was a story there in her life, but again, he didn't ask.

The Hell's Bastards were a club, not a place to share all your feelings. He wasn't interested in anything other than loyalty.

"Time will tell with my wife. Until then, be careful." He stretched up, feeling his body ache in places he didn't even know fucking existed.

"I'm taking her out tonight," Raven said.

"That will be interesting."

"I'm going to dress her up to look real nice. You want to see her? She's a big woman, but those curves in the right outfit are bangin'."

He laughed. "Nah, thanks. Got shit I need to do."

"You're just going to leave her at your house?" Raven asked.

Ugly Beast stood at the door of his president's office and looked over at the woman. Rubbing at his eyes, he wanted nothing more than to go back to bed. As it was, he had to go and check out the porn shots. It was his turn to go and visit the sex den.

"What else do you want me to do? I married her. Presented the bloodstained sheets. I don't love her, Raven. Don't mistake me for actually giving a fuck because the truth is, I don't. She's a means to an end." He saw the anger on Raven's face and smiled. "This is why men are different. You care too much, and one day, that kind of caring, it's going to get you killed. You need to learn when to back the fuck off and to allow people to breathe."

"You could kill her if Smokey asked you to?" Raven asked.

He smiled. "Without a second's hesitation." He winked at her. "You're tough, Raven. One hell of a fighter, but you're still weak, and you're still just a woman."

Closing the door, he took off out of the clubhouse, going for his bike. His nice, warm, cozy bed would have to wait.

Hunter was heading in with a new woman on his back. Ugly Beast waited. The new woman gave him a look, and he saw the revulsion in her eyes. There were times when he saw the looks women gave him, and still made them suck his cock, or fuck him. The point of a club-whore was she serviced the club.

The bitches needed to learn to keep their emotions in check.

"It doesn't take you long to move on," Ugly Beast said.

"Yeah, well, I like variety, and I don't like club pussy that is dripping with other boys' cum. What you doing?"

"Got to go head to the shack. A couple of girls are causing some trouble, and Smokey wants one of us to be there to keep them in check and do the scenes."

Hunter laughed. "Don't forget to take the dope they want. You dangle that shit in front of them, and they will do just about anything for a high."

Ugly Beast disagreed. "I've found a bit of pain can help them make the decision. Have fun."

"Where's the wife?" Hunter asked.

"At home. Leave her alone."

"You know Raven's going to bring her around

the club, right?"

"Until that happens, I'm not going to give a fuck." He straddled his bike, turning over the ignition and stopping all conversation. He wasn't interested in talking about his wife or Raven.

They were causing more trouble than they were worth, and he had other things to deal with.

Pulling out of the parking lot, he headed toward the shack, which was an hour's drive from the clubhouse. He didn't mind being on the open road. It was when he was forced to stay for weeks on end in the clubhouse that he started to go stir crazy.

He needed the open road, and to stay the fuck out of everyone's way. Sticking around the clubhouse for too long, he was always tempted to kill someone. The open road provided him an outlet, helping him get rid of any steam that had built up inside him.

Right now, his wife was causing him a lot of fucking trouble.

He didn't want Abriana.

She was there regardless of if he wanted her or not, but that didn't stop Smokey from making his move. His president wanted to start a war with Garofalo over their territory, but he also wanted some of the Capos onboard, and to extend his power as well. Their rivals were neck-deep in with the cartels, and one day, there was going to be a war. Smokey wanted to secure their place, and to make sure the cartels couldn't take them over.

The ride didn't last him nearly as long as he wanted to clear his head.

Parking his bike, he climbed off, seeing several cars already in place. Entering the shack, he heard the moans the moment he entered. They had six blocks within the warehouse. The main center was where the cameras were set in place.

Bill, one of the cameramen, nodded at him, fist bumping as he passed. He glanced into the scene Bill was filming to see a man and woman fucking. The guy was pounding the girl's pussy, and the camera was right up close to her.

Ugly Beast moved along each scene until he found the waiting couch. When he dropped down, Tiffany, one of the girls who liked to scene but also service the boys, was there. She sat beside him, her fingers running up and down his jacket.

"Would you like me to take care of your little problem, Ugly?" she asked.

"No. Go and do what you do best. When are the troublemakers due?"

"Three."

"Okay. When they arrive, I want a word with them."

"Will do, Ugly."

He watched Tiffany go with a shake of his head. Up until he got married, women often avoided him. Now they were all fucking over him. Word had certainly spread, and right now, he couldn't give two fucks about the kind of pussy that was on offer, especially with the one he had at home.

Running a hand down his face to try to clear the fog from his brain, it was no good. He really needed to get his shit together.

****

Abriana sat perfectly still as Raven applied her lipstick.

For the past hour, she had been forced to change into five different outfits before Raven settled on a black number that molded to her breasts and ass. Then she was forced to try to not scream as her hair was curled into ringlets. Raven didn't take kindly to random squeals as the hot hair iron pressed to her head.

If this was the kind of pain for beauty, Abriana would stick to only doing it for special occasions.

Now, she had to sit perfectly still. If she even breathed too hard, Raven grabbed her face and kept her into position. Raven was the boss and was clearly used to getting what she wanted.

Abriana, well, she was used to being bossed around.

Fortunately, no one had hit her yet, so she was considering that a plus. No pain and she was a happy girl.

"Where are we going tonight? The clubhouse?"

"Nah, there's a bar near the town that the boys visit often. They're not going to be there, so I figured we could have some fun with the locals. Dance, that kind of thing."

"I don't think I should." She wasn't allowed to dance with men.

"Abriana, he's not here, and the last time I heard, he was at the shack."

"The shack?"

Raven cursed. "Let's just say it's a place that women are willing to fuck anything with a dick. You're not a mafia princess anymore. You're club, and we're giving you some experiences your teenage ass should be enjoying."

"If my father ever heard you say stuff like that, he'd have made an example out of you."

"You speak to your father yet?"

"No. I've not called them, and I don't know the number, why?"

"Just curious."

"I hope I never have to speak to them."

"Why?"

"I … he's not a very nice guy."

"That I can tell with the bruises. You didn't think to hit back?"

"Trying to defend yourself only makes it worse. If I take it, he gives up and the pain goes away."

Raven paused, staring at her.

"What?" she asked.

"Nothing. We're two completely different women."

"You would have kept on fighting."

"When I'm banged-up and bruised, you should be more worried about the other guy."

"What about the bruises around your neck?"

Raven's hand went to them.

Abriana wasn't going to point them out, but seeing as Raven was prying and judging, she didn't see a problem not to.

"Sometimes I don't know when to shut my mouth," Raven said.

"Did you hurt the other guy as well?"

"Let's drop this."

She had other questions, but seeing as Raven was the only person to come and visit her and to even talk to her, she was more than happy with the company and didn't want to scare her off.

"Do you have a bike? Is that how we're riding?"

Raven laughed. "I do have a bike, but no, there's no way I'd let you ride my bike wearing a dress like that. I'm not that mean. I'm done, and you're finished." Raven put her makeup down and held up a mirror.

Abriana stared at her reflection, a little taken aback. Raven had given her sexy eyes, enhancing their brown but not making them look mousy. Her hair was coiled around her face, and she looked pretty.

"You have a gift." It was nice to sit with someone

and not have them complain all the time about how ugly she was.

"They've done a real number on you, haven't they?"

She didn't know what she was talking about.

Raven got up, stretched her body, and Abriana quickly averted her gaze as the other woman stripped down.

Covering her eyes, she tried to think of something to say.

"You've got to get used to seeing a bit of flesh. The men at the clubhouse, they don't exactly hide their natures," Raven said.

Lowering her hand, she saw Raven had changed into a small shirt that showed off her cleavage and stomach. The skirt also emphasized the length of her legs with the shortness of it. Some knee-high boots and Raven looked on fire. Her long hair she left down, and she went with minimal makeup.

"You got to learn to own who you are, Abriana. Confidence is always the key." Raven winked at her.

"Come on, let's go."

"You're sure … Ugly Beast won't mind me going out?"

"You don't like saying his name, do you?" Raven asked.

She followed Raven down the stairs and they both went for the door. "No."

"Why not?"

"It doesn't suit him."

Raven's brow rose.

"I know his scars are a little…"

"Ugly."

"Scary," Abriana said. "But I don't think he's ugly. I don't think he's a beast either. He's … different.

Intense. Scary, but not, ugly."

Raven smiled. "He's not just called Ugly Beast because of the way he looks."

Abriana tilted her head to the side, feeling like she was missing the joke.

"Why is he called that?"

"You're going to have to ask him yourself. There's only so much shit I'm willing to cause. Come on, I promise we're good to go. I don't see him here ordering us not to go out."

She couldn't argue with that, so she left the house. Raven locked the door, pocketing the keys.

Abriana's nerves kicked in as she climbed into the car.

No one was around. There were no guards tailing them. Raven was driving them, and as she pulled her seatbelt on, she couldn't help but make the comparisons. Her old life was very much over.

She hadn't seen Ugly Beast since he'd brought her to his home, and he'd not even called. The only person she saw was the neighbor, who was a nice lady, but she didn't catch her name, and Raven.

That was it.

No one else.

Raven turned the radio on to some rock music that was playing. She pressed her foot to the gas.

"You drive?"

"No. I'm not allowed."

"Then we totally have got to do that as well."

"Driving?"

"Yes. It's a rite of fucking passage." Raven laughed. "Girl, we are going to have so much fun with you."

"Don't do anything that will get me in trouble."

"With the club or your family?"

"Both?"

Raven laughed. "You got to learn to live dangerously. We only have one life, and you're wasting yours." Suddenly, Raven pulled the car to a stop. "We're totally changing places."

"What? Now? No. Please, I don't want to." She held onto her seatbelt for protection.

Raven jumped out of the car, but left the motor running.

Abriana's door opened.

"Come on. You've got nothing to fear. I'll teach you."

"How many students have you taught before?"

"None. I'm a damn good driver. Come on. I'll beat your ass if you don't get out of the car."

"You're lying."

"I'm not lying. Five … four … three … two…"

"Fine, fine. I'll do it." She unbuckled her seatbelt, climbing out of the car.

"Go ahead, girl, give me the evil eye. I don't give a flying fuck."

Her heart pounded, and her hands shook as she climbed behind the wheel. Closing the door, she buckled up her seatbelt.

"This beauty is not an automatic. It's a manual. The ignition is already on. You need to press down on the pedal nearest me, and slide this bad boy into first gear."

Abriana followed the instruction and screamed as the car jerked forward.

Raven laughed. "You shouldn't take your foot off the clutch. It's fine. We'll start again."

She hated driving. Jerking the car forward every few feet, only to stall or to panic. Raven was laughing as if it was the best comedy she'd seen while Abriana's cheeks were on fire.

"Okay, okay, you so need a lot more practice. We better change places before the bar closes and we don't get to have any fun."

She was more than happy with that. Her hands were still shaking as she climbed out of the car.

"You did good, Abriana."

She nodded but knew she was a failure. Doing good at something meant she succeeded. Tonight was a failure, and no one liked that in someone.

Raven kept on talking, and Abriana listened with half an ear. She wasn't interested in anything the other woman had to say. The small driving lesson had opened up a whole load of insecurity that she wasn't ready to deal with.

Her father had liked to tell her often how much of a failure she was and how she wasn't doing something right. Nothing she ever did was good enough. She couldn't drive a car or be a good wife.

If she was a wife Ugly Beast wanted, he would have come home long before now. She was trapped again.

Only this time, she didn't know what to expect. Raven was nice, but again, could she trust the other woman? Were they going to kill her? Women were disposable in her world. When one died, another took their place.

She tried to breathe easier, but it was next to impossible. Raven didn't notice her panic attack or mini-meltdown. Abriana had learned the value of suffering in silence.

"We're here."

Stepping out of the car onto solid ground made her life a whole lot easier.

Several cars were parked outside of the bar. She

didn't get a clear view of the sign as most of the words were dull. Only an "e" and "a" were visible, and it was dark.

Raven pushed her arm through hers, and together they walked into the bar.

The moment they did, several male gazes landed on them, and Abriana wanted to run. It would be a lot easier to do.

"Come on, we'll start by having a drink."

"I'm not old enough," Abriana said.

Raven snorted. "Please, you're with me. You're old enough."

They walked toward the bar. Raven slammed her hand on the bar. "Boss boy, how is life treating you?"

The large, heavily inked man behind the bar shook his head.

"You know I don't like that, Raven."

"Come on, Ryan, you want me to call you that instead?"

"What can I get you?"

"Two beers."

Ryan nodded. "Any of your boys going to be here later?"

"Only if I start causing trouble."

"So can I expect some trouble?" Ryan asked, putting two bottles in front of Raven. She handed him some bills.

"Only if a couple of guys don't keep their hands to themselves. You know how I work."

"Yeah, dressed like that, I better get my gun ready."

Raven laughed. "Nice talking to you."

"Does he really have a gun?" Abriana asked.

"Every good barman has a gun. Shit always kicks off. Especially around pussy and dicks."

They found a small table near the dance floor.

Abriana saw several men and women wrapped around each other. This was part of her fantasy. To have a husband that would take her on dates to bars like this. Who wasn't afraid to hug her all night long if he wanted to.

"You got that dreamy look in your eye. Don't be fooled. Half of these people are not couples and are stepping out on their wives or husbands."

"They are not?"

Raven laughed. "They totally are."

"Prove it."

"Okay."

Raven looked into the crowd. "There. The guy with the hat. His hands are on her ass."

"So?"

"He's got a wedding band on. Check out the woman's hands. No ring. Cheating bastard."

Abriana looked closely, and sure enough, there was no ring.

"Fuck off, dickface."

She turned to Raven and saw two men were at their table.

"She speak for you as well, sweetheart?" the man asked.

"Yes," she said, looking to Raven.

"See, your dicks are not wanted today. Get the fuck out of our faces." The two slinked off, and Raven shook her head. "Men, they really need to know we don't think they're fucking gifts."

"You don't want anyone?"

"I'm a Hell's Bastard, Abriana. Any guy who wants me either has to be part of the club or accept I am. Club always comes first."

It was no different than the family back home.

Whenever Garofalo called, they all went running. They were loyal to the outfit, not to anyone else.

She sipped at the beer, not really liking the taste but also not wanting Raven to be upset because of it.

Raven finished her beer. "I want to dance."

Abriana was jerked to her feet and onto the dance floor with Raven. She didn't have time to pull away as the number changed to something upbeat.

"Now we're talking." Raven let out a whoop, threw her arms in the air, and began to thrust her hips from side to side in some kind of sexy number. "Dance, Abriana."

"I can't dance."

"It's really easy. Let the music show you." Raven grabbed her hips. "Stop being so tense. We're here to have fun. You've got to be willing to relax. Only then will you let it happen." Raven moved behind her with her hands still on her hips. "You really are way too tense. Calm down. Close your eyes, and if it makes you feel better, imagine I'm your dream man at your back. That's it. Relax. Now, we're going to take it slow."

Following Raven's lead, she swung her hips from side to side. At first, she was way too tense even as she tried to relax. Nothing worked. She was in a bar, with men, drinking beer, and that was so not allowed in her world.

Raven didn't give up.

It took four songs, another beer, which she only took a couple of sips from, for her to finally relax.

With that, she let go.

Her body felt good, the buzz from the alcohol helping her to finally dance with freedom.

She even laughed and giggled, and Raven didn't even have to guide her. She let the music and happiness guide her.

Chapter Seven

"Oh, yeah, fuck my pussy. I need it. Please, Kinky, give it to me."

Ugly Beast made his shot and sank another black ball into the net. It had been a day of listening and watching women take cock like a pro. Only, he had also seen the reality, and watching a woman lube up because she wasn't aroused, or having to take a break because the pounding was hurting her pussy, and yeah, he wasn't in the mood to be hearing women fake it.

He glanced over at Kinky and one of his women, but he didn't know if the girl really wanted to be used over the bar table, or if it was just wanting to have Kinky on her list of men she wanted to fuck.

Either way, he was bored.

"Bill told me you finally got those bitches to work," Smokey said, playing his shot.

"I pulled my gun on them. Told them to either fuck, get out, or die. We don't have time for bitch drama."

Smokey laughed. "You see, this is why you're good to have around. You don't have the patience to hear out all their bitchy complaints."

"It's one of the many reasons you keep me around, I know."

Smokey laughed. "How's the wife?"

"Don't know."

"You've not seen her?"

"Had no reason to." He shrugged. "Raven's probably there."

"You think we going to have a problem with her?"

"Only if she doesn't keep her mouth shut. We don't want Abriana aware of what we're doing. You heard anything from our informants or from Garofalo and Vigo?"

"Nothing. What I have heard is there is a possible meet up with another MC."

"Anyone we know?" Ugly Beast asked, taking his shot.

"Not that I know of. No one knows who the MC is, only that a meet is in place. When I get the details of the when, we can find out the why."

"You think he planning on wiping us out?" Ugly Beast asked.

Smokey laughed. "If he doesn't, I'd take it as a personal insult. We got to know who has our backs and who doesn't." He landed another ball and looked at him. "If your wife betrays us, connection or not, she's going to have to die."

"And?"

"I saw the way you hit Vigo. Something going on there I need to know?"

Ugly Beast burst out laughing. "You growing a pussy there?"

"I'm keeping an eye on my men. I need to know they're solid as fuck."

"I'm a rock, Prez. Make no doubt of that. Abriana betrays us, consider her dead and I'll be the one to slit her throat."

"Good man."

Ugly Beast's cell phone started to ring, and he saw it was Ryan at the bar they often frequented. He'd given him his cell number in case of any trouble. The Hell's Bastards took care of their own, and Ryan was the son of one of their members who was currently doing life for murder.

"Ryan, man, what's up?"

"Raven's here with some brunette chick. You

guys okay with that?"

"She causing any trouble?"

"Not yet but they're getting drunk, and a couple of guys are eyeing them up. I know Raven can handle herself, but I also know she can't back down from a fight. The other chick, she's club property, right?"

Ugly Beast gritted his teeth.

Raven wasn't supposed to take her out, and if they had gone out, he should have been the first to know about it.

"We'll be right there."

"I'll keep them safe until you arrive." Ryan hung up.

Ugly Beast cursed as he pocketed his cell. "Raven's about to cause trouble at Ryan's place. I'm heading over there."

"She on her own?" Smokey asked.

"Nah, she took my fucking wife along with her." He couldn't believe Abriana had gone with the crazy ass woman, but then, what did he expect? It wasn't like she had a backbone, was it? Raven probably didn't give his wife the chance to argue with her.

It pissed him off, but as he straddled his bike, he was aware of his brothers getting ready to ride with him.

Raven was one of their own, and they would protect her. It certainly wouldn't be the first time they had to go and help her out of a fight she had started. The woman didn't know when to leave well enough alone.

One day, she'd pick a fight with the wrong kind of guys and they wouldn't arrive in time to protect her.

Revving his engine, he took off into the night, heading toward the town where Ryan was.

Abriana wasn't supposed to be difficult. He shouldn't have to leave the clubhouse to go and help her ass.

With each mile he got nearer, his anger rose. He didn't want to marry the mafia girl, nor did he want anything to do with her. She had his home, and she could fucking stay there. If she wanted money, it was hers. He didn't understand what else she could possibly want.

Raven needed to learn her place as well. He didn't give a flying fuck what she thought, and if she even tried to cause this bullshit again, he was going to tear her a new one. Woman or not, she was still a club member, and she was under the same instructions as the rest of them.

He arrived at the town over an hour later. He'd broken every speeding and traffic law he knew to get here.

The bar, like most nights, was busy.

He didn't wait for his brothers. Parking his bike, he made his way inside, shoving a couple who were making out in front of his path, out of the way. Niceties were not his strong suit.

Entering the bar, he looked toward the dance floor and sure enough, Raven was there, but so was his wife.

She dressed for attention, and it pissed him off to see her like that. Short dress, hair coiled and looking like it needed to be pulled as he drove his dick inside her. Anger filled him as he caught sight of not one, two or three, but six guys near them, clearly wanting in on the action. Most of the guys were trying to get close to Raven, who wasn't giving them the time of day.

When one of the soon-to-be dead bastards moved in, touching Abriana's ass, he lost it.

Stepping up to the dance floor, he pulled out his knife, pressing it to the man's throat. "If you know what's good for you, you'll step the fucking hell back."

Abriana turned around, and when she caught

sight of him, she gasped.

"Dude, this chick belongs to you?" he asked.

"They both belong to us."

The boys who had followed him from the clubhouse were now on the dance floor. The town knew who they were and what they were capable of. Several people simply left, not wanting to deal with that shit.

Others, well, they simply stared down at their drinks, not giving the men the time of day.

"Fine. I don't want her ugly ass anyway."

He looked at his wife. At the asshole's comments, she'd flinched and looked miserable. He did no more than shove the bastard to his knees, gripping his hair hard. The man let out a scream. It was a little too feminine, but Ugly Beast wasn't about to have anyone disrespect her.

She belonged to him.

"Apologize now."

"Fuck you."

He drew his fist back and slammed it against the man's face. The man collapsed to the floor, but Ugly Beast wasn't done. Pulling him back up into a sitting position, he held him in place. "Apologize now."

The music that had been playing in the background went silent. Everyone in the bar was watching. Abriana had tears in her eyes.

"He doesn't have to," she said.

He stared at her, letting her know she better shut the fuck up before he turned his attention to her.

She pressed her lips together and held her hands in front of her, submitting to him. No one disrespected the club, and if he allowed that one insult to slide, it would come back on the club and send them to their ass.

"Apologize." He wasn't going to ask the man again. He had the blade pressed tightly against the man's neck, and after a gulp, the man finally let go and apologized.

"I'm sorry. I shouldn't have called you that."

"You were more than happy to grind against my wife's ass, but then insult her?" He shoved the asshole to the floor and spat on him. He fucking hated pieces of shit like him. Stepping up to Abriana, he cupped her face. Smokey already had a hold of Raven, and like the good little member, she hadn't put up a fight. It wouldn't do her any good anyway, and they always put the club's image first.

Slamming his lips down on Abriana's, he cupped the back of her neck, holding her in place as he claimed her in front of all to see. She belonged to him. They would respect her, and he wouldn't allow any of them to treat her differently.

She tensed in his arms.

"No one touches my property," he said.

With that, he took her hand, leading her out of the bar and straight toward his bike.

"Ugly Beast, I brought my car. I can take her home."

He stopped, released Abriana, and stepped up to the other woman. "You think for a single fucking second I'm going to let you fucking near her? You're drunk. If something happens to her, the entire Garofalo outfit comes down on the club." He looked toward Smokey, and he nodded at him.

This wasn't Smokey's fight, this was his.

If the president felt he had to interfere, he would.

"It was just some fun. You keep her locked up in that house and she's all alone."

"She's been with us a matter of days."

"And this is the first time you've seen her. We were having fun. It's not our fault assholes wanted to dance with us."

Ugly Beast stepped up to Raven and got right up in her face, staring into her eyes. "You will not take my fucking wife anywhere else, understand?"

Raven's jaw clenched. "Let me take her home."

"No." With that, he stepped back, and got on his bike. "Get on," he said, not looking at Abriana.

His wife didn't argue.

She climbed onto the back of his bike, and without another word to Raven, he took off. His brothers knew the drill. He was sure he wouldn't hear the end of tonight. This was the first time in all of his years being a Hell's Bastard that he'd made a public claim on any woman.

Abriana wasn't just any woman though. She belonged to fucking him, and he took that shit seriously. She was his to protect, not anyone else.

Her arms were wrapped tightly around his middle, and he ignored that ache inside his gut that told him he needed to be careful with her.

Abriana may have been a virgin, but she was no fucking innocent. There was no way she could be a Vigo and not know what this life entailed. She must have seen death at least once in her life.

It was the one thing they had in common. He was used to being shot at and looking death in the face every single fucking day.

The brothers rode at his back, and he cut off from them, taking Abriana home. The boys didn't follow him.

Turning off the engine, he waited for Abriana to climb off before he did the same, grabbing her arm and taking her back into her house.

The moment the door was closed, Abriana began to beg.

"Please, don't hurt me or Raven. It wasn't

supposed to make you angry. She said you had agreed."

She looked so small compared to him. Her hands were clasped together, and he saw she was shaking.

"I didn't give Raven permission."

"Oh." His wife frowned, and he shook his head.

"Raven is a law unto herself. I expect better from you. You're my wife."

"I'm sorry."

"Why did you go out tonight?" he asked, growling the words.

"I wanted to." She nibbled her lip.

"Don't fucking lie to me."

She shook her head.

"I mean it, Abriana. I'm fast losing my patience right now. I'm pissed off. Do you have any idea what those men could have done to you and to Raven?" He watched as she wrapped her arms around her waist, clearly shaken by the whole ordeal, but he wasn't done. Not even close to being done. "Some men won't take no for an answer, and some even get off on it. You were not fucking safe."

"You just want me to stay home? Not do anything?"

"I don't want you to be in danger. You can't be."

"Because you lose your connection to the outfit."

At that, Ugly Beast stared at her, not saying another word.

"You're mine to protect, but if something happens to you, there's nothing to stop an all-out war, Abriana."

"I didn't mean to make you upset," she said. "Those men didn't want me."

"They wanted you. Willing or not, I don't care. You're mine."

"You haven't even seen me in a few days."

"It doesn't mean you don't belong to me." He needed to get the fuck out of here. Raven had brought Abriana this dress, and it was driving him crazy. It showed off her tits to perfection.

After seeing a bunch of women fucking all day, he didn't need to stare at his wife, who was supposed to worship his cock, and not get any. He was rock-hard, and the cause of it was standing right in front of him.

Her hair even looked tempting, to have it down, and ready for him to grip as he fucked her hard and deep.

When he stepped toward her, Abriana had enough sense to step back. With each step he took, she did take one back until he stood right in front of her and the wall could no longer grant her any room to escape.

"What are you doing?" she asked.

"Are you still sore?"

She frowned at him in confusion.

He pressed his hand between her legs, the dress covering her from his touch. He wondered if she wore panties. The dress wasn't tight enough to show him that.

He watched as she licked her lips.

She shook her head.

"What are you doing?"

"Shut up," he said.

Staring down into her brown eyes, he stroked a finger from the pulse inside her neck, down to her chest.

Her tits were pressed together, and as he stroked between their silken valley, he heard a small gasp escape her.

"I've been giving you time to get accustomed to your new life, Abriana," he said. "You're not going back to Garofalo. Your father is never putting his hands on you again."

"What do you want from me?" she asked.

He pulled her away from the wall and found the

zipper that held the dress in place. She didn't fight him as he released the dress. When he pulled it from her shoulders, it fell in a heap on the floor.

She now stood before him in a pair of black lacy lingerie. The color hid way too much.

Placing his finger across the top of her breasts, he slowly lowered the cup and her breast popped out, the tight red nipple, calling to him to be sucked.

His dick was so incredibly hard.

"We want your loyalty, Abriana. To answer to the club and only to the club."

"I've never done anything wrong."

"We'll never ask you to do anything wrong. That is not what this is about," he said. He watched her eyes dilate. She probably didn't even know she was aroused.

With his other hand, he placed it on her trembling stomach. She was such a virgin in so many ways still.

Slowly, he began to slide down. When he was at the edge of her panties, he held still, waiting.

It was like she couldn't breathe, and he watched her, mesmerized by how innocent she was.

"I don't want you to hurt me," she said.

"I won't hurt you."

"Last time, you did," she said.

He smiled. "Last time doesn't count. You were a virgin, Abriana. You want me to stop and I'll stop. You don't, I'll keep on going and keep on touching you." He slid his hand into her pants, cupping her.

She let out a little startled gasp. He slid his finger between her slit, finding her clit.

She wasn't overly wet, but he had only just started to turn her on. With her tit on offer as well, he lowered his head, and flicked the top of one tit with his tongue. She closed her eyes, and another moan slipped past her lips.

Touching her clit, he stroked her gently at first, but he also wanted to make sure she was aroused.

Moving down, he teased her entrance, finding her getting wetter. Sliding inside her, he felt her tense, and still, she was aroused.

"If you're not ready, I'm going to give you this one chance to tell me to back away. You don't take it, I'm not going to stop."

"You're my husband."

"I'm not going to rape you, Abriana. This decision is yours. You don't want me to fuck you and show you how good it can be, I won't. But I won't take this choice from you. Make it now."

She nibbled her lip, and he waited.

"I don't want you to stop."

He wasn't entirely sure if that was the truth or not. Rather than argue with her, he began to rock his finger back and forth inside her. Pressing his thumb to her clit, he stroked her at the same time, feeling her cunt tighten all around him.

Abriana responded to him so sweetly.

Her moans and gasps were genuine. After spending a day with a bunch of fakers, he found her responses to be a real pleasure.

Pulling his hand from her pussy, he held it up so she could see her own arousal.

"You see this? This is how wet you are. Your body is showing me how much it wants me to be there, and I really want to be there."

Letting go of her body, he picked her up in his arms.

She wrapped her arms around his neck as he carried her upstairs to his bedroom. "Any time you want to go partying again, you'll come to the clubhouse. Do you like dancing?"

"I don't know."

Save him from sheltered women. There was a lot Abriana didn't know.

"Did you enjoy it tonight?"

"Yes. Raven had to teach me though. I'd never danced before tonight."

"You've never been to a bar before or a club?"

"No."

"You really are protected."

"Nice girls don't go to places like that. At least that was what I was told."

Again, save him from assholes like Vigo and Garofalo.

Kicking open his bedroom door, with the bed that was much larger than the one in her room, he lowered her down. Flicking the catch of her bra, he stripped her of her clothes.

"Lie back," he said.

She lowered herself back. She looked nervous, but he liked that she did as he wanted.

"Spread your legs."

At this, she hesitated.

"I want to see your sweet pussy, Abriana. Open your legs. You belong to me. This isn't wrong for me to see, and you want to please your husband, don't you?" He was using her very nice upbringing against her, but in the end, he intended for her to be completely hungover on the pleasure she was about to give her.

She opened her thighs.

Removing his leather jacket, he hung it on the doorknob. With the rest of his clothes, he stripped them down, and left them in a pile on the floor.

Stepping up to the bed, he skimmed his fingers across her ankle. That small touch was enough to have her jerking in his hands but she didn't even try to close her legs.

She looked exquisite to him.

Her sweet pussy was already wet. She had a light smattering of curls, and knowing no other man but him had been inside her, she was every man's wet dream. Slowly, he trailed his fingers from her ankle, up her legs, to her knees.

"Touch your pussy."

"What?"

"You heard me." In the past couple of days, he had been having to repeat himself. It was something he wasn't used to, and he didn't intend to keep letting Abriana or Raven off lightly.

She lowered her hands between her thighs, both of them covering the pussy he wanted to be balls deep inside.

Abriana wasn't a gorgeous woman. She wasn't even a beauty, but she was pretty. He liked her eyes. They were soft, kind, and held pain that he recognized. He also liked that she didn't flinch away from his touch. She wasn't afraid of him, nor did she try to close her eyes when he got close.

His scars didn't seem to bother her.

Reaching forward, he put her hands where he wanted her, and then opened her pussy.

"Keep yourself open for me."

He stared down at her swollen clit, creamy cunt, and his mouth watered for a taste. He wasn't known for sucking a woman's pussy, but Abriana wasn't just any woman. She was his wife, and he fucking wanted her.

Picking her hips up, he held her and pressed his face against her pussy. She cried out, but he didn't stop. Sucking her bud into his mouth, he used his teeth to create a bite of friction before sliding down her cunt to her entrance. Circling her hole, he felt her quiver, and unable to resist, he pressed forward, fucking her with his tongue.

The moans coming from her lips were going straight to his cock and making him ache in all the right places.

He wanted to hear her pant and to scream. To give herself to him completely. As he pulled away from her slightly, the angle gave him the perfect view of her ass, and he wanted nothing more than to tease that puckered hole with his tongue, but he held off. If Abriana proved her loyalty to the club, she would forever remain his wife.

There was no way Garofalo or Vigo could take her back. Besides, with the bloody sheets, he'd claimed her, and that made her useless to them. Unless she was a virgin, she was damaged goods.

In time, he could show Abriana everything she'd been missing. Every single touch, stroke, and caress. All the magical things that could make sex mind-blowing, and he wanted to be the one to show her. To see her come apart for him and him alone. He'd never been a possessive bastard. He was used to women moving from one bed to another.

With Abriana, she was his.

No other brother would touch her unless he gave them permission.

With that, he held her close, not wanting to let her go. She fucking belonged to him. Every single part of her was his to enjoy.

"Please," she said with a whisper.

He didn't even realize he'd been holding her in place, not touching her, not licking her, but staring at her perfect cunt.

"What is it?"

"I don't know."

"You're going to learn to tell me exactly what you want. I can't give it to you unless I know what it is."

"I want you to touch me."

He saw her face was a nice shade of red, and it made him smile.

Sliding his tongue between her folds, he began to tongue her again. "Is this what you want?"

"Yes."

The word was sweet to his ears, and he wanted her to scream it from the rooftops.

"Yes, please, yes," she said.

With each moan and scream, it drove him to lick her pussy harder, faster, wanting to hear her melt under the onslaught of pleasure from his tongue.

Not once did he stop as he brought her close to the edge.

She didn't beg him to stop either.

Lowering her to the bed, he used his fingers, pushing three inside her tight heat as he teased her with his tongue. Moving between her spread thighs, he began to lick and suck at her tits.

Her cream had wet his face even though she hadn't come yet. He didn't want her to. The last time he'd been inside her, he'd not taken the time to get her off. He'd found his release, done the deed that was required of him, and then gone to sleep.

Tonight would be different. He wouldn't be inside her without her first feeling pleasure before he found his own.

Biting on her nipple, he felt an answering response to his touch as her pussy tightened around his fingers.

She was wetter than the first time they'd been together, and it made his need all that much harder to deny. His cock was so fucking stiff.

He pulled back, removing his fingers from her and wrapping them around his cock, slicking up his cock with her juice. The tip was already leaking copious amounts of pre-cum. He had this overwhelming desire to fill her up, to watch his cum spilling inside her, flooding her for him to see as it dripped out of her.

Ugly Beast couldn't wait any longer. Holding his length, he didn't bother with the condom, wanting nothing more than her cunt wrapped around his dick.

He'd never gone bareback inside a woman. It went against everything he believed. Abriana hadn't been with anyone else. She was pure, and as he worked his cock inside her, it felt fucking glorious.

She was so incredibly wet.

With every single inch he filled her, she did grow tenser, and he began to stroke her clit, reaching between them, touching her.

He wanted her to come all over his cock before he finally pounded her the way he wanted to. He plunged the last inch within her, and she let out a gasp.

"It doesn't hurt, does it?" he asked.

She shook her head.

He already knew the answer. She was more than ready to take his cock, and he wanted to give it to her. He wanted to fuck all ideas of finding someone else right out of her. Would it be so wrong of him to have her completely devoted to his dick?

The change within Abriana's body was instant as he teased her. Gritting his teeth, he counted fucking sheep to keep himself in control as her body tightened up, and at the first hit of her orgasm, he was close to coming just from the feel of it.

Her cunt pulsed around his cock like it was trying to milk his cum right out of him. Her pussy was so greedy and hungry, and fuck, as soon as she finished coming, and the orgasm ebbed away, he grabbed hold of her legs, holding them open as he watched himself work his cock inside her.

In and out, he moved within her with ease, her release making it so easy for him.

As he pulled out, he saw her cum coating his cock, and he rammed back inside, needing to get as deep inside her as possible.

When that wasn't possible, he grabbed her legs, forcing them around his waist, as he took possession of her lips, fucking her harder, driving her into the bed as he took over, needing his own release.

It didn't take him long to find the pace that sent him hurtling to orgasm, to find the tightness in his balls, the tingling in his spine, and then the pleasure as he finally released all of his cum into her waiting body.

Sweat covered their bodies, but he wasn't completely done, not yet.

Usually, he pulled out of women, dealt with the condom, and left. This time, he wanted to see.

He sat up, lifted her legs, keeping them open for him, and as he pulled out, he watched as his cum followed.

It looked so fucking pretty, and it also cemented in his mind that Abriana, mafia bitch or not, wasn't going anywhere. She belonged to him.

Chapter Eight

The house was empty the following morning when Abriana woke up. She lay in bed, listening for any sign of Ugly Beast, but there wasn't one. The bed was empty, and her body ached in all different places. She felt the wetness between her legs, and she was in no doubt of what happened last night.

He had fucked her twice more, only this time hadn't been horrible like on her wedding night. This reminded her of what that dead ex-mistress had told her. Even as she lay perfectly still, trying to be the nice, proper wife like her mother had told her, she'd been at war with herself. She didn't want to just lie still while he did all the work.

She wanted to touch him, to explore his body the way he had hers. Biting her lip, she slowly let her hand touch her body starting at her tits. They felt so tender. Circling each nipple, she closed her eyes at the memory of his lips on her. Even as he bit down, he hadn't hurt her. The kind of pain he'd given her had been so … wondrous. She hadn't wanted him to stop. Slowly, she slid her hand down her stomach. Ugly Beast had pressed a kiss to her, and then she moved between her legs. With just the one touch, she still felt full from what they had done last night.

Grazing her clit, she let out a gasp at the sudden hit of pleasure and quickly removed her hand. She shouldn't be touching herself.

Climbing out of the bed, she quickly gathered the sheets. Raven had taught her how to use the washing machine yesterday. She pushed everything into the laundry basket before going to the bathroom.

She took a quick shower before returning to her room. Her pristine, unslept-in bed seemed to mock her as she stepped inside.

Ignoring it and trying to ward off the memory of Ugly Beast being inside her, she went to her closet. Finding a pair of jeans and a shirt, she pulled them on. Even as she tried to ignore what had happened last night, her body had other ideas.

She couldn't just forget as her body felt amazing and sore, and much to her shame, she wanted to do it again.

"Men have certain needs. They are going to want to use you to deal with those needs. Don't worry. Once you have a couple of kids, your husband will find another woman to fill the role. One he wants. All you've got to do is lie there, let him do his thing. If it hurts, ignore the pain. It's what we do."

Abriana paused at her mother's words. They were the complete opposite of the other woman's, and they had terrified her.

She thought about Ugly Beast and the women he had on his lap in the clubhouse. She rubbed at her chest, not liking the sting that flooded her body.

What she needed to remember was, Ugly Beast didn't belong to her. He would never be hers.

Nibbling her lip, she caught sight of her reflection. She didn't look composed or ready. She looked like she had been up to no good in bed.

Turning away from the mirror, she ran a brush through her hair, and then made her way downstairs. The house was once again empty, and she hated it. She wasn't used to being alone so much.

She stepped into the kitchen and walked toward the coffee machine. Breakfast at her family home was always served in the dining room. Her father had put her on a strict diet, and he wouldn't let her eat anything unless he was there to see.

She turned the coffee machine on, looking into the fridge. She'd never cooked a single meal in her life.

A Vigo woman wouldn't be caught dead in a kitchen. Her place was by her husband's side, or doing other trivial things.

She had seen the cookbooks in the library though. It was nowhere near to cooking, but she liked looking at the pictures. Ugly Beast didn't have anything but milk.

She tensed up as the front door opened and closed. The sound of men entering had her tensing up. Should she hide? Run? This wasn't normal for her.

Just as she was about to have a meltdown about what she was supposed to do, Ugly Beast rounded the corner with three men she recognized from the clubhouse dressed in the same leather biker cuts.

She stood perfectly still as he stared at her.

Had she done something wrong?

"This is Kinky, Hunter, and Rock. They stopped by for breakfast."

"Actually, we came to see how married life is treating him," Kinky said.

"We saw him getting breakfast and couldn't resist," Rock said.

She looked from each man, not really knowing what to say.

Finally, looking Ugly Beast, she pointed to the coffeepot. "I'm making coffee."

"You know how to make coffee?"

"Raven showed me."

All the men apart from Ugly Beast burst out laughing. "That woman doesn't know how to boil a fucking kettle let alone make a coffee," Rock said.

Heat filled her cheeks. She wanted to defend her friend, but right now she was surrounded by not one but four men, and all of them terrified her.

Locking her fingers together, she watched the men as they put bags down on the counter.

"I didn't know what you liked so I just got a whole load of food," Ugly Beast said.

The smells were amazing, and her stomach chose that moment to growl. Stepping up to the counter, she waited her turn as the men tore open packages and began eating. She went to the bag they hadn't opened and saw a bunch of fruit inside. Taking out a banana, she peeled back the skin and took a bite.

"I bought you more than fruit," Ugly Beast said. He held a carton of pancakes open. She watched him cut a slice and hold it up for her to take.

The pancake was soft and fluffy, and the syrup sweet and tasty.

She closed her eyes.

"Look at them, they are just the sweetest together," Rock said, his voice going really high-pitched.

"Next they're going to be braiding hair, and it's going to be so cute and sweet."

She didn't like hearing them talk like that. Embarrassed, she pulled away and grabbed a fork of her own. She'd thought it was really sweet Ugly Beast feeding her. Clearly, it wasn't.

"I will shoot every single one of your asses if you don't stop."

"You're not going to feed us?" Rock asked.

She looked up in time to see him batting his eyelashes, trying to be a girl. It wasn't cute.

"I'll feed you to my dogs, how about that?" he asked.

"You're no fun."

"Eat up and get the fuck out," Ugly Beast said.

Was he mad? Had she done something wrong? Did he blame her for the men teasing them?

She lost her appetite. Finishing up the bananas, she left the pancakes well enough alone. The last thing she wanted to be doing was throwing them up. The tension in her mounted as one by one, the men left.

Abriana stood in the kitchen. She'd filled the sink with water, and she was putting the cutlery they'd used inside ready to wash them up.

She stared at the leftover food as Ugly Beast entered the kitchen. He was impossible to read.

She didn't know if he was angry or not.

"What would you like me to do with the food?"

"I bought more than we needed. Save it. Put it in the fridge." He was already closing up packets.

With shaking hands, she put the food in order inside the fridge.

"Sorry about the guys."

She looked toward him.

"The way they act, you wouldn't believe they're grown-ass men."

"You're not mad?" she asked, nibbling her lip.

"Why the fuck would I be mad?" Now he looked mad at her question.

"Their teasing."

Ugly Beast burst out laughing. "If you think I'd get mad at that, you have not spent enough time around the club."

"I haven't spent any time around the club. Apart from Raven."

"You won't be going out with her again."

"I like her."

"You can visit her at the club. I'm not trusting her here anymore. She doesn't have a lick of sense, that girl."

She saw he adored the other woman.

"Do you like her?"

His laughter got harder and louder. She didn't

know what she had said that was so funny.

"I don't want Raven if that's what you're asking. She is more likely to shoot a man's dick off than suck him."

She felt her cheeks heat at the description.

"I've got to get used to how innocent you still are," he said.

"I'm fine."

"Not around me. I'm not leaving the house today. I'm cleaning up the yard. I hear there's going to be a storm in a couple of days. I want to be prepared."

"I can help."

"You ever cleared a yard before?"

"No, but I can follow instructions. I can help." She tried not to think about all the orders he'd given her last night in the bedroom. That was a whole other set of instructions. She enjoyed doing them and would happily do them again. She hoped he didn't see how much she looked forward to sharing his bed again.

"That I do know."

There was a look in his eye that made her wonder if he was talking about the yard work or sex.

They finished cleaned up the kitchen before heading out into the yard. There was a chill in the air, and Ugly Beast gave her a jacket. It wasn't his leather cut, but it smelled like him.

The yard was a mess. It hadn't been mowed in some time, and she saw furniture was strewn around the lawn as well.

"I like to have parties from time to time. I need the furniture put in the shed. If the winds pick up like they say they're going to, I don't want them damaging shit. You want to mow the lawn or pick stuff up?"

"I can mow." Some of the chairs looked particularly heavy.

He laughed. "Let's get this party started."

Ugly Beast pulled out the lawnmower and showed her how to use it. She struggled to keep it running and push it along the grass.

Every few minutes he had to come back to help her get it over a few rougher places. She finally did get the hang of it. Once the bucket for the trimmings was full, she had to go and empty them into the trash.

All the while she was making a disaster of the lawn, Ugly Beast was carrying stuff, securing the small pool he had, and putting away anything that could be a hazard. The shed he had was made of brick and looked really secure.

By the time she finished the lawn, it looked worse than when she started it.

"I'm useless," she said, not to anyone.

She didn't know Ugly Beast was standing right behind her. "You ever mowed a lawn before?"

"Never."

"Then for your first time, it ain't half bad."

"I bet you can do a better job," she said.

He chuckled. "A lot of college kids can do a better job, but that's because they're paid to do it on weekends to earn pocket money. Did your dad ever let you out of the house to do anything but shop?"

"No."

"Then stop being so hard on yourself. You don't need to be perfect about everything." They finished cleaning up the yard, and he put the mower away. She stood inside the shed and saw an old bike that looked in need of repair.

"What is it?" she asked.

"Scrap metal. It's a body, but it needs a lot of work."

"You don't work on cars?"

"I used to. Not anymore."

"How come?"

"Don't have a use for them."

"I can't drive," she said, blurting it out.

"You can't?"

"We always had a driver. I was never allowed to learn."

"You ever cooked for yourself?"

"No."

"Cleaned?"

"Like a house or my bedroom?" He nodded. "No, I haven't. We had ... cleaners for them. I'm useless to you. That's why I was given to you, right? You don't need a trophy, and they couldn't use me elsewhere so they gave me to you."

Ugly Beast didn't say anything. He didn't dispute her claim of being useless or tell her otherwise.

She couldn't help but wonder why they had given her to this man. After spending such a short time with Raven, she knew she didn't fit in. She didn't belong here. Raven was so self-sufficient. Her place was in the club. She was equal to them, part of who they were, whereas she had no place. She couldn't even make a simple cup of coffee.

Without looking at him, she turned on her heel and walked back into the house. She didn't get it. Unless she'd been sent as a sacrifice, a means to an end. The chance for the outfit to go to war with the MC, but again, that made no sense.

She didn't have a clue what was going on.

"You don't have to be upset," Ugly Beast said, following her inside.

"I've been married to you less than a week, and from the first day I knew I didn't belong. I'm not ... trained to be with you. I'm supposed to be a good woman. Someone who doesn't cause a man any trouble. That gives babies and orders cleaners and maids." She sniffled. "You don't have maids. You don't want someone at home making babies for you. I don't fit." And the more she thought about it, the more she was convinced her father had sent her here to die, to be killed. She wiped at the tears that filled her eyes and fell down her cheeks. She was so upset and angry.

She didn't even have a right to be.

"You're right, you don't fit. I have no use for you, but you're my wife, and the good thing is, if you want to fit in, we can."

"Don't lie to me," she said. "Please. Are you supposed to kill me? Is that why I've been given to you?"

She watched as Ugly Beast rubbed the back of his head and began to pace. She clenched her hands into fists, feeling sick to her stomach about what he was going to say.

"I'm not going to kill you. You remember what I told you?" he asked.

"Loyalty to the club. Only if I betray the club, will you hurt me."

"That is still the case. I have no wish or any desire to kill you, Abriana. Betray the club and I will."

"You have a reason to think I've been given to you?" Abriana asked.

He was silent.

"All of my life I've been treated like I'm not worth anything. I'm just a means to an end. A pawn in a man's world. I've got no say in what my life is like. If my husband will like me or not. I don't … I'm used to not knowing what is happening, but I can't help you if you don't tell me what you need from me." She pressed her lips together.

Still, he didn't say anything.

141

Nodding her head, knowing she would forever be in the dark, she made her way upstairs to her room.

She sat on the edge of her bed, removing her jacket, followed by her clothes. She wrapped a robe around her body and walked to the bathroom.

Turning on the shower, she waited for the water to run hot. Stepping beneath the water, she tilted her head back, closed her eyes, and released a sigh.

She would never belong.

She was stupid to even think she could ever make it in Ugly Beast's world. She was far from her father, but at the same time, he still held all the cards in her life. Had he really sent her here to die?

She let out a gasp as the shower curtain was pulled aside.

Ugly Beast stepped in. Every single inch of his tattooed self.

She tried to cover her body, but he gripped her hands, holding them away from her.

"This body is mine. Every single part of you is mine, Abriana. You don't hide from me, ever."

"What do you want?" she asked, releasing a cry as she spoke.

This was all too much. She needed time and space to compose herself for what he wanted from her. She couldn't handle all this madness right now. There had to be some way for her to keep sane.

"I don't know if your father sent you here to die, but we didn't expect them to hand us over one of their daughters. We believe your father is going to be in touch with you. He's going to try and use your connection to him and to the club to get what he wants."

"I don't know anything."

"Doesn't mean he's not going to try and accomplish it. Anyone would. You're a weak link to him.

All women in your world are weak." He reached out and tucked a curl of her hair around her ear.

"Why are you telling me this?"

"You wanted to know. I won't kill you, Abriana. Not unless you betray the club. If your father asks you to do something for him with regards to the club, I want you to come to me."

"He won't do that. My father would never trust me."

"We'll see. I'm giving you an option here, Abriana. Take or leave it. This will be the only warning I give you. Betray me and I will kill you."

****

Ortiz bowed as he threw down two men without a patch on them. "What is this?" Smokey asked.

Ugly Beast chewed on his gum as two of Ortiz's men stripped the civilians of their shirts, and lo and behold, two made men with Garofalo's mark were on their arms and backs. They were not MC. They didn't even look like MC men. They were too clean, too pretty-looking.

"What do we have here?" Smokey asked.

"We caught these two men sniffing around Tits, figured you'd like to know why they're in our territory when you didn't even get a call from Garofalo," Ortiz said.

Smokey shook Ortiz's hand. "Until next time, brother."

Ugly Beast watched the other man leave before returning his attention to the two men. When one of them reached into his boot, he stepped on the man's hands, grabbing his wrist, and twisting it.

"Hunter, check it," he said.

The VP grabbed the small knife and let out a whistle. "You planning on killing yourself or one of our boys?"

The man didn't speak.

Ugly Beast saw the emptiness in the man's eyes. A made man and a solider knew how to take a beating. They were trained to deal with pain, to not give in and to take it, not to break. Their outfit was their honor. To break that honor, to talk, to rat, to squeal, was to be filled with shame.

"Does your boss know you're a little far from home?" Smokey asked.

The other guy held his hands flat out. He wasn't shaking though, and Ugly Beast wasn't fooled.

Nodding to Kinky to grab the chairs, they had them tied to them in the next second, secured.

Both men had been roughed up a bit. Neither spoke a word.

"You think they'd talk if I fucked their ass?" Kinky asked. "I could go in his ass, and make him suck it right off."

Ugly Beast didn't say a word. It wasn't his place, not yet. This was Smokey's call. The rest of the guys, they could play around and do whatever the fuck they wanted to do. He thought about Abriana. He'd left her at home today. It was the first time in the past week he had, apart from when they were first married.

He didn't want to leave her, and he'd been working to try to help her to fit into his world.

She wasn't wrong about her father. They hadn't picked her because of her being part of their world.

With her bland looks, she wasn't any use to Vigo. No deals would be made because of her beauty. She was a pawn in their world, and she'd been placed here. From the beatings she took, he knew her father wasn't above hurting her.

Ugly Beast just needed for Abriana to show her

loyalty to the club. He would kill her if she ever tried to betray them. No doubt about it.

"Who sent you?" Smokey asked.

Silence.

"You can't talk?"

Silence.

They wouldn't talk.

Smokey looked toward him, and he raised a brow. All his president had to do was say the word. Smokey walked toward him.

"What are your thoughts?" he asked. "I've got mine, but I want to know yours."

Ugly Beast smiled. "I think these boys have been sent to us as a test to see how we'd respond. Garofalo hasn't contacted you, has he?"

"No."

"Then I say we step it up and find out what the fuck has these two ugly fucks here."

"You want to do the honors?"

"Love to." He winked at Smokey.

"You're fucking scary." Smokey slapped him on the back.

The warehouse they were at, and where they told Ortiz to bring them, was the place they dealt with club problems.

He walked toward the closet at the far end of the warehouse, and, opening up the safe, he removed the tools he'd spent a hell of a lot of time cleaning.

Kinky put a table near the two men, and he opened up his case, holding up a scalpel to inspect. The blade was sharp. All of his tools were. He didn't believe in doing anything by halves. He was a master in this world.

Rolling up the sleeves of his cut, he stepped toward the first man, the one who tried to hurt them or who thought it would be a good idea to do it.

"You want to tell me who you work for?"

Silence.

Ugly Beast stared at the man tied to a chair. Torture was never fun when his victim was already unable to fight back. However, he couldn't exactly take the time to have some fun with fighting and winning.

He could slash the guy. Add a couple of extra scars to the man's face and body. His chest was exposed.

Maybe grab a tit, and slice? So much could be done. So many decisions.

He opted for the eye.

When it came to Garofalo and Vigo, Ugly Beast had no patience.

These men were sent to spy on them, in their territory, and right now, he was really fucking insulted by the complete lack of respect.

The men screamed out as the blade pierced his eye.

The pained noise filled the room, echoing off the walls.

"I'm guessing as made men, you need the use of both of your eyes, right? Otherwise you're damaged goods."

"You're fucking insane," the other man finally spoke.

Removing the blade from the man's eye, he stepped up to the other.

"Why are you here?"

Silence.

Looking back at Smokey, his president shrugged. This was his call, his show.

Smokey wanted to know why they were there.

Ugly Beast stabbed the man in the eye. He now had two partially blind made men, and he waited as one of them started to talk.

What came out of his mouth, he didn't expect, and finding out they were a distraction didn't bode well for Ugly Beast.

"We were to be a distraction so he could see her."

"Who?"

"Gable Vigo wanted to see his daughter without any of the Hell's Bastards listening in."

Abriana was home alone, and Ugly Beast had just given Vigo the chance to turn his daughter against them.

Chapter Nine

Abriana stared at the cookbook Ugly Beast had given her and checked through the list of ingredients again. She then read through the instructions, and again, it all was the same. She had followed everything.

Only the roast chicken was black on the outside and still raw in the center. Cooking shouldn't be this hard. She'd watched a few of the celebrity chefs, and they made it look super easy.

"What did I do wrong?"

She sniffled, upset that nothing was working. Every night Ugly Beast arrived home, she had no choice but to order takeout. He didn't offer to take her to his club, and she didn't ask to go.

Since her little meltdown, she had tried to keep her distance. He'd also not tried to sleep with her.

"Can't cook. Can't socialize. I can't even keep him happy in the bedroom." The only thing he had complimented was her ability to clean. She could make a room sparkle, that was for sure.

Raven hadn't been by to see her in the past week. She figured that had something to do with Ugly Beast being with her. Since their trip to the bar, she hadn't really been alone. When he got the call a few hours ago, he looked unsure to leave her here. She didn't mind being left here.

She wasn't going to burn his house down.

The bird had caught fire. Pressing her hands to her face, she tried to breathe, but it was no good.

Picking up the oven tray, she let out a gasp, as the pan was also too hot.

Just as she was about to use the oven gloves, there was a knock at the door.

If it was Ugly Beast, he'd walk on in. Even

Raven didn't wait for the door to be opened. Nursing her burning hand, she walked toward the door, and when she saw her father on the other side, she panicked.

He was waiting for her to answer, and she'd not been quiet about approaching the door. He could probably hear her from the other side.

"Stop being a baby, Abriana. Open the fucking door."

She didn't cry.

Opening the door, she cried out as he shoved it open, taking her by surprise. The force of him opening it caused her to collide with the wall.

Falling to the floor, she gasped as her father's fingers suddenly went around her neck, pulling her up from the floor.

She grabbed his arm, stopping him, but he'd cut off her air supply and panic flooded her. She hadn't been this afraid in what felt like a lifetime.

Ugly Beast didn't raise his hand to her, or make her scared.

Sure, he had this scary look, but that was when he was deep in thought. She also knew her husband had nightmares. She heard him cry out at night, and minutes later he'd go downstairs to have a drink. She had tried to talk to him the first time, but he told her to go to bed and not to come to him when he did cry out.

She left him alone. There was no point in disturbing him or disobeying him.

Abriana started to see stars, and her father finally released her.

She collapsed to the floor with a gasp, one hand holding the floor as the other went to her neck.

"Well, well, well, I see you think you're free here. I should have known the ugly bastard wouldn't know how to deal with you."

She braced for the kick that didn't come. She squeezed her eyes tight and whimpered as he placed a hand on her shoulder.

"Look at me, whore," Gable said.

Opening her eyes, she was still taking deep breaths.

"You need to remember you're a Vigo, and that means your loyalty runs to Garofalo."

"Ugly Beast—"

He slapped her face, silencing her.

Her hands shook, and tears sprang to her eyes at the explosion of pain. She hadn't missed this. Hadn't missed anything about her old life.

She would take feeling out of place rather than being back under his rule.

You never really left it.

You're at his mercy now.

He could kill you.

"We want to know everything," Gable said. "We want to know what move they're going to make. If you have to, fuck the entire club to find out what moves they're making."

She flinched as he reached into his pocket and pulled out a phone.

"You will call me the moment you know of anything. Do not think for a second that because you wear that pig's ring, you are free. You will never be free. You are my blood, and I will find you, Abriana. I will make you suffer."

"What do I say if he asks about my face?" she asked.

"You're fucking ugly. Bruises make it an improvement." Gable stood up. "Do not disappoint me."

With that, he was gone.

The phone was in her hand.

If she wasn't loyal to her father and to Garofalo, they would kill her. If she wasn't loyal to Ugly Beast and the Hell's Bastards, they would kill her?

Sitting with her back against the wall, she stared down at the phone.

She didn't want this.

Tears filled her eyes, and she couldn't stop the sobs. She hated being weak. This was what she was. This was what her family had made her.

She was weak. Useless. Not worthy of being part of them.

She didn't know how much time had passed before the door opened.

Abriana hadn't moved.

She looked up at Ugly Beast.

Three of his men were there. She recognized Smokey, and the other was Kinky. She couldn't remember the man with the VP badge.

He started to talk, and she stared at the phone. These were the choices she didn't want to make.

Her father demanded her loyalty and would beat her for his own personal pleasure. Ugly Beast … ignored her or … she didn't even know what the past week had been about.

Staring up at him through tear-filled eyes, she didn't know what to do.

"Ugly, dude, I think she's in shock."

She didn't even flinch as Ugly Beast touched her neck.

"He was here," Ugly Beast said.

She licked her lips, and suddenly breaking out of the haze, she stared up at her husband. "He wants me to tell them everything you do." She pressed her lips together, knowing in one way or another she had signed her death certificate. She held out the cell phone. "He wants to know every single detail of the club. What you're doing. He wants me to make sure you all trust me and to report back to him." Her voice hurt from where he strangled her. "I ... here you go."

She placed the cell phone in his hands, and stepping away from him, she made her way to the kitchen. Turning off the oven, she did a double take. She had put the oven on way too hot. It was why the bird had cooked on the outside and not within.

Without looking back at the men, she made her way upstairs to her bedroom. She didn't sit on the end of the bed. She stepped into the small closet, closed the door, and lay down on the rough carpeted floor.

Right now, she wanted to be safe, and nowhere she went, offered her any comfort.

She didn't want to be Abriana Vigo.

More than anything, she wanted to be no one.

Where no men could hurt her and she didn't have to make choices. By telling Ugly Beast the truth, her father would find out.

One day soon, she would die. Probably by his own hand. Maybe Ugly Beast would show her some mercy and do the deed quickly.

Wiping away the tears, she stared across the closet floor. Counting inside her head, her eyes went heavy, and she finally fell asleep.

****

The cell phone Abriana handed to him was a shitty one. There was a single cell phone number, and Ugly Beast looked toward the stairs where he caught sight of her seconds ago. The house smelled like burnt chicken, and he was so fucking angry.

Staring at his president, he saw the wheels in his mind turning. The moment one of those made men had spilled the fucking truth, he'd been on his bike as fast as he fucking could.

Only, it hadn't been fast enough.

He wasn't here to protect Abriana.

"She needs to start having a guard here. I don't want her to be vulnerable again," he said.

"You do know she just picked you," Hunter said.

He turned to the other guy with a glare. "What?"

"She handed you the phone, told you the truth, and now it's up to you to keep her safe. Vigo finds out what she's done, he'll kill her."

"If she betrayed the club, I'd kill her," he said.

"See what she has done here, brother," Hunter said.

Right now, he was really struggling to keep his anger in check. "I need to deal with those bastards."

Smokey shook his head, putting a hand on his shoulder. "Not tonight."

"Did you know this was going to happen?" Ugly Beast asked.

"Did I know Vigo would step on my turf and attack club property? No. I didn't. You think I take their threat lightly?"

"Be careful," Hunter said.

Kinky even raised his brow.

"I'm sorry. Shit, I'm fucking sorry."

"For a guy that doesn't give a shit about his wife, you're taking this really fucking badly," Smokey said.

"I don't love her. I could never love her. She's my problem to deal with. My weak link. The club cannot afford to have someone who is weak." He paced the length of his hallway, which really wasn't fucking long enough for him to deal with all this pent-up frustration and anger. The cell phone was a big fucking problem.

"We need to know their play," Smokey said. "We're going to need to use Abriana as well. Hunter, notify everyone. This Sunday, it's church. Bring your wife. She can hang out at the club. We don't have time to divide our men. From now on, where you go, she goes," Smokey said. "Deal with her. Get her on our team. We'll handle Garofalo. Are you willing to make an arrangement to see Drago?"

Ugly Beast gritted his teeth as he stared at his president.

"That's not necessary."

Smokey held up the cell phone. "This is a problem. Reach out to him. Arrange a meet. I don't give a fuck how you do it, just do it." Smokey stood up. "We'll leave you to deal with your woman. Get the job done. I don't want any loose ends."

Ugly Beast closed the door behind them.

Alone in his home with his wife, he'd rather take on a fucking army of enemies than go upstairs to her.

He put the phone her father had given her on the cabinet near the door, and made his way upstairs to her bedroom.

Leaning against the doorframe, he stared into the room. She stared down at her hands, and he saw the tear tracks. When he got his hand on Vigo, that bastard better pray for death.

"Why did you do that?" Ugly Beast asked.

She looked up. She never wore any makeup, and he got to see all the puffiness of her face from crying.

He hated seeing women cry. It wasn't a pretty sight.

With Abriana, he felt a twist in his gut and an overwhelming need to hurt something.

"Do what?"

"Give me that cell phone."

She sniffled. Her lips pressed together. He wasn't trying to be a dick, even though that did come naturally to him. Folding his arms, he waited.

Abriana wiped at her eyes. "I don't want to die. We're married, and that's got to mean something."

"You're a mafia princess."

She snorted. "I'm more like the mafia dog. I'm no princess."

"By giving us to each other, they tried to insult us." He stepped into the room, and moved to sit beside her on the edge of the bed.

"I'm sorry," she said.

"It's not your fault. I don't feel insulted about our marriage. Do you?"

"I don't think about it."

"You should. You just picked a side down there, Abriana. You need to know how to deal with doing something like that."

She laughed. It was forced and slightly hysterical. "Are you mad at me because I gave you the cell phone? Do you want to kill me, is that it? Now that I've shown my side, you can't get rid of me. You can divorce me. It wouldn't matter."

"Abriana, I'm not going to divorce your ass, nor am I going to kill it. I'm going to keep you alive. However, what this does mean is if your father or Garofalo ever find out, they will hurt you. I want you protected at all times."

"What does that even mean?"

"You're about to have a shadow everywhere you go. The clubhouse, even for drinks, and coming home. You won't be alone. I will do whatever it takes to make sure you stay alive. You're my wife, and by doing this, you're now under club protection as well. Smokey will tell everyone that you're to be protected at all costs."

"I'm not worth it."

He took hold of her hand, turning her to face him.

Unable to stop himself from touching her, he cupped her cheek. "You are worth it, Abriana. Do not let those bastards get you down."

She pressed her face against his hand, and he hated how fucking broken she looked.

"What did you try to kill in this house?" he asked.

"What?"

"The smell? Did you try to set your father on fire?"

She started to laugh even with tears rolling down her cheeks. He didn't know what it was, but he was starting to see little parts of her that were beautiful. Especially when she smiled. There was a happiness within her gaze that called to him.

"Chicken. I tried to cook some chicken. It wasn't edible. I had the oven on too high. It burned on the outside and was raw in the center."

"First things first, we so need to get you some lessons on cooking."

"Do you know anyone?"

"Not a clue, but we've got the cooking channel."

"I tried that," she said.

"We got this. If all else fails we've got noodles or takeout."

She moved away from his hand and rested her head on his shoulder. "Thank you."

"You don't have to thank me for anything."

She fell silent, and he stared across the room, waiting for her to speak.

"I hate him," she said. It was a mere whisper, but he heard it. "I want him to die."

"One day, I'll kill him for you."

"Do you promise?"

"I'll even let you watch if you think you can handle it."

"I want to see it happen. Does that make me a bad person?"

"To some, maybe. Not to me."

"How come?"

"I'm used to the sickness in this world. I'm used to the fucked-up shit."

"Does that make me fucked up?"

Hearing her swear was the cutest thing.

"No. You're not fucked up."

"I don't want to be some scared woman afraid of her own shadow anymore, Ugly Beast. I want to be … someone you can be proud of."

He frowned and leaned back so she had no choice but to sit up. "What makes you think I'm not proud right now?"

"You shouldn't be proud of someone like me. I'm weak."

This time, he cupped her face with both hands. "In a world dominated by men, you are still walking. Still talking. You're strong. Vigo didn't break you. This world has not broken you."

"I'm nothing like Raven."

"Raven is one of a kind. Believe me, I don't *want* you to be like her. I want you to be like yourself. Now, I think dinner tonight is a lost cause. Get changed, I'm going to take you out to the bar. We're going to enjoy some wings and some dancing."

"We are?"

"Why not?"

"It'll be our first official date."

He saw it made her nervous to say.

"Then you better get ready. A few of the boys will join us for sure, but I don't have a problem with that." He pulled her to her feet. Staring down at her clothes, he pressed his lips together, thinking. "Do I need to call Raven here to pick you out a fresh outfit?"

She glanced down at herself. "She left some clothes behind."

"We're good then. Don't worry about it. Come on, chop, chop. We're going to have some fun."

He left the bedroom to give her a chance to get ready. Pulling out his cell phone, he sent Smokey and the boys a text. Not all of them would be able to make it to Ryan's place, but some of them would, and he wanted Abriana to have a night that was filled with fun. He also didn't want to have guys breathing down her neck, looking for some pussy.

Chapter Ten

Abriana sat tense at the table while Ugly Beast went and got them some food.

"You really need to relax," Raven said.

Her new friend had arrived at the house just as she and Ugly Beast were leaving. She was shocked when he invited Raven, especially as he seemed to blow hot and cold with the other woman.

"I'm fine."

"I heard what happened. You need to learn to kick your dad in the nuts, or grab them really hard, and pull. It'll keep every single man away from you."

She hated that so many people knew her father hated her. He despised her enough to hurt her where he could leave marks. She touched her neck. Did he do it on purpose because of Ugly Beast? Thinking her new husband was more than likely to leave marks on her flesh.

She stared down at the table, feeling the greatest wave of shame.

Stop it. He doesn't want you to feel that way.

Taking a deep breath, she forced herself to look up.

"That's the spirit," Raven said. "You got to stop worrying about what people think."

"Is that what you do?" Abriana asked.

"I'm a biker chick, sweetheart. I've been judged on everything. Whether I fuck the club, the men out of it. Believe me I've been called so many names. All of them make me laugh. Bitch, whore, slut, fucker, ho, you name it, I've been called it." Raven shrugged. "You got to learn to put on your armor. People only fuck with you if they think they can."

"I wish it was that easy."

"True, I wasn't brainwashed to think of myself as lesser of a person. Your guys do a number on you, huh?"

"I don't think I know. I guess. I mean, we're not required to do a whole lot of things, you know. We're too stupid to know family business, or not bright enough to pick our own husbands." She hated it.

Raven placed a hand over hers. "In a way you can count yourself lucky. You got out. No one here is ever going to force you to do shit you don't want to do. If they do, I'll kick their ass."

"And Raven terrifies most of the male populace. I have a feeling she's switching teams. You trying to seduce my wife?"

"Please, it wouldn't be that hard. I know how to arouse and pleasure a woman." Raven stroked a finger down her arm.

Abriana looked to Ugly Beast, but he seemed more amused than anything else.

"You brought the wings with you?" Raven asked, taking one.

Abriana waited for Ugly Beast to take one before having her turn.

"Have one, Abriana. Be warned, they are spicy as fuck!"

Raven moaned. "So good. You got more food than this, right? I'm dancing, and I'm going to need my strength for whatever fight breaks out."

"You have one," Abriana said.

"I won't have one until you do." Ugly Beast waited for her, and seeing he was going to starve if she didn't take one, she reached in, taking a wing. "See, that wasn't so hard."

"Why do I feel this is a big deal?" Raven asked.

"The men in her world are used to being served first. The women wait their turn," Ugly Beast said.

"Wow, fucking wow." Raven shook her head. "Is it wrong of me to want to be in their world and fuck with their heads?"

Abriana smiled.

"I see that look, honey. You know I'd cause trouble, right?"

"They wouldn't have a clue what to do with you." Abriana glanced over at Ugly Beast.

"Take a bite."

She rolled her eyes. Sinking her teeth into the flesh, she took a bite. An explosion of flavor hit her tongue, and she closed her eyes, enjoying the taste.

When she opened her eyes, she saw Ugly Beast was already devouring one, and Raven reached for another.

The chicken was good. By the time they finished one pile, Ugly Beast went to grab another.

He also brought fries with the second order, and they were covered in melted cheese. It all looked so delicious. Ugly Beast even got her a beer as well. He promised to monitor her beer, but she didn't mind. Just sitting around, enjoying food and listening to the banter between Raven and Ugly Beast was fun.

She knew he cared about her new friend a lot. When others from the Hell's Bastards joined, she saw they were a real family, a unit, a team. Even though Raven was loud and boisterous, the guys adored her. Whenever someone tried to get close, they would gather around her, keeping the guys at bay. She noticed it, and it made her appreciate the club so much more.

Once all the food was gone, Ugly Beast bought her back another beer. She had taken a few sips when he held his hand out. "Let's dance."

There was a loud cheer from the club, and her cheeks heated.

The song was fast-paced, and she had no idea what she was doing. Ugly Beast didn't seem to care, and she followed him, trying to copy her moves.

By the time the song ended and turned to a slow number, she was relieved. Only they didn't leave the dance floor. Ugly Beast grabbed her hand and pulled her in close. Their bodies melded together.

Abriana didn't like how good it felt to be in his arms. Even though this man was her husband, she still felt a real threat from him. He would kill her if it ever came down between her and the club. She knew that, and even as it terrified her, she couldn't mistake the longing she felt for him to look at her the way some of the men stared at the women.

It wasn't even love.

It was desire.

They wanted each other, and she wasn't a fool to believe Ugly Beast didn't feel desire. She knew he did. She had felt the power of him thrusting inside her, and she wanted it again.

"The wings were pretty good, right?"

She smiled against his chest. "Yes."

"And the weather we've been having."

"It's been all right."

"Do you like Christmas?"

She lifted her head up and looked at him. "Are you trying to find things out about me?"

"Yeah, I'm not exactly being subtle about it."

"What do you want to know?" No one had ever paid her any attention growing up. They didn't care what she liked or disliked.

"Everything."

"That's a pretty long list."

"Tell me. I don't mind."

She glanced toward the table. Raven was no

longer there, but looking past Ugly Beast's shoulder, Abriana saw she was in the arms of another man.

"I like Christmas. Who doesn't? I love decorating the tree. I also love Halloween. It can be a lot of fun."

"Partying is fun around those times. The club is always filled to bursting."

She started to notice as he stroked the base of her back. It was just a light caress at first, but it gradually started to build. She liked his touch. Her body grew warm, and she wanted nothing more than for him to keep on going. This was the first time she'd really felt like this, especially in a room full of people.

"Would I be able to go to one of these parties?" she asked.

"It's about time you asked. Yes, your ass is going to be there."

Abriana couldn't allow herself to be too happy. Her father would one day be calling. "What do I do about my dad?"

"We'll deal with him."

"Killing a Capo will get you all killed, Ugly Beast."

He smirked. "How about I worry about the killing? We've got this handled."

"But—"

"Tonight is about you and only you. Stop thinking about your dad and about all the bullshit. Just enjoy. It's what we're doing." His hand moved down to her ass, gripping the flesh. He pulled her against him, and she felt the undeniable press of his arousal against her stomach.

"What are you doing?"

"Easy. I'm preparing you for what I want."

She licked her dry lips. "What do you want?"

"Oh, Abriana, you really don't know me at all."

"But I want to."

"What?"

"I want to get to know you." It suddenly struck her hard how much she really wanted to know him, and it wasn't just so he wouldn't kill her either. She really did want to know who he was and what made him tick.

"I think you've had enough dancing with the woman. Give me a turn." Smokey intervened, taking her away from Ugly Beast.

She couldn't argue. It wasn't right for her to say no. Putting her hand on Smokey's shoulders, she watched Ugly Beast as he walked back to the table.

"Don't worry about him. He knows I won't hurt you."

"Why would you want to dance with me?"

"Why not?"

"I'm not a very beautiful woman."

"And you think I only want to be with beautiful women?"

"Why not? Most men do."

"I'm not most men, sweetheart."

"I'm confused right now."

He chuckled. "You came good for the club. Against your father, that couldn't have been easy. We're all grateful for what you did."

"It wasn't a lot though."

"No, it was something. It was more than a lot would give."

She stared at his chest. Her heart raced, and she didn't want to be dancing with Smokey but she also didn't want him to be angry with her.

"Ugly Beast is my husband, and well, I'm loyal to him and the club."

"You're fucking terrified though, right?"

"I know the damage my family can do. I'm

scared."

"It's good to be afraid, Abriana. It lets you know you're alive, but don't insult the club by thinking we can't take care of ourselves. We can. Believe me. I want this fight with Garofalo."

"You do?"

"One day, honey, you're going to realize some things are not what they appear." The dance had ended, and Smokey escorted her back to the table.

For the remainder of the night, she danced with several members of the club, but only with Ugly Beast's permission. She didn't want to, but she also didn't want to offend anyone. The only person she was interested in was Ugly Beast.

Raven hugged her hard and promised to stop by later in the week. Abriana climbed on the back of Ugly Beast's bike, giving her friend a wave. She wanted to be alone with Ugly Beast, and right now, that didn't make a lot of sense to her.

****

Ugly Beast was starving. He'd already taken a shower, and now he needed to eat. Opening his fridge, he marveled at all the new ingredients that were stacked up. Grabbing some cheese and pickles, he started to make himself a sandwich just as Abriana entered he kitchen.

She came to a stop in the doorway. She wore one of those sexy negligees that showed off a great deal of flesh but also hung on her so he could see how big her tits were. The fabric didn't do anything to hide her body from sight, and his cock thickened.

He'd hated sharing her with his brothers, letting them have a turn dancing with her, but it had all been for a reason. A very important reason. He wanted all the guys to know her, to take care of her.

She'd picked sides and was willing to go against

her family in order to be loyal to the club. That had to be rewarded, and in doing so, he needed to keep her safe. There was no way he was ever letting anyone get to her to hurt her. He'd kill every single fucking man before he let that happen.

"Hungry?"

"Yes. I thought I ate enough wings, but clearly not."

She looked so nervous. He didn't want her to be nervous.

"Cheese and pickle?"

"I can eat that."

She stepped into the kitchen. Her hands were pressed together, enhancing the rounded curves of her tits.

Again, he wanted to fuck her. He wanted to take his wife and discover every single inch of her. She stared into his eyes, not glaring at his face, or making him aware of the scars.

He wore a pair of sweatpants, no briefs underneath, and he wanted to fuck her. He wanted to take her so fucking hard and make her his.

She was his wife. Why wouldn't he want to fuck her?

"Couldn't sleep?" she asked.

"I've not even tried yet."

"What are you doing tomorrow?" She tucked her hair behind her ear.

"What are *you* doing tomorrow?"

Her cheeks were on fire. "I was going to attempt that chicken again. I think I know what I did wrong."

"Then I guess I'm going to be praying that I don't get food poisoning."

"You don't have to eat it."

"Oh, yeah, I do." He winked at her. "Here's your

cheese and pickle sandwich." He pushed the small plate toward her.

She took it, and he saw her nerves.

"But, what if it's awful?"

"Only one way to find out."

"You're not doing anything else tomorrow?"

"Nothing of any importance, no." Smokey had already told him he had to stay home. To keep her safe and to get her used to going to the club.

In a way, he had to train a full-grown woman how to live without the constant orders and instructions of the club. While he was doing that, Smokey and several of the guys were meeting up with their contact about Garofalo's recent new best friends.

They needed more details before they could allow Abriana to answer a call from her father. He had no idea when it was going to ring. The cell phone was in his possession, which was why his wife now had to stay by his side at all times. The information they wanted Vigo to know would come to them soon enough.

"Do you want to fuck?" he asked.

She started to cough, her hand rubbing at her chest. Her face was a beautiful shade of red.

"What?"

"You keep staring at my body. You want to fuck?"

"How can you ask me something like that?" She pulled apart her sandwich, but he noticed she didn't dispute what she wanted.

She was horny. Her nipples pressed against the negligee, and they were far too fucking distracting for him.

He moved around the counter so that he was standing right in front of her. He pulled out the chair just far enough so she didn't have any choice but to look at him. With the way she was sitting, her legs were spread, and he made sure to press his against the stool so she wouldn't be able to get away easily.

He liked watching her like this. Trapped. Helpless. At his mercy.

She needed to know he was the one in charge of what happened to her. No one was coming to her rescue. At least, not today.

She shouldn't have to be rescued though. There's no way he could rape the willing.

"You like to unnerve me," she said.

"I want to do more than unnerve you." He reached out, fingering the strap of her negligee. "This looks really pretty on you."

"I'm not used to something like this."

"I know, which is why it's going to be a lot of fun to show you what you can now have." He slowly lowered the strap of her negligee, and he saw her breath catch.

The fabric stayed over her nipple, but all it would take was a quick swipe of his finger and her tit would be exposed. She didn't fight him.

"Tell me, Abriana, is your pussy wet?" he asked.

"I don't know."

"Then touch yourself. Let's see if that pretty pussy is ready for my cock."

He let her go and watched her. The hesitation. The nerves. The indecision.

"Tell me what to do," she said.

"Put your hand between your legs." He watched her. "Are you wearing any panties?" She surprised him with a shake of the head. "Now touch your pussy. Stroke your slit."

She let out a gasp.

"You like that?"

She bit her lip and nodded her head.

Ugly Beast went to his knees in front of her. Putting his hands on her thighs, he gathered up the silk, pushing it out of his way so he could clearly see her. Her hand covered her pussy.

Taking her wrist, he pulled her fingers away and saw the evidence of her arousal. She was slick.

Taking each digit into his mouth, one after the other, he sucked them clean. She tasted amazing.

He didn't think it was possible to be aroused by his wife, or the fact he was the only guy she'd ever been with, but he felt this overwhelming need to keep her, to make her his own, and to never let her go or let another man know how tight and wet she always was for him.

When her fingers were clean, he moved her so she sat on the edge of the seat.

Lifting up her negligee, he made her hold it up, and returned his attention to her pussy.

The light dusting of curls was wet, and as he opened her sweet pussy, he saw how fucking slick she was. Keeping her lips open, he slid his tongue between her slit, teasing her clit before sucking the nub into his mouth.

She let out a beautiful cry, and he wanted to hear more. He didn't want her to stop. Letting go of her lip, he slid a single finger inside her cunt, then two. Spreading her open, he pumped inside her, filling her. Each thrust had her arching up.

"Take your tits out," he said.

She eased the cups of her negligee down, and her tits were finally free for his gaze. His cock was so hard he wanted to do nothing more than to fuck her into oblivion. Instead, he held himself in check. There would be time enough for him to play.

When she took three of his fingers with ease, he used his thumb to tease her clit, watching her.

Her eyes were closed, and she held her negligee out of the way. He wondered if she even realized she was rocking against him.

She looked like a siren, her need overtaking her sensibilities. He wanted that. To see her lose control. To break the chains her parents had put in place. He didn't want her bound by anything but need. Uncontrollable desire for him and him alone.

Her cunt was like a suction, and he fucking relished it. He was pumping inside her exactly how his cock was going to be in a short time. He wanted to see his cum once again sliding out of her, to know his was the only one there.

She let out a little moan.

Taking her clit into his mouth once again, he brought her to orgasm, hearing that slight gasp, and then a moan that echoed around his kitchen as he gave her what she wanted. There would come a time when he'd get to see her come apart. Until then, he had to make do with what he could get.

He brought her down over the peak and placed a kiss to her pussy, watching her shake a little with each indrawn breath.

"I love it when you do that," she said.

"I can give it to you every time you want it." He gripped her thighs, standing up, and pressing a kiss to her lips. She tried to pull away, and he shook his head. "Kiss me."

She did. It was quick, and she pulled away.

"I don't have no room for a prim and proper girl in my bed, Abriana."

"Who says I want to be in your bed?" She looked nervous. He liked it.

"You want my dick in your pussy, right now. You can deny it all you want, but we both know it's my dick you want." He stroked a finger between her sodden curls. "You can deny it. However, if you don't join me in my sitting room, I'll never make you come again. You won't find pleasure with another man either. You even think to do that, and I'll kill them. I'll kill every man you look at because no one has what belongs to me. No one gets to taste what is mine."

He stood up, not hiding the fact he was so fucking hard right now. Pushing his sweatpants down, he threw them into her lap, before heading into the sitting room.

If she didn't turn up, he'd put on some porn and take care of business himself. He had no doubt that behind Abriana's prim exterior there was a wanton woman who wished to break the chains her family kept locked around her.

He had no problem with her portraying the part of sweet, innocent virgin to the outside world. She would always be his sweet little virgin. That was where the fucking image stopped. When they were alone, he wanted a slut, a whore, a woman who was willing to take his cock, and to do every single dirty thing he could imagine. He wouldn't share her.

No other man would ever get to know just how fucking precious she was.

His newfound feelings for her wouldn't stop him from putting a bullet inside her head if the time came for it. Until then, he wanted her, and he was going to take her every single chance he got.

She'd become like a drug to his system, and he couldn't stop it. He didn't *want* to stop it.

Not once did she flinch away from his scars, or look at him as if he was a lesser being. He wasn't above admitting it was fucking heady to have a woman finally look at him and want him.

And he saw her want each time she looked at

him. There were nerves, like there always were, but this went deeper.

Like he knew she would, she entered the sitting room. Her hands were clenched at her sides, and she looked really unsure of herself.

"Take your clothes off. Coming in here, I want you naked." He looked toward her, wrapping his fingers around his length, waiting.

Her hands were shaking, but she did as he asked without a single complaint, and she was fucking beautiful.

He loved her curves. Some of the bitches at the clubhouse were all skin and bone, their drug habit not exactly helping their figure.

With Abriana, to some, she was fat and wouldn't be attractive. To him, he loved the added pounds of flesh. The way her tits were nice, full, round, and the large nipples. Her waist narrowed in, only to flare out to full hips. Baby-making hips.

He wasn't going to think about a baby.

Not now.

His life didn't accommodate a child.

Her thighs were strong, full, juicy, and they could wrap around him and take the pounding he wanted to give. Her long hair fell around her face, and to him, in that moment, she looked like a goddess.

His own personal goddess.

"Come here."

She stepped in front of him. Her gaze went from his face to his dick then back again. He was making her nervous, but he didn't have a problem with that.

"Do you want to touch me?"

"Yes."

"Get comfortable." He threw a pillow to the floor and watched her lower herself onto the pillow, to get comfortable. Once she was, he held out his hand for her to take, waiting for her to do as he asked.

She placed hers inside his, and he was patient, letting her get calm and relaxed. He understood her nerves, but he had no time for it here, even though he tried to give it to her.

Wrapping her fingers around his length, he showed her exactly what he liked. Moving her hand fast, gripping him tightly, he hissed at the pleasure. It had been a long time since he'd let a woman touch him like this.

Sure, he'd allowed women to blow him, but he'd only let their mouths on him. Physical touch had been out of the question. He didn't like their hands on him. Most of the women were repulsed by his face, so getting them to physically touch him, he didn't like.

Abriana's tits grazed his knees, and he watched her, waiting. She didn't move away, and he felt the hardness of her nipples.

He let go of her hand, watching her ministrations on his dick. He tightened around her, moving rapidly up and down, then slowing. The tip was leaking copious amounts of pre-cum.

"Can I…" She stopped.

"Can you what?" he asked.

"It doesn't matter."

"I want to know what it is you want so I can know if I can give it to you or not."

She licked her lips, and her gaze landed on his cock.

"You want to suck my dick?" he asked.

"I want to taste you, like you taste me."

He smiled. "I'm not going to have a problem with you tasting me."

She moved in close, and the anticipation was the

fucking key. Only, she stopped. "Have you been with anyone else?"

"Huh?"

"Since we've been married. Have you been with anyone else?"

"No."

"You're sure?"

"I don't make a habit of banging chicks I don't remember. Look at my face."

"That didn't seem to stop them when we arrived. You had a lot of dancers more than willing to give you what you wanted."

He stared at her. "Are you jealous?"

"No."

"I don't know. How you're reacting is a lot like jealousy."

"I don't have to do this."

She made to get up, but he caught her wrist. "First, don't walk away from me, ever. I mean it, Abriana. I don't play fucking games."

She slowly lowered herself back down, and he waited for her to relax before he continued.

"Second, those bitches only wanted me because I was now taken. Look at my face. I'm a fucked-up monster, and I scare them half the time."

"You don't scare me," she said. "I like your scars."

"Those women, before I brought you home to me, couldn't give me the time of day unless I demanded it of them."

"You can do that?"

"They're club pussy. They're not owned by a member. They're not an old lady. I can do whatever the hell I want to them. It's why they signed up to be club pussy. Any guy, anytime, anywhere."

"They agreed to that."

"Yep, and believe me, a lot of them love it as well. They love the variety of serving a lot of dicks."

"I couldn't do that."

"Babe, you won't be fucking doing that. I mean it. Any man touches you, I'll fucking kill them."

"I had a lot of your boys dancing with me tonight, including Smokey." She smiled at him, and he saw she was happy.

"They were dancing with you because I let them. Make no mistake, Abriana, I'm the one that decides what happens to you. I won't share you. Not now, not ever. You belong to me, and only to me."

"You don't want to share me?"

"No. My dick hasn't been near a single pussy or mouth since we married. Those chicks were only dancing. I wouldn't fuck them even if they begged me to." He cupped her cheek, needing to touch her. "Got me?"

"I got it." She gripped his cock, not too firmly, and he moaned as she licked the tip of him.

Her actions were nervous but unhurried, and he had no wish to stop her from exploring all that she wanted.

When she took the tip of him into her mouth and sucked, he had to utter out a warning for no teeth, but she followed his instruction, and feeling the warmth of her lips, it felt fucking amazing.

He didn't want her to stop.

Wrapping her hair around his fist, he held her tightly and began to rock into her mouth, going deeper.

Ugly Beast couldn't look away. She was sheer fucking perfection, and his cock was coated in her saliva.

It wasn't the best blowjob, but her innocence and lack of experience were more than a turn-on.

She drove him wild, and he couldn't help but pump into her mouth, and as she moaned around his length, he did it again.

He hit the back of her throat, and he couldn't take it anymore. He pulled out of her mouth, needing to regain his control.

"Did I do something wrong?" she asked, wiping her saliva off her chin.

"No. You did everything right. Everything I needed." He tugged her up, onto his lap. "I'm not going to come into your mouth. Not yet. Not when I can use this pussy and get it acquainted with my dick." He put one hand on her hip. She held onto his shoulders, and he lined his cock up with her entrance, and he couldn't look away as he guided her down. Each inch inside her was heaven.

She was so wet that he didn't need to use extra lube or get her more aroused.

She arched her back, thrusting her tits out. When he had more than half his length within her, he gripped her hips and slammed her down, hearing her cry of pleasure.

"I don't want you to hold back. Whenever we're together, I don't want to see my prim and proper wife, Abriana."

"What do you want?" she asked.

"I want to see a woman who wants to fuck my cock. Who has no problem showing me her body, and wants to feel this with me."

"I do."

He could give her the fucking world, and all he wanted in return was her loyalty. "I can show you everything you've only ever dreamed of, and so much you never even knew existed."

"Yes."

Ugly Beast held her hips and began to rock her up and down his length. She cried out as he shoved her down, going as deep as he could. He knew he was causing her a slight pulse of pain, but there was also pleasure. He'd hit the very hilt inside her.

Her nipples were so hard, and she didn't fight to get away from him. He took her, fucking her, driving her wild, and taking everything he wanted and more.

Seeing her tits bounce with every hard thrust was a fucking dream. He wasn't going to last, not this time. He was too primed and ready from having her lips wrapped around him.

Abriana held his shoulders and moved up and down his length. He was no longer guiding her, but showing her what she wanted as well as him.

Leaning forward, he took one of her tits into his mouth, sucking on the beaded nipples. She cried out, crushing her chest to his face, and he lapped it up, desperate and hungry for more. Moving onto her second nipple, he did the same, feeling his orgasm.

Taking over, he fucked her hard, thrusting up within her body as he pulled her down, making her take him. They were both panting, the sounds of their pleasure echoing around the room.

With one final thrust upward, and drawing her down, Ugly Beast closed his eyes and groaned, sending wave upon wave of his cum deep within her.

"I could get used to this," she said.

He knew he felt the same.

Chapter Eleven

"How many chickens have you wasted so far in your experiments to cook?" Raven asked.

Abriana stared into the oven, willing this one to work. "This is my tenth."

"Really? You didn't give up?"

"Why would I want to give up?"

Raven jumped off the kitchen counter and held up the takeout leaflets. "That's why the good old world invented these. So women no longer had to cook."

"I like cooking."

"You do?"

She did, but nothing she cooked had been a success. She'd even failed to make mashed potatoes. She hadn't boiled them for long enough, and they had been lumpy and horrible. Ugly Beast had started to eat them, but she couldn't let him do that. He went out to work, every single day, and she wanted to make him a meal for when he got home. Most days, he took her with him. She'd be at the club with him, waiting for him to deal business. If she couldn't be with him, he'd leave her with one of his members, be it a prospect or one of the club brothers.

Raven was with her the most.

"I do. I mean, one day, I hope to be good at it."

"Come on, Abriana, what is this about?"

She shrugged. "It's not about anything. Really." She went to check the vegetables. They were cooked, and they no longer looked like she'd burnt them. They were bright green, with a slight crunch, and tasted like a vegetable.

The gravy needed the pan drippings, and the mashed potatoes were keeping warm in the other oven, on low, really low. They were not lumpy, or gloopy. So far, dinner had taken her five hours, but she had nothing else to do.

"What's with the need to do something? Aren't you supposed to like, shop, or knit, or do whatever it is mafia princesses do?"

Abriana sighed.

"See, that noise right there. You can pretend nothing is bothering you, but I know something is."

"I never wanted to be someone who just shopped or knitted, or read. When my husband comes home, I wanted to be someone who mattered. I wanted to be someone he wanted to come home to. Food, and a nice home, isn't that something? Ugly Beast earns a living. He keeps me safe, and the least I could do, is something. I don't want him to spend his entire life eating takeout. Meals are supposed to mean something. Otherwise, I'm a waste of space. I can't be that." She felt tears fill her eyes.

"We're home," Ugly Beast said.

She quickly got her emotions in check, and the timer for the chicken went off.

"You're many things, Abriana, but a waste of space is not one of them," Raven said.

Abriana hoped no one heard their conversation.

Ugly Beast entered the kitchen. "You tested it yet?"

"I'm about to."

She opened the oven, but Ugly Beast took the oven gloves away from her, and took out the large roasting tin.

Glancing around the kitchen, she did a quick head count and saw five of his club brothers would be joining them.

"Will you want dinner?" she asked.

Ugly Beast chuckled. "They will stay as long as

you tell us this is cooked." He placed the roasting tin onto the counter. She grabbed her thermometer and sent a prayer to the kitchen gods.

With the men in the room, she felt an overwhelming sense of pressure. So far, she hadn't been able to give them anything, not even the safety of knowing they were going to be taken care of. Her family was against them and had shown their cards with that damn phone, and her own father attacking her. For once, she wanted to be useful.

The moment the thermometer beeped the right temperature, she was so thrilled. It meant it was cooked inside and out. The skin looked golden and crispy. When she pulled the thermometer out of the chicken, the juices ran clear.

There were juices.

Raven helped her to serve, and they all sat around Ugly Beast's table. She placed the chicken in front of him to carve as she served. She wasn't nervous. She was happy to have finally accomplished something for herself.

The meat looked amazing as Ugly Beast served it up on plates.

Once they were seated, she waited a few seconds, watching everyone dive in.

Ugly Beast didn't.

"Start eating," he said.

"Please, just, let me see you try it." She nibbled her lip, nervous for him to like something that she cooked. He rolled his eyes but also took the time to try her food. She held her breath, waiting, unsure, if he was going to like it or not.

"You did good, Abriana."

She did good!

Smiling at his praise, she tasted it herself. For her

first homecooked meal that was edible, she was so happy.

"We're all having a cookout tomorrow," Smokey said. "Lewis and Verge are coming in."

She watched the conversation among the men, knowing something was going on that she wasn't privy to. Even Raven had gone silent, listening.

Eating her food, she served up seconds, and by the time they were all finished, there was no food left. She got to her feet to clear away the dishes when Ugly Beast put a hand on her arm.

"Kinky, Raven, Hunter, clean up while I talk with Abriana," Smokey said.

She looked toward Raven, but the other woman didn't look in her direction. Had she done something wrong?

With her hands in her lap, she waited for whatever he was about to say.

Smokey pressed his fingers together on the table. At least he wasn't reaching for a gun.

"We have reason to believe your father will be calling you tomorrow during the cookout."

"How do you know that?" she asked.

"Abriana," Ugly Beast said in warning.

"I'm sorry." She stared at the table.

"You have a right to know. You're going to help us. I want you to tell him we've got chapters coming up from the south as well as some of our boys traveling from the UK," Smokey said.

"I don't think she should give that much intel on the first phone call," Ugly Beast said.

"Why not?"

"You think about it, it's suspicious. I rarely include women in my work. Why would she know everything all of a sudden? It makes no sense."

She looked from one man to the other.

"Okay," Smokey said. "You tell him nothing. You say that Ugly Beast hasn't said anything, and the cookout tomorrow is the first time you've seen him for long time."

It was a mixture of a lie and truth. She saw him every single day and she spent a great deal of time at the clubhouse, but Ugly Beast never talked about the club.

"I can do that."

"I need for you to be convincing," Smokey said.

"I can. I promise."

"Cool. Tell me what you're going to say."

"I don't know anything. Ugly Beast doesn't tell me anything."

Smokey stared at her.

"It'll work," Ugly Beast said.

"Will one of you be with me when he calls?" she asked, looking between the two.

"Yes," Ugly Beast said. "If he threatens you with anything, we need to know."

"The next phone call, you start feeding intel," Smokey said. He knocked on the door. "Done for the day. I'm out of here."

She watched as one by one the men left, followed by Raven, leaving her alone with Ugly Beast.

"You're nervous."

"Just a little."

"You ever lied to your dad?"

"No."

"Do you have a problem with us asking you this?"

She shook her head. "It's … I want to do good. I don't want to screw this up for you guys."

"It's impossible to screw this up. Now, that was a fine meal, Abriana."

"Thanks."

"Let's head out. I want to show you something." He got to his feet, and she followed him out of the house. It was warm, and she saw a couple of kids down the street playing in their driveway.

Ugly Beast moved to a car, opening up the passenger door. "Get in."

"You own a car?"

"Yep, and I want to take you for a drive."

She was a little disappointed, as she rather liked holding onto him on the back of his bike. Climbing into the car, she buckled her seatbelt as Ugly Beast got settled behind the wheel.

"Do you think one day you'll ever tell me your name?"

"Maybe. One day." He winked at her, and she liked that.

They'd been married for a little over a month, and in that time, she had felt him opening up to her a little. It wasn't an overnight thing, but since she handed him the cell phone and pledged her loyalty to the Hell's Bastards, it had been a lot easier.

"Where are we going?" she asked.

"You'll see."

He pulled out of the street. Several of the kids waved at him, but he didn't wave back. He never did.

Sitting back, she looked at the mirror, seeing their house slowly disappear.

The small built up town was nothing more than a dot as he sped up out on the open road. They passed the clubhouse, that she recognized, and came to a large dirt ground with a fence all around.

Ugly Beast pulled the car to a stop and went to the metal fence, opening up the padlock on it.

When he came back, he drove into the fenced off

area, locked the gate, and then turned toward her.

"It's time to give you some driving lessons."

"Here?"

"There's no better place. Come on." He tapped her leg before he got out. The motor was still running.

With shaking hands, she released the seatbelt and climbed out of the car. As they passed each other, Ugly Beast captured her face, tilting her head back to look at him. "You've got this. You've got nothing to be afraid of."

"What if I trash your car?"

"You won't."

"I don't like this."

"You've got to learn one way or another. I didn't figure you'd want to risk killing a kid?"

"I don't want to hurt anyone."

He ran his thumb across her bottom lip. "I know."

She saw the heat in his gaze, and it called to her and begged for her to explore whatever this was with him.

As quickly as it appeared, he pulled away, leaving her feeling so alone.

"Get behind the wheel."

She didn't argue. Sitting behind the wheel, she buckled up the seatbelt, gripping the steering wheel in her hands.

She could do this.

It was easy, right? Piece of cake. Just as easy as riding a bike.

Only, she'd never ridden a bike before.

It didn't matter.

"You get a feel for the car?"

"Sure."

He laughed.

"I totally know what all these things are about,

and how to work them, because that's what I do."

She turned to him just as he rolled his eyes.

"This one's the clutch, the brake, the gas. The clutch you press to change gears. I'm a manual kind of guy. None of this automatic shit. So, I want you to put your foot on the clutch. Good, now, put the gear stick into first." She did that and immediately took her foot off the pedal and the car came to a sudden jerk.

She let out a scream, grasping the wheel even tighter.

Ugly Beast burst out laughing. "No, you've got to press a little on the gas and slowly bring your foot of the clutch."

"This is too much."

"Babe, you're going to learn how to drive a car."

"I don't want to."

"You want to be completely dependent on a guy just like your dad wants?"

"But you can drive."

"And what if I end up in prison? Or dead? What are you going to do then?"

She hated the thought of anything happening to him. Instead of saying anything, she stared straight ahead.

"See, not so fucking bad when you got a reason to keep on fighting. You ready to go again?"

She kept stalling the car three more times before finally rolling forward. All afternoon Ugly Beast was patient with her as she kept bringing the car to a sudden stop and stall, jerking it forward, letting out screams.

She hated every second of the two-hour driving lesson. By the time the sun was going down, she was more than ready to call it a day, and fortunately, Ugly Beast agreed.

On the way back to the house, she felt exhausted.

Between making dinner and driving, she was ready for bed.

"I don't think you're useless."

"What?"

"I like the idea of having a homecooked meal, but I don't think you're useless. If you can't ever be a good cook, I don't mind."

"You heard what I said?"

"All of the guys heard, baby. You're not useless."

"You don't even know if I can handle this thing with my dad."

"I know you can. You're a lot stronger than you give yourself credit for."

****

"Do you have no physical attraction to her at all?"

"Fuck off, Raven."

"I saw her bedroom. She still sleeps in it, and I've got to say, I'm confused. You're married."

Ugly Beast took a swig of his beer and glared at the soon to be dead only female member of the club. "Why are you bugging me about this?"

"You like her, I know you do."

He raised his brow. "Are you starting to have feelings, Raven? You know, those pesky human emotions that bother everyone else and you always claim to be immune to."

"I am immune to them."

"You're a fucking liar."

"I'm not."

"Then why do you want to beat down on his ass if you're immune to them?" Ugly Beast asked.

"You're changing the point, making me angry."

"She's in her own bedroom to give her space. Now leave me the fuck alone." Ugly Beast grabbed one of the bottled juices and headed out. He wasn't surprised to see Abriana on her own. He'd come to see in the past month she rarely approached anyone. Raven was the one to always find her, or himself.

She tended to keep to herself, and he didn't know if he liked that or not.

"I got you a drink," he said, handing it to her.

"Thanks."

Several of the old ladies and club bitches were in residence today. They were getting along as per Smokey's instructions. Lewis and Verge from their southern chapters had arrived last night, bringing in extra men, just in case.

He had arranged a meet with Sebastian Drago. It was a secret meet, one he had to take Abriana to, but she couldn't know about the meet at the same time. It was due to take place at the rally all the bikers attended. With so many men, women, and children around, it was the perfect opportunity to arrange the meet up without anyone paying attention.

He'd not seen Drago in over fifteen years, maybe even longer, and he had no desire to see him now, but the needs of the club far outweighed his own needs.

"You want to dance?" he asked, looking toward a couple of the bitches. He couldn't remember their names.

Since his marriage, a few of the faces of the women had changed, and he had a hard time keeping up. One of them he recognized from the porno set, but he doubted her real name was Swallow.

"It's fine."

The women were sexy dancing, and Abriana looked away, staring down at her hands. She was out of place, and it wasn't just the way she dressed either. She wasn't used to seeing women so overtly sexy and open about what they wanted.

"Have you ever been around a woman that likes

sex?"

Her head lifted up, her eyes looking a little wild at his question. "Excuse me?"

"It's a pretty reasonable fucking question. You have a place right here, and you're nervous. Why?"

"I'm not used to … being part of something like this."

"One of them works for us. Does porn," he said.

"Oh."

"Didn't your mom or anyone else talk to you about this? About sex and stuff?"

She looked away. "Not my mother."

"Someone did," he said. "You're never shocked by what I tell you. Sure, you're a little nervous all the time, but when you sucked my cock, you weren't afraid."

"Should we really be talking about this here?"

"I'm not a mafia prince, princess. I say and do whatever the fuck I want. The boys hear me, they know to keep their mouths shut around you. They won't say shit. That's what being loyal means. You're my woman. They can look at you, so long as I don't mind the way they look. Touching, I'll break their fingers, and if they try anything else, I'll kill them. Be honest with me."

He sat back and waited.

The guys moved around, none of them paying attention to him or to Abriana.

"It wasn't my mom that told me about sex and what was expected of me on my wedding night. It was a woman. I don't know her name or anything. I know she's dead. She was in my parents' home, and I stumbled onto her. I believe she died from stealing from someone. I'm not really sure. She's the one to tell me about sex and men."

"What did she say?"

"A lot. Actually. She talked about my first time.

She advised I get some lube if the guy I was with didn't know what he was doing. She said the first time would always be the worst, but after that, given time, it would be amazing. Depending on the guy. She told me about blowjobs, and what men want. How men want it. Erm, other things."

He saw her cheeks heat up, and he wanted to know what made her like that. "What else did she say?" He leaned in close.

"I don't want to talk."

"I'm your husband, Abriana. Tell me."

"Anal." The word was whispered. "She said with the right guy and time, it was amazing."

He burst out laughing. "I'm surprised this chick didn't scar you for life."

Abriana shrugged. "My mother didn't think I was important enough to warn. After the wedding night, she doubted any husband I had would want me, so why get into talking about something that won't happen." She shrugged.

"Do you like when I touch you?"

"Yes."

"Good."

The cell phone he'd been carrying in his pocket rang.

Abriana looked startled, but he held his hand up. It was the cell phone her father had given her.

"Let's take this some place private. I want it on speaker to hear."

They rushed inside, going straight to Smokey's office. Abriana let out a gasp as he had a woman riding him behind his desk. Smokey instantly put his hand across the woman's mouth, whispering something to her.

"Answer it," Smokey said.

Handing the cell phone to her, he pointed at the

speaker, and she clicked accept, and beeped it again so they all could hear.

"What took you so fucking long?" Vigo asked.

"I'm sorry. I was outside, and I didn't know if you wanted me to answer in front of everyone. Ugly Beast doesn't know I've got a cell phone."

He nodded at her.

"Fucking useless."

Ugly Beast tensed up.

"What do you know? What are they planning? We got word that Smokey's got men coming in all over the place."

"Erm, nothing, I don't know anything."

"So help me God, Abriana. Just fucking think, you worthless piece of shit."

She didn't cry, but he saw how her father's words were affecting her. He wanted to end the call, but they needed her to play along, even as it was annoying him to see her treated like this.

Get a grip. She's just a pawn.

"I don't know anything. I rarely see him. I mean it. I don't have much to do with the club."

"He's probably fucking some prettier piece of ass. I want answers, Abriana, and fast. I'll call you next Saturday. You better learn something or you'll be sorry."

"What exactly do you want me to do?"

"You've got a pussy, work him. Get him to fuck you. I don't care what. Work his president if that ugly scarred fuck won't give you something. I want details. If I don't get them, you're not needed."

The line went dead.

"Get the fuck out," Smokey said, shoving to one side the woman he had on his dick.

Abriana handed him the cell phone. "Can I please be excused?" she asked.

She wouldn't look at him, and Ugly Beast didn't like it.

"Go," Smokey said.

She was gone before he could dispute it.

"You okay, Ugly?" Smokey asked.

"Yes."

"You look like you want to go and tear Vigo a new one."

"I'm fine."

"It's okay to care."

"What the fuck?"

"She's your wife. I have to say, I don't like that shit he was saying about her, either," Smokey said. "I wonder if she's put up with that shit all of her life."

Ugly Beast didn't need to wonder; he knew she had. It's why she felt useless.

"They're getting desperate."

"You need to bring the meeting with Drago forward. We need to end this shit once and for all," Smokey said.

"I'm on it." Ugly Beast nodded at his president before leaving the room. The woman that been riding Smokey's dick was outside the office, smoking a cigarette, looking desperate to go back inside. He didn't even want to get into that shit.

Before he called Drago, he made his way upstairs and found his wife sitting on the floor near his bed, knees drawn up, and she wiped at her tears as he walked inside.

"I'm sorry for running off like that."

"Your dad speak to you all the time like that?"

"It's fine. It's nothing."

"It didn't sound like nothing to me." he said, closing the door.

He sat on the floor beside her, hating the sniffles that came from her.

"One day I'm going to kill your dad."

She laughed. "Good luck with that."

"You don't believe me."

"You're not the first guy who has wanted to kill him." She shrugged. "You won't be the last."

He took her hand. It was so soft and small against his own. Opening his hand up, he waited for her to spread her hand out. He waited, and his patience was rewarded. Holding her hand tightly, he turned her hand over so his was on top.

"I'm not like most guys, Abriana. He's made you cry one too many times. He'll die at the right time."

He rolled his head toward her, and she was staring at him. The silence in the bedroom spread out. She nibbled on her fat bottom lip, and he wanted to tug it between his own teeth.

"Will you make me one promise?"

"What?"

"Will you promise?"

"I don't make promises I can't keep. I need to know more before I give my word."

"Stay alive," she said. "Don't get yourself killed dealing with him."

"I won't get myself killed. I promise you that."

She smiled, and she rested her head against his shoulder.

Chapter Twelve

"You're wearing way too many clothes," Raven said, removing the jacket she wore.

The party at the clubhouse hadn't ended on the first night, but it was now Saturday and with all the kids gone for the night, things were heating up.

Abriana chuckled. Raven had sneaked her a beer and a shot of whiskey, and she was already starting to feel the buzz of the alcohol she'd consumed. She'd never been much of a drinker.

"Hey, I like that jacket," she said as Raven tossed it into the fire.

"It's an ugly ass jacket."

The shirt she wore was suddenly torn, showing off her arms. Out of nowhere Raven had a knife and was cutting at her jeans. It was way too warm anyway. Ugly Beast had warned her about the heat, but she hadn't listened. Most of the women that stayed at the club were in bikinis. They had all looked so comfortable. She wished she'd listened, but right now with Raven helping her, she felt more herself.

"Ow," she said, rubbing at her head. Raven had pulled the band out of her hair. "I could have done that."

"Girl, you need to know how to work your body."

Abriana glanced over at the men, but more specifically one man, Ugly Beast. He was sitting with the club, many of whom she didn't recognize, but the women there were getting a hell of a lot of attention.

She hated the spike of jealousy at seeing him watch them. Did he want them? Running fingers through her hair, she turned to Raven. "Why?"

"You think I can't see right through you. You're upset, and you don't even have a clue how to show it. It's pitiful. These men and even the whores will walk all over you if you don't stand up for yourself." Raven stepped back and clapped. "Perfect."

"Wait, this is stupid. I need to go back to his room." She walked a few steps, thinking about the night before. Talking with her father always made her feel like shit. He had that natural ability to always make her feel like less of a person. When Ugly Beast had come to see her, she had felt … something. He came to his room to see her, to make sure she was okay. That had to mean something, right?

Ugh, she was so confused.

They didn't have sex last night, or this morning.

She hated all of the questions and confusion. She wasn't used to being like this, or being nervous.

Raven grabbed her arm, stopping her from escaping. "No, you don't."

"This isn't me, Raven. I don't know what the hell I'm doing. If he wants to be with all those women, he can be. It's not up to me to stop him."

She took another step away, but Raven wouldn't let her move.

"I get it. You're not used to fighting for what you want. Abriana, you're not in your old world anymore. You don't have to ignore shit because you don't like it. Do you trust me?" She looked at her friend and nodded her head. "Good. Follow my lead."

"He doesn't like me like that!" She pulled her hand away.

"No, then why are you still here, huh? He'd have packed your ass off home. He likes you, Abriana, but like all stubborn fuckers, you're determined to do your own thing." Raven pulled her close. "We're just going to have some fun, do some dancing. Trust me."

The music suddenly became louder, and Raven pulled her into her arms.

"This is wrong."

"What? We're having some fun."

"Has he slept with any of those women?" Abriana asked.

"I don't know."

"You don't have to lie to me. I can take it."

Raven sighed. "Yes, he probably has fucked them all, Abriana. Don't take it personally."

"I'm not." She hated to know the women were getting all the attention. With her bland looks and body, she had always been ignored. Not a moment in her life had she been special. "I want to go to my room."

"Not happening, princess," Raven said. "I want to dance, and you're dancing with me."

The only light from the night was that created by the fire. Raven pulled her across the yard to where the other women were. Several of them were already completely naked and grinding on each other.

Much to Abriana's embarrassment, Raven pushed them out of the way. The moment the other women realized it was Raven, they backed down. Suddenly, Raven grabbed her ass, and with a little yelp, she had Raven's leg between her thighs.

"Don't look at them. Think about me."

"I shouldn't be doing this."

"Yes, you should. Have fun. Let go, Abriana. No one here is going to punish you for having fun and loving it. Let your hair down." Raven sank her fingers into her hair, and drew her close. They were a breath apart, and if she moved less than an inch, they could have kissed.

The song changed, and Raven, with all of her strength, pulled her back, twirling her. Letting go was not something she was used to. The last time she allowed herself to let go, sing, and dance, her father had punished her for the embarrassment she caused. She had thought she was home alone, and she'd played her music loud in her bedroom. He'd been there, and afterward she wasn't allowed her music. He had controlled every element of her life.

He's not here now.

Dance.

What do you want?

Your dad's approval or Ugly Beast's gaze on you?

Closing her eyes, she allowed herself to let go, giving up everything she'd been trained. Dancing with Raven, she wrapped her arms around the other woman's neck, swinging her hips in the way she'd seen in the music videos she loved so much.

She spun Raven around, holding her as they danced together. Everyone faded away as she focused all of her energy on Raven and their dance.

The heat of the moment was making her warm all over. She wanted Ugly Beast's hands, especially between her thighs.

She heard several cheers and applause as someone stood behind her. Before she could move to see who it was, a hand splayed across her stomach. He didn't try to turn her around, but she knew it was Ugly Beast without turning. He'd come to be with her. She didn't let Raven go even as his lips grazed her neck.

"What are you doing?" he asked.

"Dancing."

Raven spun around and laughed. "See, I knew he couldn't resist you. No one can resist two chicks dancing."

"Go away, Raven," Ugly Beast said.

"Not a chance. I'm having this dance."

Abriana laughed as she was pulled out of Ugly Beast's hands, and suddenly Raven was between them.

She danced along for a few seconds before moving out of Raven's hands. Her gaze was on Ugly Beast with Raven still between them. Taking Raven's advice, she allowed herself the chance to dance, and hoped she was tempting him.

Lifting her hands, she teased and tempted him, knowing her breasts were pressed against the shirt, and hoping she was enough to draw him close.

Ugly Beast did no more than lift Raven out of his way, dumping her on her ass so he could come to Abriana.

He wrapped his arm around her waist, and she laughed as he twirled her around. Feeling his arms around her thrilled her. She'd never known jealousy in her life, but with Ugly Beast and those women, she hated they'd been able to touch him, to feel him inside them, even before she was there.

Banding her arms around his neck, she stared into his blue eyes. They were so shockingly bright and mesmerizing. She had no doubt Ugly Beast had been a looker before his scars. She loved his scars. They didn't frighten her.

"Want to tell me what you were doing with Raven?" he asked.

"Dancing."

"Just dancing?"

"What else was it supposed to be?"

"I don't know. I saw the way she pushed those women aside."

"Did you want to keep watching them?" she asked.

Removing her hands from his neck, she went to move away. He caught her hips, and she cried out as his knee moved between her thighs, touching against her jean-clad pussy.

He leaned in close so his lips were against her ear. The music was still so incredibly loud.

"You're jealous."

Clenching her hands into fists at her sides, she stared at him, hating how right he was. She didn't want to be jealous of anyone, and yet, she was.

"Do you want them?" she asked.

"Excuse me?"

"Those women. Do you want them?"

"No."

"You've had them before."

"Before. Not since and not after."

"How can I believe you?" she asked.

He took hold of her hands, putting them around his neck before gripping her waist, and swinging her down to the floor before pulling her up against him.

"You can't believe me. I don't answer to anyone."

She hated him.

"But you can go and ask them if it will make you feel better. I've not been with anyone but you. I've no interest to be with anyone else."

"Then why haven't you?"

"Why haven't I what?"

She licked her lips, suddenly nervous. She shouldn't have drunk that beer or shot. *Crap.* "Why haven't you been with me?"

"Just over a month ago you were a virgin. You'd never known a cock." He kissed her cheek, and she felt a shiver work up her spine. "What I'm being, baby, is a gentleman. I'm really fucking trying to do the right thing, but dressed like this, dancing the way you do, you're making my job real fucking hard. You have no idea what I want to do to you."

She wanted to know more. How could she not?

He finally admitted he wanted her, and with all of these sexier, slender women around, it sent a thrill down her spine.

"What do you want to do to me?" she asked. Abriana had no idea where this woman had come from, but she loved it. She loved the ability to ask questions and to know she wasn't going to get hit at the end of it.

"How about I show you?"

Before she could protest, not that she wanted to, he held her hand and walked her further away from the clubhouse. Now this confused her. When he pressed her up against the shed, they were shrouded in darkness, but one look over his shoulder and she saw the men gathered around their fire and the music still so clear to hear.

"You like to dance?" he asked.

She stared into his eyes. For a split second, she was afraid. Her father had once asked the same question, only he'd punched her in the stomach afterward.

He's not my father.

"Yes." Her voice was a whisper, and she hated how afraid she still was of the man who was supposed to have loved her.

Ugly Beast put his hands on her waist, holding her steady. "I liked watching you dance."

She held her breath as he worked the button of her jeans and slowly began to work them down her body. She put her hands on them in an attempt to stop them.

"Trust me," he said.

Slowly, she let them go, staring into his blue eyes as her torn jeans fell to the ground at her feet. Her heart sped up. She stood outside in the warm heat with only the torn shirt and panties to keep her company.

"Anyone could see."

"No one will see you."

"How do you know that?" she asked.

"Because I'm not going to move and I cover your entire body. None of the brothers are allowed to see what is mine. You belong to me, Abriana. No one else. No one will ever be allowed to know how your virgin body looks."

"I'm not a virgin anymore."

"You'll always be my virgin." His fingertips skimmed up her thigh, and she licked her dry lips, feeling her need escalate as he slowly teased them toward her pussy. The moment he touched her, she couldn't contain her moan anymore. "I've never had a woman be jealous over me." He gripped her panties and yanked them from her body. She jerked a little from the force of his grip, but she liked it. She didn't want him to stop.

Sinking her teeth into her lip, she waited, anticipating what was about to come. When he cupped her pussy, it was the best feeling in the world, especially as he slid a finger between her slit.

Gripping his shoulders, she closed her eyes, loving the feel of his fingers as they filled her pussy. He pumped them inside, once, twice, three times, before pulling out to stroke over her clit.

"I love how wet you are, Abriana. You were jealous of those women?"

"Yes."

With his other hand, he cupped her face, tilting her head back so she had no choice but to look at him. "You really think I'd want them."

"They're beautiful women," she said.

"They're cum dumps. They go from brother to brother, taking dick whenever they want to. You think you have to compete with that."

"I … I don't like the way you look at them. I know you didn't want me, Ugly Beast, and one day when you've done what you need to do, you'll get rid of me…"

She never got to finish as he slammed his lips down on hers, silencing any protest she might have.

He finger-fucked her at the same time. His other hand went to her hair, gripping the back of her head, holding her in place for his kiss. At the same time, he pressed his cock against her stomach, and she felt his arousal.

"I'm not getting rid of you, Abriana. You belong to me. Those women don't hold a candle to you. This pussy is mine. Every single part of you belongs to me. You don't want me to look, I won't look, but you've got to make sure you're close by at all times, because it's you I want to look at. The moment you and Raven were on the floor, my eyes were on you. They will always be on fucking you."

He kissed her again. This time harder, more brutal, and she loved it. The sweet taste of him as he deepened the kiss made her want so much.

"I want you, Ugly Beast," she said.

"You want my dick?"

"Yes."

He pulled his fingers from her pussy, and she watched him take his cock out of his jeans. They were still fastened around his waist, and in the next second, he had her back pressed against the shed. "Wrap your legs around me." She did as he said, and he placed the tip of his cock at her entrance. Biting her lip, she waited, anticipating.

Every inch he sank down inside her felt so incredible. She didn't want him to stop. On the last inch, he gripped her hips and slammed her down. Sinking her nails into his leather cut, she tried to contain the moans. "I want to hear how much you love having my cock inside you. Don't hold fucking back, Abriana, let them hear it. I want to hear you. I want to fucking fill you.

You've got the best pussy, and it answers to my cock only."

She cupped his face, kissing him back, needing him even more as he began to thrust within her.

The pleasure was intense, and knowing they were outside, it only added to her arousal. Opening her eyes, she stared across the yard, and yes, she saw the fire still burning bright. The women were dancing, the men finally joining in, but they couldn't have Ugly Beast. She didn't mind the women being at the club, but this man, the one between her thighs, he belonged to her, and she didn't want to give him up.

He was hers.

Ugly Beast held her ass even tighter as his thrusts got harder and deeper. She felt how close he was and heard the change in his voice as he came. He sucked on the pulse at her neck, and she closed her eyes, giving herself over to the pleasure of the moment. After he finished, she expected him to zip up and leave. Only, he didn't.

He put her on her feet, and seeing his cum running down her inner thighs, he pressed a finger between her legs. He pushed two inside her, and drawing his cum up to her clit, he began to stroke her, drawing her close to orgasm. "You think I'm going to let you go without? I love seeing you come, Abriana. Now, give me my reward."

She felt open as he stared at her, watching, waiting, anticipating her release. Her entire body was alive and in need of his touch, desperate to feel him. When her orgasm finally came, he never stopped looking at her. He slowed his strokes down to a pace to draw out her release.

He kissed her lips, and she watched as he smiled. "Always the best sight to see."

****

"You know this is really fucking dangerous to meet here," Sebastian Drago said, taking a seat in the booth. The town was nowhere near were the Hell's Bastards were located, and Ugly Beast had even gone without a leather cut.

He had no choice but to bring the meeting forward.

"No one's associated here."

"Look at your face. Anyone who is anyone will remember you." Drago shook his head, muttering. He picked up the menu and sneered. "Seriously. You brought me to a burger joint." He dropped the menu.

"Get the stick out of your ass. I'm here alone, and you have four guards waiting for you back at your car. I told you to come alone."

"I only allowed my most trusted men, loyal. What couldn't wait two weeks, Umberto?"

"Don't call me that," Ugly Beast said.

Drago held his hands up. "Fine, fine. You don't want to remember. What was so important?"

"Gable Vigo paid a visit to my wife the other day." Ugly Beast watched as Drago sat up. "You didn't know."

"I … didn't."

"He ordered her to give him information regarding the Hell's Bastards. He wanted to know every single detail."

"I'm not aware of this."

"You are aware though of them meeting with another club, right?"

Drago's fingers drummed on the counter top.

"Can I get you anything?" the waitress asked.

The waitress was Raven. They had paid the management team handsomely to allow her to be present for this meeting. Smokey didn't want him going in alone, and seeing as most of the waitresses were female, it seemed like the perfect plan.

"Yes, thank you."

She leaned over, pouring out a cup, and then to Ugly Beast, she poured him a cup. Neither of them kept eye contact. She turned on her heel and left.

"You really think I don't know she's one of your club members?" Drago asked. "You're not dealing with an amateur here. I was the one to advise the consigliere of the benefit of doing business with the Hell's Bastards. I'm a little disappointed in you, Umberto."

He gripped the cup.

"You know the workings of Garofalo's businesses more than anyone. If I recall, you made it your business."

"Smokey wants to know what he's doing."

"We all know it's obvious. Garofalo wants you gone. Vigo didn't put much stock in that daughter of his. He always said she was too ugly and stupid, and he'd need to sell her to a thick, blind man. Instead, he got you."

"If you continue to insult my wife, I will end you." He tapped the point of the blade beneath the table on Drago's knee. "All of your men wouldn't make it to save you."

"I'm simply stating the facts when it comes to Vigo and Abriana. She's worthless to him, unless she can provide the information he clearly wants. The other MC, they're demanding more turf and want to expand the drug use. If their deal goes down, Garofalo will look weak. Weaker than he does with the way he reached out to the Hell's Bastards." Drago opened his jacket. "Can I give you a file?"

"You want me to read shit?"

"You better be able to read. I paid a fortune for your education, Umberto."

If this fucker kept on calling him that, he wasn't going to be able to hold back from beating the living shit out of him.

Drago pulled out a slender file and slid it across the table. "It's time for the boss to go."

Putting his knife away, Ugly Beast opened the file and looked at the few pictures and the paperwork attached to them. "What is this?"

"Garofalo has an interest in young girls … underage girls."

Ugly Beast looked up at him. "This is Abriana's sister."

"Yes, and from what I've been made aware of, Garofalo has been with her since she was fourteen years old. The girl thinks he's in love with her. When the truth is, he's got an entire harem of underage girls across the city. Each one is being paid to service him. Some have been taken from families, stolen so he could enjoy the fruits of their virginity."

There were several explicit pictures, which only served to turn his stomach. "Why are you giving me this? It's your problem, not mine."

"Now, it's your problem. I need for the Hell's Bastards to take care of Vigo and Garofalo, but it also needs to be done when they're both servicing their own needs, not the good of the outfit." Drago pointed down at the file. "They need to go."

"Why are you giving this to me and not Smokey?"

"You'll give it to Smokey, and you'll deal with it. Until then, I've got to keep Garofalo happy. I'd also be careful. Abriana, if she doesn't come through with what Vigo wants, he will find a way to send a message to her."

Drago nodded at him and was about to climb out of the booth.

"Why did you save me?" Ugly Beast asked.

Drago paused, turning to look at him. "Excuse me?"

"You didn't have to save me, and yet you did." Ugly Beast waited.

"I had my reasons. Enjoy the rest of your day, Umberto."

With that, Drago got up and left.

Raven slid into the booth afterward. She changed out of the waitressing uniform and was back in her club kit.

"He knew who you were."

"Of course he did. What's with the file?" she asked.

He slid it over to her.

"Wow, dirty old men like young girls. What's the deal?" She slammed the file closed, and he ran his fingers through his hair, trying to think.

"I don't know. He wants us to get rid of Vigo and Garofalo."

"I've got no problems with that. If we do it and he doesn't show his hand, we're at war with the outfit."

"Exactly."

"Do you think you can trust him?" Raven asked.

"I don't trust anyone but the club." He tapped his fingers on the counter top. "Fuck!"

"You were hoping for some answers?"

"I knew what was coming today. I didn't want to fucking think about it. Come on, let's get back to the clubhouse. We've got to update Smokey."

Smokey didn't like the information he presented him with either, once they arrived three hours later.

"What's our next move?"

"I've got to think," Smokey said.

"We need to know what's going to happen," Ugly Beast said. "Vigo is calling on Saturday."

"Until she proves her loyalty to us, we've not got a problem with them finding out we know." Smokey opened the file again and shook his head. "Tell me, Ugly Beast, what does this really mean? We know the world is a fucked-up place."

"Even the outfit has certain standards," Ugly Beast said. "This, right here, is a sure sign of weakness. Someone was able to picture him doing this stuff to underage girls."

"Save me from fucking men in suits." Smokey dropped the file and began to pace his office. "I should have let you kill this fucker when you had the chance."

Ugly Beast said nothing. He would always do what was good for the club, not his own personal enjoyment.

Just as he was about to say so, gunfire erupted across the clubhouse parking lot. Screams followed.

"Abriana!"

Rushing out of the clubhouse, gun in his hand, he made it clear of the parking lot. He saw the three bikers, each with a gun pointed at the clubhouse. Bodies were on the ground, and he saw some with blood.

He spotted Abriana with Raven, who gave him a thumbs up.

The bikers took off, and he didn't hesitate. Grabbing his bike, he straddled his machine, knowing several of the club brothers were following on behind him.

There was no way cops would get called, as they didn't live close to any developed area.

Spotting the first guy, he held his gun, took aim, and fired at the tire. The guy was flung off his motor.

His club would take them back to the clubhouse where they would be dealt with. They would be killed. He fired again, but the other biker swerved and he missed. The biker in front of him however, caught the bullet, and as his bike swerved out from under him, it took the third biker down. Riding past them, he spun around and turned to face them all.

The Hell's Bastards were already there, picking them up. The leather cut all three men were wearing stated they were prospects, and it pissed him off to know their rivals had sent boys to do a man's job.

On the way back to the clubhouse, he saw the doctor's car in the lot, but also, a couple of brothers with pensive faces.

"What is it?" Smokey asked.

"Raven got hit in the stomach. She's refusing to go to the hospital."

His thoughts were on Abriana, and he rushed into the clubhouse going to the backroom where they all got stitched up.

Raven was on the table, passed out.

Abriana sat on a chair, stroking the woman's head. Tears were running down her face.

"Thank God, maybe you could make her see reason. I can't do everything here. The wound is too deep. She has to go to a hospital."

Ugly Beast let Smokey handle it. He walked up to his wife, stroking a hand down her hair, holding her shoulder.

"She hates hospitals. If she wakes up in one, all hell will break loose."

"She's losing too much blood, and I can't operate. The bullet didn't come out. This isn't a through and through, and she could have internal bleeding. Her only chance of surviving is in the hospital."

"Fuck!" Smokey slammed his fist against the wall, and Abriana jumped. "Pieces of fucking shit."

His gaze turned to Abriana. "Did you know? Did you fucking know?" Smokey advanced on her.

This was the first time Ugly Beast had ever gotten in his president's way. He stood in front of Smokey. "You know she didn't do this."

"It's her fucking family that did this. We don't need to interrogate those fucking dweebs. We know the truth. Pieces of shit!"

"She showed her loyalty."

"I swear I didn't do this," Abriana said. "Please, can we take her to the hospital? I'll sit with her. I don't want her to die."

Smokey stepped away, and paced. "She's going to the hospital. She's not fucking dying on my watch. One of the boys will watch her though."

Abriana tensed at his side, and Smokey looked at her.

"You don't have what it takes to protect the both of you. As far as I'm concerned, Garofalo has just shown his hand, and his days are numbered."

Hunter and Kinky were to take the first shift in keeping Raven safe.

All of the brothers were pissed they hadn't done a better job in protecting them. It was rare for a drive-by shooting but not unheard of. This was their turf, and as yet, they weren't in a war over land or fuck all.

They all stayed at the hospital while Raven was in surgery.

Several of the people had moved when he took a seat with Abriana. They looked at his face in disgust. Abriana held his hand though. She was pressed close to him, almost as if she was afraid he'd leave.

Time ticked slowly by, and they were all aware of

the three men chained in their basement.

Those men were about to get a lot of anger thrown down on them.

All it required was one word from them, and they were going to fucking slaughter the outfit.

"I'm going to use the bathroom," Abriana said.

She let out a little sniffle, and he watched her go.

He waited a couple of minutes before following her to the bathroom. Opening the door slowly as to not to alert her of his presence, he saw her gripping the sinks, crying.

Entering the room, he gripped her neck, hearing her gasp as he pulled her against him.

"What are you doing?"

"It's not your fault," he said.

"How can you say that? She's dying."

"She's not dying. You're not the one to pull the trigger or organize the attack. We'll deal with it. We'll handle it."

"It's really happening, isn't it? We're all going to die."

"You need to have a little more faith in us than that." He cupped her face, pressing her up against the sink and his hard body. "We're not going to die. I'm not going to let anything happen to you."

"I don't care about me, Ugly Beast. Raven is … she's the first person to treat me like a friend. I don't want to lose her. Not ever. It probably sounds silly and childish."

"It's not." He assured her.

She tried to pull away from him, but he wouldn't let her go.

"Please. I don't want you to see me like this."

"See you what?"

"Like this. I … I'm useless, okay? I can't help

her, and I don't know how to help you. I'm so lost right now, and you need to go back to your club."

He pressed his lips against hers. "You're not useless."

"You don't have to try and say nice things to me. I know I'm not good at anything."

"Do I strike you as the kind of man that'll lie to you? I won't lie. You're not useless, and I won't have you saying otherwise. Cry. Scream. Rant. Rave. I don't care. You're hurting because you care. I care."

"Why are you not crying?"

"Because I don't deal with my hurt the same way. I'm fucking infuriated that those pieces of shit thought they could deal with us in this way. I'm going to kill Garofalo, Abriana, and I'm going to take care of your dad. They won't be able to identify the bodies when I'm through with them. That's the kind of monster I am. The one you were given to."

"You're not a monster." She cupped his cheek.

She hadn't seen him kill. One day, she would, and she'd see who she really married.

Chapter Thirteen

Raven had lost a lot of blood, too much. She had to stay in the hospital for a couple of days before they would even consider allowing her to leave. Kinky and Hunter had to each stop her from trying to leave. She had 'round the clock care and security to guarantee her safety.

Abriana was up in his room at the club. He wanted the club together, stronger, and sending her home he'd have to get a brother to stay with her, and Ugly Beast didn't want her too far away.

When Vigo and his men showed up, he was going to be ready for them.

He stood back, watching as Smokey took out his aggression on the three men who were chained to chairs. They'd already pissed themselves, and from the smell, one or all had shit themselves as well.

They were prospects, and this was the job they'd signed up for. Even to be taken, they had to handle interrogation.

"We're not talking." The one who had declared himself leader of the prospects, spat. There were piss stains on his pants, but clearly he thought he was a big, tough guy.

Rocky, Verge, and Lewis all laughed.

Ugly Beast kept his arms folded, leaning against the wall, waiting to see what they'd say. They all knew what this was about, and once they got the information, they'd plan their next move.

No one had died in the shootout. Raven had been the closest to death, but the prospects had been bad shots, and the only damage they really caused was to a couple of the bikes. They couldn't be ridden again until they got the all clear of their safety.

Smokey stepped back.

"We know who you work for. We know your orders. So why don't you save us all this pain and confusion and just tell us," Smokey said.

"Fuck you. Your piece of shit club is going down. All of you bastards are going six feet under, and we'll be riding your whores and making them wish for death before we're finished."

"I'm going to call him One," Ugly Beast said.

"One?" Smokey asked.

"Yeah, One. He's their little leader. The one to his left, Two, and the one that looks like he wants the floor to open up and swallow him, Three," Ugly Beast said. "I love a good countdown."

Smokey smirked. "So, Three, what brings you here?"

He dragged a seat over to number three, who let out a little whimper.

Ugly Beast had been in this position as well. Another club, another time. One scar after another had appeared on his body and face for his loyalty to his patch.

Smokey wrapped his fingers around the man's neck, and he let out a terrified scream. It was a very feminine sound, but there was no mistaking the guy was a dude.

"Please, don't hurt me. I didn't want this. I just wanted to have some fun. Fuck some chicks. I don't want this. Please, please. We were to kill as many of you as possible." He began to sob.

"Shut the fuck up," one said, yelling.

"I don't want to die. I just wanted my dick sucked, and you've seen the kind of bitches they have. They are always willing to fuck." He was shaking so bad.

The sound of piss hitting the floor rang out in the

basement.

"I'll fucking kill you if you tell these assholes anything. I fucking swear to you. I'll fucking kill you."

Ugly Beast had enough. Nodding at Smokey, he got his president's approval before he walked over to One and slashed his fucking throat.

The sound of gurgling filled the room.

Three began to shriek in terror, and just as he figured, number two started to talk. They didn't know everything, but they knew enough for Smokey and the club to fill in the blanks. Once they were done, they wrapped all three of the bodies, threw them in the back of the truck, and Rock took them to be disposed of.

Ugly Beast left the basement and made his way toward the bathroom.

Entering the room without knocking, he saw Abriana staring at her reflection in the mirror. She looked pale. A little too pale.

He didn't say anything as he washed the knife in the sink and his hands, which were covered in blood. He felt her eyes on him.

When all the blood was gone down the sink, he reached over to the door and flicked the lock in place.

Turning toward Abriana, he removed his clothes, piece by piece. His leather cut, he hung up on the doorknob. His jeans and shirt would go to be burned.

"You killed them?" she asked.

"Does that surprise you?"

"Not really. They hurt Raven."

"They were boys pretending to be men," Ugly Beast said.

"Why kill them then?"

"They opened fire on our clubhouse. There's no way for us to strike a deal or create peace afterward. If we let them go, we look weak, and after seeing Raven on

Doc's table. I wasn't going to let it happen."

"So you just killed them."

"I didn't have a choice." He looked at her. "I don't care that I killed them either. They hurt Raven. You could have been killed there. An experienced man would have killed you."

"It's my dad, isn't it?" she asked.

He didn't say a word. Reaching for her, he expected her to flinch away from him, so it shocked him as she stepped up close to him, her hands going to his inked chest.

"You're not going to tell me."

"There is shit you don't need to know."

"You're going to kill him?" she asked.

"I told you I would."

She nodded. "Raven's going to be okay."

"She's going to be okay." He stared down at her pretty, plump lips. "I need to shower."

"Okay."

"Join me."

He opened the belt of her robe, and pulled the nightshirt she wore from her body. They wouldn't be disturbed, and even if they were, the door was now locked. Turning on the water, he stepped beneath the cold spray and pulled Abriana into the tub with him.

She gasped. "It's cold."

"I know." He needed the chill right now. He needed something to take his mind off of killing.

Staring at Abriana, he felt his dick harden. Her tits looked heavy and thick. He wanted to fuck her, to take her and drive his cock inside her.

"I can't be gentle tonight."

"You don't have to be gentle with me. I won't break."

He cupped her face. His hands were so big. He

could crush her head so easily. With his hands, he was used to causing death. He was good at it. "You shouldn't say that to me. I'm not a good man, Abriana."

"You've been good to me. You didn't want me, and yet, you've been good to me."

"What makes you think I didn't want you?"

"Look at me, Ugly Beast."

He chuckled. "Look at me, Abriana. I'm a fucking monster. I kill, and I don't care. Those men, those boys, they got in the way of the club, and I took care of them. I will always protect the club."

"I know your loyalty will always be to them."

He slammed his lips down on hers, pressing her up against the opposite wall, away from the spray of the water. Taking hold of her hands, he pressed them above her head. "If you need me to stop, just tell me."

"I won't break."

Ugly Beast couldn't help but doubt her claim. She didn't have a fucking clue what he wanted.

Drawing her hands up above her head, he kept them locked in place within one of his. With his other hand, he slowly slid it down her body, touching each of her tits in turn. Cupping one mound, he slid his thumb across the extended peak. Her nipple hardened, and he stared into her eyes, watching the pleasure flash across her face. It only served to heighten his arousal for more of her.

Moving to her second breast, he did the same before caressing down her body to stroke her pussy.

He kicked open her legs and pushed two fingers inside her, stretching out her tight cunt. He wasn't going to go easy on her tonight, so he needed for her to be prepared to take a pounding from his cock.

Spreading his fingers apart, he worked in a third finger, and this time pressed his thumb to her clit, watching her. He repeated this for a couple of minutes, feeling her cream soak his fingers.

Pulling out of her, he spun her around.

"Keep your hands above your head. Don't fucking move," he said.

Her hands pressed flat against the tile, and he let her go, waiting to see if she'd disobey him.

Her hands stayed on the wall. Sliding his hands down her back, he moved them to the front, holding her tits as he kissed her neck. Sucking on her pulse hard, he bit down, knowing he'd leave a mark on her flesh.

Trailing his lips down her back, he moved to the base just above her ass, flicking his tongue across the small indent. He cupped her ass, pressing the cheeks together and spreading them apart. He moved her body so her ass was sticking out, and he got the perfect view of her anus and cunt.

She was wet but not nearly wet enough, not enough to satisfy him. When he took her, he wanted her dripping, hungry, desperate.

Spitting on his fingers, he teased her entrance, watching her take his finger. He leaned in close and slid his tongue around her hole, teasing her. He circled her cunt before plunging inside.

She cried out, and he held her ass apart to take all of his tongue.

"Let go of the wall," he said. "I want you to hold your ass open."

He saw her hands were shaking, but she didn't stop him as she held her ass open. With his hands free, he fucked her pussy with his tongue, and stroked over her clit with his fingers, feeling her get even more wet.

With his other hand, he began to stroke over her puckered anus. The first stroke had her tensing up. He didn't stop, nor did he let up in his ministrations. He worked her body for his pleasure, wanting to touch every single part of her.

All of her firsts belonged to him.

He fucking owned her, and he was going to take every single one of them. It was his duty, his fucking right.

When he pushed against her tight muscles, she let out a gasp, and he pressed the tip of his finger inside her, feeling her shake against him. It felt fucking amazing to have her in this place. As his own little fuck toy.

She was his wife, and he needed her in more ways than he ever wished to admit.

He drew her close to orgasm but didn't push her over the edge. He wasn't ready for her to come just yet, but he wanted her body primed for him.

With the finger in her ass, he pumped inside her, teasing, tormenting. After she started to rock back against him, he gave her more, sliding more of his finger into her ass.

"Oh, my," she said.

"You like that?" he asked.

"I don't know."

"I'm going to fuck your ass, Abriana. You're going to take my cock because you belong to me. Every single part of you belongs to me." He turned her in the shower so the side of her body was against the tile wall. She stared down at him, and with his gaze on her, he pushed two fingers in her ass and in her pussy, penetrating her.

She closed her eyes, licking her lips, and he saw the frown across her face.

"Fucking look at me. I'm the one inside your body. No one else. This body belongs to me, only mine."

"Yes!"

"I'll fuck this pussy and this ass, and you're

going to like it. You don't want me looking at other women, you give me what I want, and in return." He stood, pulling his fingers out of her holes. "I'll give you what you fucking want."

He claimed her lips, pressing her against the wall as he roughly gripped her ass. Lifting her up, he found her entrance and slammed in deep.

She cried out, but he wouldn't let her move away from the kiss. He consumed her, fucking owned her lips, and not a part of her would he let her go. Breaking from the kiss, he stared down at his cock and watched as she opened up around him, taking his cock. Up and down her worked her cunt on him, his cock slick with her cream.

Even if she was afraid, she was also incredibly aroused, and so was he. He couldn't stop. All he wanted to do was bounce her on his dick, to flood her pussy with his cum. He wanted it to last though.

When he drove his cock inside her, she gripped his shoulders, holding on as he made her tits bounce with every forced thrust. Over and over, he took over, fucking her.

When he nearly came, he pulled out of her, and moved her beneath the spray of the water. Grabbing the soap, he lathered up her body.

"Ugly Beast?" she asked.

"Shut up."

He washed her body, followed by her hair. Once he finished with her, he handed her the bar of soap to take care of him. Watching her, he felt how nervous she was. Her hands held a little tremor with each stroke of the soap.

He watched her though, hungry to be inside her pussy.

Hungry to take every part of her as his own.

Abriana handed him back the soap, and next he

knelt down in the shower and allowed her to do his hair.

She did so, gently, with care, and by the time she finished, he was ready.

Turning off the shower, he climbed out of the bathtub and held out his hand. There was only one towel, and he held it out to her.

She quickly wrapped it around her body, and as he went to the door, she tugged on his hand. "What about you?"

"There's nothing to worry about with me." He opened the door, and even with club brothers in the hallway, none of them stopped him.

A couple paused to watch him as he pulled his way down the short corridor to his room.

He slammed the door closed, and pressed her against it.

"You've got one chance to leave now."

"I'm not going anywhere."

"I want to fuck you so you know who you belong to."

"I know who I belong to. I want this. I want you. I'm not leaving. I'm not stopping."

He grabbed her tit and squeezed it. At the same time, he removed the towel covering her and moved her toward the bed.

Bending her over, he drew her to her knees so she was at the perfect angle. Spreading the cheeks of her ass, he slid in deep, feeling her pussy tighten around his length.

They both moaned.

Gripping her hips, he started out slow, watching his cock fill her pussy. She coated in his dick in her arousal, and he wanted her sodden. Pulling out of her pussy, he flipped her over onto her stomach. Lifting her legs up, so they were over his shoulder, he thrust back inside her, staring down into her brown gaze.

"Watch my dick, Abriana. Watch me fuck you. This is what I want. I want you, only fucking you."

He gripped her hips and fucked her hard. The sounds of flesh slapping against flesh and their groans filled the room.

It wasn't enough; he wanted to get deeper. He moved her to the headboard. He put her hands on the wall, angled her ass, and fucked her. Pulling her back against him, he tilted her head so he could take her lips. Running his hand down the front of her body, he found her pussy, stroking her clit.

"Come for me, Abriana. Come on my dick." He fucked her, and as he teased her body, he felt her began to tighten. Her body was ready for him. She came, and he swallowed the sounds of her screams, loving as she gave herself to him.

With his cock covered in her orgasm, he moved so she was on her stomach, pushing a couple of pillows under her. Ugly Beast ordered her to spread her ass wide. Going to his drawer, he used some extra lubrication on her anus.

Abriana didn't protest, but he felt her tense up.

He wasn't going to hurt her, just fuck her until she couldn't think straight. Throwing the lube out of the way, he moved over her thighs, keeping them together but her ass stuck in the air at the perfect angle.

Pressing the tip of his hard cock to her puckered anus, he began to fill her. She let out a little cry, and he paused, giving her time. Stroking the base of her back, he slowly, inch by inch, took the final piece of her virginity.

Sinking balls deep inside her ass, he stayed perfectly still. Her hands touched him from where she held her ass open, and with his cock now inside her, he took hold of her hands, placing them on the bed. Locking their fingers together, he pressed her down to the bed and began to rock inside her.

Building up his tempo, he felt the change in her, and when she could finally handle what he wanted, he fucked her, taking her deeper, working his cock. He kissed her neck, trailing down to her lips, and kissing her harder, consuming himself with all that was Abriana.

When he came, he did so crying her name, the sound echoing around the room as he took his pleasure from her body.

****

"I hate the hospital," Raven said.

"I doubt anyone doesn't."

"You ever been in the hospital?"

"No."

"Ugh. I feel like a child."

"Stop acting like one." Abriana looked up from the magazine Raven had thrown at the nurse and raised her brow at her friend. "You're being waited on hand and foot. Why can't you enjoy that?"

"I hate being poked and prodded. They don't have a fucking clue what they're doing. No doctor does. They're a waste of fucking space."

Abriana closed the magazine and moved to the bed, taking Raven's hand. "It's okay to be scared."

Raven pulled her hand out of her grip. "I'm not fucking afraid."

She sighed. "Okay, then what is the big deal?"

"I hate hospitals. It's not a big deal."

"There's got to be a reason for hating them."

Raven shook her head and looked away.

Abriana didn't walk away. She stared around the sterile room. "I don't like hospitals either. They give me the creeps."

"I don't trust anyone to take care of me."

"Why not?"

"Because, my place in the club is because I'm strong, Abriana. If I appear weak, I lose my spot, and I can't do that. I can't lose the Hell's Bastards. They mean everything to me."

"You're not weak. You don't even look weak. You've got to stop freaking out and learn to relax. If you keep this up, you're not ever going to get out of here. You keep busting stitches open."

"Can't I come and stay with you guys?" she asked.

"Nope," Ugly Beast said, biting into an apple as he entered the room. He was supposed to be getting them some coffee. He tossed her an apple as he took a seat in the corner of the room.

It had been three days since they had … sex. When she woke up the following morning after their fuck session, Ugly Beast had been gone, and she didn't know who to talk to about everything. He'd taken her ass and walked right across the hall to wash himself. He'd brought back a washcloth for her. Ugly Beast hadn't been done with her though. He'd only been getting started.

She'd not been able to talk to him. By the time he came to bed, she was out cold, if he even made it to bed. It was like they weren't married.

"Why not?"

"I know what kind of a bitch you are as a patient. You think I'm going to put my wife through that shit? I wasn't born yesterday."

"Ugh! This is so unfair."

"Get over it," Smokey said, entering the room. "If you stopped stressing and being a stubborn bitch, you'd be out already. The doctors said all is fine. It's because you won't rest and relax and allow those stitches to heal."

"I don't see what the big deal is. You guys can walk right out after being stitched up," Raven said.

Abriana took a bite of her apple.

She felt a tingling down her spine, and as she looked behind her, she saw Ugly Beast was staring right at her.

"There is a big difference between getting shot in the arm and shot in the gut. All of us would still be in the hospital."

Abriana looked away from Ugly Beast, taking another bite of her apple, more aware of the way he kept on looking at her.

"If Abriana can take care of me…" Raven said.

"No. She's busy, and I'm not going to be cruel. You're staying here. Just be thankful I brought her along this time," Ugly Beast said.

Raven sighed and collapsed back, giving an oof as she pulled her stitches. The guys were right; she really was stubborn and wouldn't take no for an answer.

"Fine. Fine. Moving on to easier stuff. Get me up to speed?"

At the silence, Abriana looked behind her again. Ugly Beast and Smokey were sharing a look.

"Oh, come on. You tell me I can't leave the hospital, and now I can't know what the fuck is going on."

"We're being careful. You make it out of here alive in one piece, we'll talk," Smokey said.

Abriana's stomach grumbled as she ate the apple.

"It's time for Abriana and me to go. I've got to feed her."

"You heading back to the clubhouse?" Smokey asked.

"Nah, going home. Got a few things I need to

take care of."

"All right, brother."

"Don't leave me here to die," Raven said.

"You're not going to die. You've got to learn to relax and be a good little girl," Abriana said.

"I don't like you. What happened to my sweet friend?"

She didn't look toward Ugly Beast. She couldn't.

Abriana had wanted to come and see her friend today, but she'd also been a little scared in case Raven could see how nervous she was.

Leaving the hospital, Ugly Beast didn't take the elevator but the stairs. She followed behind him, as doctors were passing and other patients and their family and friends.

When they got outside, he took hold of her hand, leading her toward his car.

"Am I getting another driving lesson?"

"Not yet."

"Oh." He'd not taken her for a driving lesson since the last one. She didn't need to be told the club was on edge since the shooting. During the past couple of days, she'd noticed an increase in the bikers arriving. None of whom she recognized but each one saying the same. They were Hell's Bastards, only from a different charter.

"When all the shit blows over, we'll start your teaching again."

"Okay."

She climbed into the car and buckled her seatbelt.

The silence in the car was deafening. She didn't know how to stop it.

Pressing her lips together, she tried to think of something funny or witty, and instead, her mind went blank.

"Do you know what you want me to say to my dad when he calls?" she asked.

Ugly Beast drove out of the parking lot and headed in the direction of home. Was it her home?

"Yes. He wants you to mention the shootout, but he wants you to tell him we had a couple of men die. We captured the prospects who shot at us and you've not heard from them."

"I can do that."

Again, more silence.

She stared out of the window, wishing she could say whatever was on her mind. Running her hands up and down her thighs, she felt incredibly nervous. "Why did you leave?" she asked.

"Abriana, we don't have to do this."

"I want to do this."

"Why?"

"We had … sex, and you just left. We had a lot of sex."

"And?"

"Did I do something wrong? I didn't think I did anything wrong. You had a good time. I had a good time. I don't know what I did wrong. I'm so confused."

"You didn't do anything wrong."

"Then why did you leave?" she asked. "We shared … something, and you just got up and walked away."

He burst out laughing. "What exactly did we share, Abriana?"

"We … you know … we…" She couldn't finish it and her cheeks heated. She hated how stupid she was being. This man was her husband. He'd taken every single part of her, and at his own words, she belonged to him so why couldn't she just say the damn words.

"We fucked, Abriana. I took your pussy and your

ass. I blew my load in your ass, and I watched it drip out. It was fucking dirty and sexy as fuck. That's what I did."

"So why did you leave? What did I do? It's what you wanted."

He pulled onto the drive. "For fuck's sake, Abriana. It was fucking. That's all it was. Plain, cold fucking. I needed a pussy or an ass. You gave me both. You're my fucking wife, but I didn't ask for this. I didn't want a wife. I don't deal with women. They are nothing more than holes for me to deal with! I don't do cuddles or any of the other bullshit. It's not my job to make you feel better."

His words cut her to the core. They served to remind her of her place. Ugly Beast was right. They weren't in a relationship. They weren't in anything. This was her problem, not his. She had believed and hoped for something more.

"Thank you for clarifying that for me."

She unbuckled her seatbelt, rushed out of the car, and went straight to her room. She heard Ugly Beast enter a few minutes later. The door to the front of the house slammed shut. She flinched at the sound but made no move to leave, no move to do anything other than sit on her bed. Clenching her hands together, she let the tears come.

Her father was always right. No man would ever want her. She was unlovable, and nothing she could do would ever change that. No one would ever love a bland face, no matter how kind the person was.

When all of this was over with her father and she didn't need to keep looking over her shoulder, she'd leave. Ugly Beast wouldn't have to put up with her any more than he had to.

Chapter Fourteen

Abriana turned the phone off after giving her father the message he'd asked her to. She stood in Smokey's office, and he watched her. She placed the cell phone within his hands and without another word, left the office. The door clicked silently behind her.

He knew where she was going without looking out of the window. Raven had finally gotten her own way, and after relaxing enough to heal, the doctors had granted her wish. She was still on bedrest, but Abriana was taking care of her, helping the woman get around in the wheelchair that had been provided.

"Want to tell me what that was all about?" Smokey asked.

"It's nothing."

Smokey laughed. "I know pussy, and your wife is hurting."

Ugly Beast raised a brow. "You care?"

"She's your wife. She's showing her loyalty to the club, so yeah, I care."

"I put her in her place the day of the hospital. She didn't like it. Not my problem." Neither of them had spoken since that day. He'd taken her home with every intention of fucking her again. Only, after their argument, she didn't come downstairs for food. She did eat something as the pizza he ordered had missing slices the next morning. Since then, they'd stayed at the clubhouse. They shared a bed, but she huddled as far away from him as possible. She never came to him if she needed anything, and always kept to herself. Since Raven had returned home, she had some company. Without Raven, she simply read, and never bothered anyone. There had been no dancing. When the bitches tried to lighten the mood, Abriana would get up and leave.

"Really, what is her place?"

"She's my wife in name. She wants more. It's not going to happen."

Smokey. "You do know in order for her to be in name only, you shouldn't have fucked her."

"My marriage is of no concern. What's the next plan?"

"With Raven out of the hospital and Vigo and Garofalo believing we're distracted, I think it's time we found these lovely young ladies."

"You want to go and kill his young harem?" Ugly Beast asked.

"No. I want to unleash them. I want to make sure Garofalo loses them. If what Drago says is true, he's not going to admit to having them, is he? I want to piss him off. He thinks he can take from me, it's time he learns his lesson."

"I think it's lame," Ugly Beast said.

"I know, but these girls need to go. I'm not going to let them keep being abused."

"What about Chantel, Abriana's sister?"

"That one is tricky." Smokey tossed him his cell phone. "Check out the last text message."

Ugly Beast opened up the phone. "Chantel's pregnant."

"Yes, and I'm guessing it's Garofalo's brat. Wouldn't that make you—"

"Shut the fuck, Smokey."

His president laughed, holding up his hands. "I'm just the messenger. Don't get pissed at me. Personally, I've always been interested in aged pussy, but hey, I guess I'm picky."

"I don't want Chantel near Abriana."

"Why not?" Smokey asked.

"The last conversation the two sisters had, I

didn't like. I don't want them in the same room."

"You're getting soft on me, Ugly Beast."

"No, your plan is getting soft."

"Oh, did I also happen to mention that our trip will take us on the turf of the very MC that tried to fucking end us?" Smokey said.

Ugly Beast tossed the cell phone back to Smokey. "It will?"

"Yeah, and I've got it on good authority that tomorrow night, there's going to be one hell of a party. You know how I love to crash a party. Gather the men. Go and get Raven. I want church right now to talk through my plan."

"On it."

Ugly Beast rounded up the men, saving Raven until last.

Heading outside, he found Abriana sitting on the ground near the wheelchair. Raven wore her leather cut, and she must have told his wife he was heading their way. She closed the book she'd been reading and stood up.

"It's time for church," he said.

"Awesome. Wheel me in."

"Should you be going to church? You're injured," Abriana said.

"Injured I may be. My ears still work perfectly fine."

"And your mouth," Ugly Beast said.

"Okay. I'll see you in a bit." Abriana turned on her heel and left.

Raven let out a whistle. "What did you do, man?"

"I didn't do anything."

"I've known Abriana as long as you have, and not once has she tried to get out of anyone's company as quickly as she tries to yours."

"Mind your own fucking business."

Raven laughed. "It's official. You totally did something wrong."

"I didn't do anything wrong. You want to be in church, you'll shut your damn mouth."

"My lips are sealed." He pushed Raven into the house and through to church where most of the guys were gathered. The main club was seated, but there were also the presidents of the other charters as well.

He took his seat close to Hunter, who was the club VP. Sitting back, he listened to Smokey arrange the details for the following night. They were going to hit five of the homes where Garofalo kept his girls. Smokey already had their cops on standby and ready to take the girls home.

From there, they were heading to the MC who wanted their turf. The plan was simple. They had the explosives Kinky had obtained. Go in, place the explosives, get out, boom. Quick, simple, and effective.

The Hell's Bastards were not known for keeping any prisoners. They were known for sending their enemies straight to hell.

Once everyone knew what was going on and their details, he left the room, leaving someone else to deal with Raven.

He went to his room, and Abriana wasn't there. Going to the window overlooking the garden, he found her leaning against the shed, reading one of those fucking books she always had in her hand. When the men filed out of the clubhouse, she stopped reading to watch them. He spotted a couple of the club-whores who were smoking pot. They were scantily clad, and Abriana looked at them before averting her gaze. He noticed she pulled on her shirt. What was going on inside her head? Why did he even fucking care?

She meant nothing to him. They were not going to be in a relationship for long, and once they took care of her father, she would be free to live her own life. She wouldn't be forced to live with him or to be married to him. He didn't need a woman anyway. He never had.

Shaking his head, pissed off at himself, he left the room, grabbing everything he'd need to be ready for the coming day's drive.

Garofalo had what was coming to him. For too long that son of a bitch had been at the very top. He'd vowed to see the man fall. This was the start of that fall, and he intended to relish every single moment of it.

****

Abriana stared at the parking lot. Men and women were gathered around. She held the handles of the wheelchair, knowing Raven was pissed she couldn't go.

"I should be riding with them," Raven said.

"You'll get to go soon enough." The men were preparing for something. She didn't know what was happening. Last night, Ugly Beast had been in the room waiting for her. She'd taken a shower first, and when she entered his room, she'd been so surprised she'd simply stood there, watching him. She hated this.

The women were throwing themselves around the men, telling them to ride safe and to come back in one piece. She kept on staring, not really knowing what to do.

After her and Ugly Beast's … conversation, she didn't know where she stood. They were not a married couple, not really. He put up with her because it was who he was.

"You take care of her," Smokey said, coming toward them.

"I will."

"I can ride."

"You can also have my foot up your ass, but I don't see you volunteering for that," Smokey said.

Raven cursed and slumped back. Smokey ruffled her hair, and she shoved his hand away. Abriana smiled, watching the two.

Her happiness dropped when she caught sight of Ugly Beast. He'd already strapped a bag to his bike, and as he approached, she felt the ache in her stomach.

"You want me to leave?" Raven asked.

She gripped the handles tighter.

"Take care of yourself and Raven."

"I will," she said. "Ride safely."

He nodded.

Neither of them spoke, merely staring at each other. Part of her wanted to run into his arms and beg him not to go. She'd heard the women talking about missions and rides being extremely dangerous.

He doesn't want you.

You're a nuisance to him.

"This is getting kind of creepy, and I really don't know what to do right now," Raven said. "Do you two want to go and have a quick fuck session? Jump each other's bones. Pretend you don't hate each other."

Abriana pulled her away. "I'll see you when we get back."

She didn't wait for a response and began wheeling Raven away from the parking lot. She didn't go back into the clubhouse but took her friend out toward the tree where they sat most days.

"When I'm able, I'm cutting this fucking thing down."

"Why would you do that?" Abriana asked.

"I've never been so fucking sick and tired of seeing the same thing." Raven shook her head. "You want to tell me what all the staring was about?"

"Nothing."

"You've been miserable for a couple of days. You spend most of your time in a book or with me. When the whores come out to play, you go off to your room to hide. No offense, that's not nothing. I smell bullshit from a mile away, and you, girl, stink."

Abriana laughed. "Okay, something happened, but in a way, it reminded me about something important."

"Well, come on, spill."

"Ugly Beast and I, we're … not the same. You know. We both were forced together in marriage, and well, we're going to be over it soon."

"Wait, over it?"

"Divorce."

"I didn't think mafia peeps could get divorced."

"Ugly Beast is not mafia, and I don't want to go back to it either. I'm done. I'm finished. It's all over."

"Abriana, can I ask you a question?"

"Of course."

"Do you … love Ugly Beast?"

Abriana paused. "I don't know." She shrugged. "I've never known love."

"Okay, okay, let me think. Do you care about him?"

"I guess."

"If, for whatever reason Ugly Beast didn't come home, would you care?"

"Of course I'd care. Why wouldn't I care? Is it dangerous?" she asked.

Raven pressed her lips together. "Yes, Abriana, it's dangerous. There is a chance of one or more not making it home."

"Why do they have to do this if it's such a high risk?" She couldn't allow her tears to fall. It would show too much of a weakness. The thought of Ugly Beast not returning filled her with so much pain and anger.

"This is club life. With it comes risks, but you live by the club and die by it. Ugly Beast, he's fierce. One of the best men I've ever known."

She couldn't handle the thought of him being hurt, especially after their last words together. She'd been such a bitch to him, and she just couldn't handle the thought of hurting him.

"I've got to head back to the house," she said. Abriana stood up.

"What? You can't go anywhere."

"I just need to pick something up. Please, I won't be that long. I promise."

"It's against the rules," Raven said. "You've got to stay here to keep you safe."

Abriana ran fingers through her hair. "Please, Raven, you know I won't do anything stupid, and besides, I'm not exactly wanted or anything. I just need some air."

"I don't like this."

"I won't tell anyone you let me go."

Raven blew out a breath. "Prospect," she said, calling to the guy in the leather jacket scrubbing the floors. He had "Prospect" on his leather jacket.

She had to get out of the clubhouse and far away from all the pain she was being flooded with. Ugly Beast didn't want her, but she couldn't help but feel scared for him. Their marriage was one of convenience, but that didn't for a second mean she didn't care about him.

"What's up?" the guy asked, holding onto the map.

"Take her to her place. Wait with her to pack up whatever she needs, then bring her straight here, you understand?"

"Got it."

Raven paused. "Who are you? I don't recognize you."

"I've been here two months. I mostly work the bar."

"Huh?" Raven kept staring at him. "Okay. You owe me."

Abriana threw her arms around her friend. "Thank you."

"You know this means you love him, right?" Abriana tensed up. "You can try to pretend all you want. I know the truth, and so do you. Feeling this need for air and scared as you are, it means one thing; you're in love with him. It's okay. I'll keep your secret. You're not ready to share it yet." Raven patted her leg. "Hurry up before I have to lie to Ugly Beast when he calls." Raven winked at her.

Abriana followed the prospect out to his car. She didn't know his name, and she climbed into the passenger seat. As they pulled out of the parking lot, she let out a sigh of relief. She didn't want to leave the clubhouse, but staying there was just too hard.

What if something happened to Ugly Beast?

What happened if he died?

She had so many questions and no way of answering them.

She closed her eyes for a few minutes, taking a deep breath, trying to calm her nerves. Nothing was helping.

Opening her eyes, she frowned as she realized they were not heading toward her home, but in the opposite direction.

"You're going the wron—" She cried out as his fist connected with her face. The back of her head was grabbed, and before she could stop him, he slammed her head against the front of the dashboard.

Pain exploded across her face and behind her eyes, and she felt sick to her stomach.

"Fucking ugly bitch. You think we weren't watching you. Bastard MCs think they can get one up on us."

The prospect pulled against the side of the road. She tried to work the door to get away. He was already there, pulling the door open. She screamed as he tugged on her hair, dragging her out of the vehicle. She curled into a ball as he kicked her in the stomach several times.

The pain just kept on coming until he finally lifted her up and shoved her in the trunk of the car.

He had to get one more hit in. "This is from your father. He's not very happy with you."

He slammed the trunk down, and Abriana knew she was going to die, without a doubt.

Chapter Fifteen

Ugly Beast blew out a lungful of smoke as he pulled out his cell phone. Dialing Raven's number, he waited for her to answer the call. They had broken into three of the homes Garofalo had in his possession, and the girls had been taken to special homes to help them. They were drugged up to shit, and most of them didn't even know their own name.

It angered him to think what that fucker had done to them. One day he would kill Garofalo and laugh at the mess he caused. He looked forward to the blood he was going to spill, and every single drop of it would be done with him laughing, relishing every beg and plea.

"Hello," Raven said.

There was something in her tone that instantly put him on alert. "What's going on?" Ugly Beast asked.

Smokey chose the same moment to take a seat on his bike, along with a couple of his brothers.

"Erm, it's probably nothing."

"Raven, just fucking tell me."

"Have we had a prospect join the club in the last couple of months?" Raven asked.

Ugly Beast asked Smokey.

"You know all the prospects we've had. The last one is six months in, why?" Smokey asked.

"No, we haven't."

"Oh, fuck," Raven said.

"Okay, the suspense is now starting to piss me off."

"I think her father planted someone here, watching us, watching her," Raven said.

Ugly Beast stood up, alert. "Where's Abriana?"

Silence met his question.

"She's been taken, Ugly Beast. I think Vigo has

her, but I don't know. She left hours ago. She was so worried about you and just needed some space. I told her these rides were always a risk, and it freaked her out."

"For fuck's sake, Raven." He hung up the cell phone and slammed it to the ground, watching it shatter.

As if on magical cue, Smokey's phone began to ring.

Smokey was watching him as he answered the call. "Garofalo, what a surprise it is to hear from you."

There was a pause.

"He's with me."

Another pause.

"You can talk to me."

Smokey gritted his teeth, turning the cell phone onto speaker. "He wants to talk to you."

"Hello," Ugly Beast said, without taking the phone. His heart was pounding. He didn't know how fucking quickly his life could get this messed up. There's no way Vigo or Garofalo had anyone in the club watching them. They would have noticed.

"Umberto," Garofalo said. "Nice name. I like it."

Ugly Beast tensed up.

"I see you've been frequenting a few of my places. I wouldn't do that if I was you." Before he could say anything, he heard a scream.

"Stop. Please, stop."

It was Abriana's voice.

"Oh, dear, you see, Ugly Beast, you think you can take on me and my boys, make your demands, and think you know who is in charge. You MCs are all the same. You don't see what's right in front of your nose. You will return my girls to me, or I'm going to start removing shit from your wife. By the way, she's taken a pregnancy test. I will remove your fucking spawn from her cunt. You have an hour."

Garofalo hung up, and Ugly Beast stared at Smokey.

"We've got to stop." He looked toward Smokey. Abriana was pregnant with his kid. There was no way he could put her in danger. He had fucked up.

"I'm not stopping, Ugly Beast. This is your fight to get Abriana back, but I'm taking out Garofalo," Smokey said. "We back down now, we lose this fight."

Ugly Beast knew he was right.

"We split," Hunter said. "Garofalo is going to assume Ugly goes for his woman. Why not go for his woman, *and* we continue with what we started? This is what we live for right? Ride or die. I say I'd rather die than let that fucker win."

There was a round of cheers.

Smokey looked at Ugly Beast.

"She's pregnant, Smokey. I promised I'd protect her."

"I know. I'm trying to think what is the best way of doing this." Smokey ran a hand down his face. "Splitting up is not an option. We divide, we lose."

"I can't let her get hurt any more than she is being right now."

"He could be lying about her being pregnant?"

"I didn't use rubbers," Ugly Beast said, staring at his president. "I do everything you ask of me. Don't ask me to do this."

"We all go together. Garofalo doesn't want me getting his girls, the fucking pedophile, fine, we all go to him." Smokey threw his cell phone at Ugly Beast. "We need to know where he's hiding, Ugly, and we need to know now."

Ugly Beast stared down at the cell phone. He was in fucking shock, had to be. He dialed the number, putting the cell to his ear.

If Abriana was truly pregnant, it meant he was going to be a daddy.

He helped to bring a child into this world.

Him.

A monster.

The scarred fuck with a past he didn't want anyone to know about.

The man on the other end answered the call.

"Drago, where is he?"

"Don't do this," Sebastian Drago said.

"He's got Abriana." Drago cursed. "I'm not going to let her get hurt because of the club. I need to know where he and Vigo would take someone they're torturing." His hands were shaking, but not with nerves. He was pissed off. Drago didn't answer. "I don't care if this causes war, I will fucking murder every single one of you, do you understand me?"

"Umberto!"

"Tell me where he is," he said. His voice was calm. He would see through his threat. Abriana was his responsibility. He had left her at the clubhouse believing she was safe, and she was anything but. Now he was pissed off, angry, and was ready to fight to get what he wanted.

With the club at his back, it was now or never. They had played their cards tonight, and Garofalo had counteracted it with his own. Now it was time to take the fight to him. To kill him on his own turf.

Besides, Garofalo had just given him a good reason for the war, and why he could take him out. The agreement they signed with the outfit was with the understanding of marriage. Unless Garofalo made it aware of his love of underage girls, he'd broken their treaty, not them.

Ugly Beast waited.

"You don't give me the answers I need, I will slaughter everyone you hold dear. I've got nothing left to lose, remember that."

Drago sighed. "I hope your wife is okay." Drago gave him a location that was on the outskirts of the city. It was a boarded up old junkyard. It had gone out of business years ago. The land never been bought up.

He hung up and handed the cell phone back to Smokey.

"I've got to do this," he said, looking at Smokey.

"You want to tell me what this means?"

He looked at his president without flinching. "It means I've got to go and get my wife."

"For a guy who didn't give a shit about her, you're rushing off to defend her."

"I made the vow to the club, but I promised to keep her safe. She put the club first." He wasn't about to tell Smokey he felt guilty. They hadn't parted on the best terms, and she probably expected him to let her die.

He was so fucking angry at Raven for letting Abriana out of her sight. He'd deal with her when they got to the clubhouse.

Smokey nodded. "Give me the location."

Ugly Beast told him the location, and as they gathered around, he listened to the plan with half an ear. He rarely did what he was told. As the Sergeant at Arms, it was his role to make sure they all got out with their lives intact. He didn't have time to make friends or follow instructions.

With their orders in place, they all climbed onto their bikes, revving the machines, ready to take off.

"Are you ready for this?" Smokey asked.

"No."

"You know you'll get to kill him tonight. This will be your only chance. You let this fall through your fingers, you'll never get another."

"I know what this means, and I'm ready. You don't have to worry about me."

Gunning his engine, he took off into the night, following the rest of the club. They all had his back, every single one of them willing to fight for him.

Abriana hadn't been his woman for long, but she didn't deserve to suffer because of him. He would save her, and if she was pregnant with his kid, he would make sure she was always taken care of.

****

"Stop crying, you fucking useless cunt."

Abriana flinched, expecting the lash of her father's belt, but it didn't come. They had already beaten her, and she believed her arm was broken. The pain in her abdomen was unlike anything she'd ever felt before.

Blood coated the thighs of her jeans, and she knew the pregnancy she had, was gone. The baby that had been growing inside her had been beaten out of her.

If they didn't take her to a hospital soon, she was going to die. Her body was shaking, and she felt clammy.

The prospect who'd brought her to her father and Vigo was dead on the floor, his brains blown out. He'd been a plant for some time, always avoiding suspicion as he'd been made to blend in when necessary.

Also … her sister … Chantel.

She covered her face, wishing the past couple of hours hadn't come. Her sister had always been difficult, but she never wanted her sister to die.

Her sister was dead, and she knew Ugly Beast wasn't coming for her. Why would he? They were not in love. She didn't belong to him, not really. They were married for a deal, a deal that was now broken.

Her father dropped onto the bed where she lay.

He lifted up her hair and winced. "You know,

even battered and bruised, you're still the ugliest fucking thing on this planet. Your mother must have fucked someone else. There's no way I'd spawn something so ugly." He grabbed her face hard, and she whimpered. She didn't think it was possible to still feel any kind of pain, and yet, here she was, hurting all over.

"Please, stop."

"Please, stop. Ouch, it hurts." Her father mimicked her voice, throwing her back to the bed. He didn't stop there. He grabbed a fistful of her hair, tugging her head back. "You've always been such a big disappointment to me. I hate things I can't use, and you're nothing but a useless, pathetic thing."

He got up from the spot on the mattress, and she just wanted one of them to kill her. To stop the pain.

In a matter of hours, she had lost everything. The one thing she wanted to be was taken from her. She would have loved her baby, regardless of who the father was. Ugly Beast, she didn't know if he wanted kids or not, but she would have loved their baby.

Closing her eyes, she wished to just die. This was all too much for her.

Garofalo and Vigo had gone mad; they had to have. They wanted to put the blame of Chantel's death, and hers, on the Hell's Bastards. To make it look like they tried to take their territory, raped Chantel before killing her, even though she was already pregnant. Yes, she'd been shocked to hear Chantel was pregnant, but it was with Garofalo's baby, not anyone else's.

They were going to frame them by using men from the MC club, only it wasn't the full club. During her beatings here, she had learned the men her father and Garofalo had were once part of the Twisted Bastards MC. She was in no state to point out that her husband's MC had "bastard" in the title, and it seemed rather rude.

The men wanted the association with the mafia, and the drugs and power they offered. Twisted Bastards MC had nothing to do with Garofalo, and it wasn't their fight. Tonight, Garofalo hoped to use the men from the MC he had in his power to kill Smokey and his crew, and use them to make it look like they were responsible for killing her sister, her, the made man, and breaking the treaty. With this show of disrespect, Garofalo could take over Hell's Bastards MC turf, and he wouldn't have to be indebted to the club.

She hoped Ugly Beast didn't come.

She hoped he finished what he started and exposed Garofalo to all of the outfit, so all of them would turn their backs on them. Vigo and Garofalo would then be handled by the outfit, and they would die. She knew it. At least, she hoped they would get what was coming to them.

Would it be so wrong to wish for a horrible, prolonged death on both of these men? There's no way she could see Vigo as her father. He'd laughed when Chantel begged for her life. He'd called her a whore and slut, and yet, she was still his daughter, and he mocked her. How could anyone do that? Chantel had been in love with Garofalo. Abriana had seen it, even with her black eyes.

Now her sister was dead.

The man who had beaten her before even getting to this junkyard was also dead. He didn't get a chance to beg for his life though.

She squeezed her eyes tightly as another wave of cramps flooded her stomach.

I can do this.

It's fine.

I'm so sorry, my baby. My darling.

She sniffled, hating everything.

When she heard the unmistakable sound of motorbikes, she heard the laughter in Garofalo's voice, and the victory in Vigo's.

Ugly Beast had walked right into their trap.

Opening her eyes, all she saw was her sister, turned to face her, lifeless. There was nothing in her eyes, no recognition.

It broke her heart. No matter how much they quarreled, they were still sisters, and she loved her sister.

Always would.

She would have loved to have been an auntie.

If only Chantel had confided in her, she would have been able to keep her sister safe. Not now. Not anymore.

There was no keeping her sister safe.

"Well, well, well, what do we have here?" Garofalo asked, looking toward the entrance to the junkyard.

Smokey, Ugly Beast, Hunter, Kinky, and so many others of the Hell's Bastards stood there, staring. To Abriana, they looked terrifying. All of them were focused on the men who stood, looking rather smug.

The monsters who had taken so much from her. Tears swam in her vision, and she bit her lip to try to contain the sobs that threatened to spill.

"So, you think you can take us?" Garofalo asked. "You have no idea what you're messing with."

"Oh, I know what I'm messing with," Smokey said, taking a step forward. "You took club property."

"My daughter isn't club property. She's a traitor and has been treated exactly how her kind is supposed to be." Vigo pointed in her direction.

She stared at Ugly Beast. He looked ready to kill, to slaughter, to murder.

In a weird way, the look on his face offered her a

little comfort. He wanted to protect her, and she wanted to be protected.

Touching her stomach, she closed her eyes, trying to stop the pain, but it wouldn't stop. Even her lips were hurting.

"You made a mistake taking her," Ugly Beast said.

She opened her eyes as he stepped forward, shocked by the sheer rage she heard in his voice.

His gaze was on her, not once staring at the men.

If he didn't care about her, why did it look like he wanted to murder them? She could barely move.

"You're willing to risk all-out war over this slut?" Vigo asked.

"Close your eyes, Abriana, baby. I'll be done soon. No matter what, you don't open them."

She nodded her head, and he waited.

Closing her eyes, squeezing them tight, she heard the fighting. The screams, the yells, the sudden fighting, and the gunshots. She didn't know what was going on, but she trusted Ugly Beast. He promised to protect her.

She covered her face with her hand so she wasn't even tempted, hoping and praying he'd make it.

Finally, after what felt like an eternity, someone slowly picked her up.

She screamed.

"It's me," Ugly Beast said.

"I want to die. Please, kill me."

"I'm not going to kill you."

She cried. "I'm worthless. I lost it. I know I lost it. Please, Ugly Beast, I'm not worth it."

"You belong to me, Abriana."

"I'm not strong enough."

She knew the club was silent as he carried her across the junkyard. What surprised her was when

Sebastian Drago stopped them.

"I'm so sorry, Abriana," he said.

"Kill me, please. Someone, kill me. I want to die." She couldn't fight Ugly Beast as he carried her away, ignoring her pleas for death.

She's lost the only good thing in this world, her baby.

What was the point of living?

The pain finally consumed her, and she was able to fall into blissful peace.

Chapter Sixteen

"She looks a fucking mess," Ugly Beast said, staring into the hospital room where his wife was hooked up to tubes.

She'd lost too much blood, suffered a broken arm, shattered ankle, a miscarriage, and a concussion. Her face was covered in bruises, not to mention her body. Not a part of her wasn't hurt in some way.

So far, she'd slept through most of the pain, which he was relieved about.

Smokey grabbed his shoulder. "We're all here for you, brother. She's part of the club. You need to get some rest."

"Not happening."

"Ugly Beast."

"No. You heard what she said. She wants to die because she knows what she lost. I'm not leaving her. Not now."

"You don't have to stay married to her," Smokey said. "This didn't end the way I wanted it to, but there's no reason for you to stay married to her."

"What the fuck was your plan?" Ugly Beast asked. He'd done what Smokey had said, and look what happened. Abriana had been hurt, and their child was dead.

"I had every intention of forming an allegiance with Garofalo's people. By binding our club with his made men, it made our territory stronger. I had no idea he'd reach out to the Twisted Bastards. We know how volatile they can be."

"What did you want?"

"More power, more turf, and a permanent alliance with Garofalo's outfit, even if we killed him, would have guaranteed that. It was a long shot, but the Twisted

Bastards have been gaining power for some time. They could be a problem for us."

"So you did have a reason for the alliance."

"I did. It's over now though. You're free. I knew you'd do anything for the club, and well, Abriana seemed like a nice girl."

"I'm not giving her back, Smokey."

Silence met his words. He didn't look away from his wife. She looked too pale. His wife would never be a looker, but she was his, and he liked that.

He'd fucked up big time with her, and now ... the baby? Fuck, his chest felt so tight just thinking about seeing her on the mattress where she'd been dumped, blood coating her jeans as she struggled to keep the pain at bay. They'd made her lose the baby, beaten her so fucking badly.

The elevator doors opened down the long corridor.

"How is she?"

Ugly Beast looked to see Raven being pushed by Hunter toward them. The brothers had kept a vigil in the main reception while he stayed with Abriana.

He didn't know how far gone she was, and if she would willingly risk ending her life. There's no way he could let her do that. Just thinking of finding her dead scared him. After everything he'd experienced, the last ten hours had been the most harrowing of his life.

Raven gasped as she got a look at Abriana.

"Oh, my."

"She'll be fine," he said. "I'll make sure she will make a full recovery."

"She ... was pregnant?" Raven asked.

"I told her," Hunter said.

"Yes, she was. She's not anymore." He clenched his teeth together, breaking inside, shattering. Every time he said it, the reality hit him even harder. Never had he imagined he'd be a father. Looking at him, he should never father a child, and yet, he had, only for it to be taken from the both of them.

Raven grabbed his hand. "I'm so sorry."

"It's not my body."

"No, but it's your kid too. I can't imagine what she's going through."

No one mentioned how she wanted to die.

The elevator doors opened again, and Ugly Beast growled as he saw Sebastian Drago step off.

"You're not fucking welcome here. Get the fuck out of here, now!" He didn't care how he was drawing attention from the staff and other patients. There is no way in hell he would ever let any of those bastards near his woman again. He would murder every single one of them.

He got the pleasure out of killing Garofalo, but not Vigo, and not the prospect who thought he could infiltrate them. That little shit had been dead when they hit the junkyard last night.

Garofalo and Vigo had men all around the junkyard, which was why it took him so long to get to his woman, to get her to the hospital.

Drago held his hands up. "I'm not here to make waves. I assure you."

"Then what the fuck are you doing here?" Ugly Beast wanted to rip his throat out.

"I've come here hoping for peace, and also for you to listen to reason."

"You've got to go," Smokey said.

"You're Garofalo's only heir."

Ugly Beast grabbed Drago and slammed him up against the wall. In the distance he heard someone scream for security. It wasn't going to work. His men would deal with anyone who tried to stop him.

"Umberto Garofalo is dead. He died a long time ago. When are you going to get that through your thick skull?"

"You're the boss, Umberto. You can take his place."

"I've got my place. My name is Ugly Beast, and I'm not a Garofalo, never have been, never will be." He let Drago go, turning to Smokey. "Make sure he leaves."

His president was already on it, and Hunter was escorting Raven away. With no one to keep him away, he entered his wife's private room, sat down in the chair beside her, and watched her.

She looked so peaceful in sleep.

All he wanted to do was hold her and let her know it was going to be okay.

The minutes passed, turning into hours. Nighttime fell, and still, he kept watch over her. It was lunchtime the following day before she finally woke up, and she did so with a whimper.

She turned her head, left and right, then back again before her gaze landed on him.

Neither of them spoke, but he watched as she put her hands on her stomach. "Is it really gone?"

"Yes."

She sobbed, and he moved from the chair to the bed. He tried to hold her the best way he could without hurting her. She was covered in bruises. They had strapped up her hand, and put a cast on her ankle. For a long time after she got out of the hospital, she'd need more care. He didn't mind taking care of her.

"It's fine."

"I'm sorry."

"It's not your fault."

"I had no idea."

Tears filled his eyes, and he squeezed them tightly shut. She shouldn't be apologizing to him for losing the baby. He knew who was responsible for this, and as far as he was concerned, he'd dealt with the slight that had been dealt to them.

"I wanted that baby," Abriana said. "So much."

"It's okay." He stroked her hair with a light touch.

"I wanted something to love and hopefully, one day, it would love me back."

He really wanted to squeeze her tighter, but he didn't, afraid of hurting her. "I took care of it."

"Of what?"

"Of Garofalo. Vigo. They're dead." He pulled away to look into her eyes. They were flooded with tears.

"I watched them kill my sister. They mocked her love for Garofalo. She was in love with him, and he'd been sleeping with her for years. He's a monster."

"Was. He's not anymore." He gently cupped her cheek, knowing he needed to tell her something.

"Have you started a war? Is this it? The end? Raven told me there was a risk you'd die."

"I'm not dead. There's no war. Drago made sure of that."

"Drago?"

"There's something I've got to tell you. Something only a few people in the club know."

She frowned, watching him.

He gritted his teeth, struggling to find the words. "My name … is Umberto Garofalo." Her eyes went wide. "Nico Garofalo was my father."

"That's not possible."

"My mother was underage when she had me. Garofalo didn't want to deal with what he'd done. She was sixteen, terrified, and I do know she left me on church steps. She gave me his name, hoping one day I'd clearly find him. I grew up in foster care, as the church couldn't keep me. They were broke, and I think they were petrified of finding out who my father was."

"I'm so sorry."

"One day when I was ten years old, Drago came to the foster home. He'd heard about an Umberto Garofalo, and he told me I needed to drop the name. If Garofalo was to ever find out who I was, he'd kill me, wiping away all evidence of his little scandal. There can never be any evidence. My mother was supposed to abort me. That's what he paid to happen. Instead, she gave birth to me, and put me into care. I didn't stop using the name. In fact, I didn't stop using the name until my eighteenth birthday."

"What happened?"

"I got into a lot of fights. I was angry. I'd never been placed in a home for long, and I liked to fight. It … grounded me. I ended up in one of Garofalo's organized fights, and that's the name I went by."

"Wow," she said.

"Yeah. Let's say by the end of the night, I looked more bruised than you do." He was going to say terrible, but he didn't want to hurt her feelings. Her bruises would fade away. "I realized to Garofalo, I was something to be ashamed of. He tried to kill me. Wanted me dead, but with Drago's help, I made it out alive."

"You found the MC."

"Umberto Garofalo died a long time ago, Abriana. I'm Ugly Beast. I know you hate calling me that." He cleared his throat and pulled out his license. "I had my name changed years ago." He held up his license, and she squinted to see.

"Eric Dickson."

"That's me. My name."

"Why that name?"

"I liked it. Now, I just go by Ugly Beast." He knew she hated saying the name though, always with a little wrinkle in her nose, or she tried to avoid his name. "I respond to Eric."

"Are you going to kill me?"

"No."

"Why not?"

"You're my wife."

"I'm mafia."

"No, you're not mafia. I'm not sending you back there. We're done with the mafia. Drago will find someone else to replace Garofalo. The Hell's Bastards are my life, my club."

"You hate me."

"I don't hate you."

"I hate myself. I ... failed."

He took her good hand, still being careful in case he hurt her, and cupped her other. "You're not a failure. You'll never be a failure. Not now, not ever. It's not possible." He pressed a gentle kiss to her lips. "You need to rest though."

He helped her to get comfortable.

"Thank you for telling me your story."

"Thank you for listening." He leaned over her, staring into her eyes. "I'm sorry I didn't get there in time."

"It's fine."

"It's not fine. I wish I could rid all the memories you have so you never have to think of what those bastards did."

She closed her eyes, and for several minutes, he watched her sleep, not caring in the slightest how creepy he looked.

Stroking her cheek with the backs of his fingers,

he watched her, amazed at how he felt about her. He nearly lost her last night, and he could still lose her. The power of those emotions unsettled him. He'd never been one to be led in by his emotions, and yet, here he was, terrified for her.

"I'll always take care of you."

****

Three months later

Finally, without any crutches, Abriana walked out of the hospital feeling … alone. No one had come with her to her appointment. She ended up getting a cab to finally have the cast on both her wrist and ankle removed.

Her joints and muscles were weak from the prolonged binding she had to undergo. The first cast hadn't been set properly, so she had to go in for extended treatment.

Folding her arms across her chest, she stood at the curb waiting for the cab to arrive. She'd called him from inside the hospital. All she wanted to do was go home and go to bed. In the past three months since she'd been taken and her baby had been beaten from her, all she'd wanted to do was go to bed.

Ugly Beast, Raven, and several men from the club including Smokey, wouldn't let her. They'd forced her to participate at Thanksgiving, Christmas, the New Year, and with Valentine's Day fast approaching, even Raven was getting into the swing of things, decorating the club for a dance they were holding. Raven had told her the women were going to be stripping, competing in wet t-shirt contests, followed by sex games where they all had to win at something.

Abriana didn't want to know.

She knew her time with Ugly Beast was limited.

With their connection to the mafia over with, her

place in their world was no longer needed.

Wrapping her arms around herself, she still felt the dull ache in her joints. The pain had subsided quite a bit, but she would never get full function back. The doctor had insisted she would be able to carry another baby, and they'd carefully monitor her, but she didn't know if she was ever going to have another baby.

Ugly Beast was her husband, and he'd not even looked in her direction since before the attack. After three months, she imagined he was already getting something from the club. Glancing at the time, she saw it was getting closer to five, and she'd been waiting for nearly thirty-five minutes.

She didn't have a cell phone, and just as she was about to head inside, a car pulled up beside her. Ugly Beast climbed out. "I missed it, didn't I?"

Abriana tucked some hair behind her ear, nodding. "It's fine."

"It's not fine. I was trying to … I want to show you something."

"What do you mean?"

"I had every intention of coming with you today." He rounded the car and opened the door, being the perfect gentleman. She climbed in without a second thought. He closed the door before moving to his own side and climbing in.

"What did the doctor say?" he asked.

"It's all healed. I'm going to need to do some exercises and possible therapy to help regain more movement, but other than that, it's all good."

"I'm glad." He took her hand, placing a kiss to her flesh. "I hated seeing you in pain."

"I'm fine now."

She pulled her hand away, and Ugly Beast drove them away from the hospital, toward the club. "I'd really like to go home."

"It's not happening."

"Then can we talk about our impending divorce?"

"That's not happening either."

"What?"

"I'm not going to divorce you, Abriana."

"But you don't need me."

"I've never needed you. I was always planning to kill Garofalo. I've not needed you for anything."

"Oh." Pain struck her head, and she stared down at her lap.

Ugly Beast sighed and pulled into the parking lot of the clubhouse. "I'm not good with words. I never have been. I … I didn't want to marry you. I did what I had to for the club and the club alone."

"I know."

"But I want to *stay* married to you. I enjoy having you around, and I don't want to … let you go."

He took her hand, pressing a kiss to her wrist before his hand moved to her stomach. She tensed up but saw the pain in his eyes.

"I'm the one sorry for not getting to you in time. You're my wife. I should have been there to protect you."

"It's not your fault."

"It's not your fault either."

"You were … happy I was pregnant?"

"For a few blissful moments, yeah, I really was because I would get to be a dad but also, I'd have an excuse to keep you."

"Ugly Beast?"

"I'm not good. I'm not a good guy. In fact, I'd pretty much say I'm an evil fucking bastard. With you, you make me feel everything. Not a day goes by I don't think about you." He lifted the hand from her stomach to cup her cheek.

"What are you trying to say?"

"Forgive me. Give me another chance to prove to you I can do this."

"You could have any woman."

"I know my face is scarred to shit. You're the only woman I want."

"I'm ugly."

"To me, you're beautiful. To me, Abriana, you're everything." Tears spilled down her cheeks, and she bit her lip. "I don't want to make you cry."

"Maybe you should stop saying nice things."

He chuckled. "Hearing you were gone, I wanted to kill Raven for being so stupid with your safety. You're the only precious thing in my entire world. I can't give you up. I don't want to give you up, and I'm not giving you back. You're mine, and I will destroy any man who thinks they can take you away from me."

She reached out, touching his cheek. His skin was rough with a couple of days' growth. "I have nowhere else I'd rather be."

They both jumped as someone knocked on her window.

"Lovebirds, come on," Raven said. "We're all waiting for you inside. Don't make me vomit."

Abriana smiled, pulling away from Ugly Beast. Wiping the tears from her eyes, she waited. "We better go inside."

Ugly Beast climbed out, and she was already on her feet. He placed a hand at her back, and it was then she realized he was wearing a wedding band. Pausing, she turned to him, grabbing his left hand, and sure enough, he was wearing a ring.

"You're wearing a ring?"

He'd refused to have one at their wedding.

"I feel it's only appropriate." He stroked the curve of her hip. "Come on, I want to show you something."

He guided her toward the clubhouse, and as she entered the main room, she came to a stop.

There were streamers and banners, welcoming her home.

She was already an emotional wreck, but seeing this and the Hell's Bastards all there, she was overcome with happiness.

Ugly Beast turned her toward him, cupping her face as he slowly got down on one knee.

"What are you doing?" she asked.

"Trust it," Raven said.

Staring down at Ugly Beast, on his knees before her, it kind of scared her. "I married you to get closer to Garofalo. Smokey knew why I wanted to kill him, and so do many members of the club. To do what I wanted, we had to plan. We had to make sure Garofalo would give us something. He gave me you. I didn't want to marry you. Once all of this was over, I was going to let you go. I can't do that, Abriana. I've got to go back on my word. With the club as my witness, I'm about to tell you something I've never said to another living soul."

She didn't know what was going on. Her heart was pounding, and as he said his next words, she knew she was never going to be the same again.

"I'm in love with you. I want to be with you. I want you as my old lady, by my side, wearing my ring, and my patch."

She turned her head to see Smokey holding out a leather jacket. He turned it around for her to see the inscription on the back.

Ugly Beast's Old Lady, Hell's Bastards.

"I'm claiming you as mine. I'm not telling you

this will be easy. Far from it, in fact. You're mine, and I love you." Ugly Beast got to his feet, holding the jacket. "Belong to me, Abriana. Be mine. I will make up for all the crap I put you through."

With tears falling down her cheeks, she stared at the man she'd been scared of, turned on by, and then broken because she knew there was no chance of him ever loving her. Only, he'd just admitted to loving her.

Silence fell in the clubhouse, and she cupped Ugly Beast's face. The scarred mess that she actually found so incredibly beautiful. He wasn't perfect, yet neither was she.

"I never wanted the prince growing up, I always had a thing for the beast," she said, throwing her arms around him, pressing her lips against hers.

He wrapped his arms around her.

She heard the clubhouse erupt with applause.

They were not perfect. In fact, they were monsters in leather, but to her, they were family. More family than she had ever known in her entire life.

Her loyalty was to them, and it would remain so.

"Welcome to the club," Smokey said, gripping her shoulder as Ugly Beast finally let her go. He kept hold of her hand, and she smiled, loving the deep connection she felt with him.

Bottles of beer were opened and sprayed all around them, and Raven pulled her into a hug. Still, Ugly Beast didn't let her go.

The music was turned up loud. She couldn't even think. He wouldn't let her go, and she ended up resting her head against his shoulder as they made their way around the clubhouse. The party spilled into the backyard. Fires were lit, as were the barbeque pits.

Ugly Beast didn't take her outside though. He kept hold of her hand, leading her upstairs to their bedroom.

Once they were inside his room, he pulled her toward the bed, holding her on his lap. "I know I've shocked you."

"Do you really love me?" she asked.

"Yes."

"Really, really?"

He laughed. He moved her so that she straddled him. She felt the hard evidence of his cock as it pressed against her core. "I never thought I was capable of love. You, Abriana, you got under my skin, and I couldn't say no to you. I couldn't give you up." He ran his hands up her back, sinking into her hair. "You drive me so fucking wild, and I don't know how to control it. I don't want any man to know how good you are. How sweet you look, how amazing you taste. I want it all to myself. Do you think that's selfish?"

"I don't want you to go with another woman." She took his hand, placing it against her stomach. "I want you to put another baby inside me. I … I love you too."

He slammed his lips down on hers as he pulled off her leather jacket. His fell to the bed, and they tore at each other's clothes, needing to get naked.

Once they were naked, Ugly Beast pressed her to the bed, and he slid her thighs open wide. She cried out his name as he licked at her pussy, opening the lips of her sex, and keeping her wide and exposed for his pleasure alone.

"You taste so damn good." He plundered her cunt with his tongue before sliding up to circle her clit. He repeated the action, drawing her closer to orgasm, and she felt this need curling deep inside her for him to not stop, to not ever stop.

The pleasure was so intense, and as she came, Ugly Beast pressed his face between her thighs, tasting her, prolonging the bliss he was creating with his tongue. He began to kiss up her body. His face wet from her pussy, he trailed his lips up until he got to her tits, sucking each bud into his mouth.

"You're going to breastfeed our kid. I want to watch you."

"Ugly," she said, moaning his name.

"Yes. I know what you want." He found her entrance, and she cried out as he slammed in deep.

The pleasure was intense as he took her hard, the bed hitting the wall with the force of his thrusts, driving inside her.

She wanted him more than anything else in her life.

"Look at us, Abriana."

She looked down at where they were joined. His cock was slick with her cum as he rocked inside her. She thrust up to meet him, needing more.

Ugly Beast took her hands, pressing them above her head so she was locked against him with nowhere else for her to go, not that she wanted to. He angled his hips, and he pressed deeper inside her, making her cry out.

"I love you, Abriana. I've never loved anyone in my fucking life, but you, you're mine. I've never been a possessive bastard, but I can't have anyone else near you. You're mine. All mine."

She shocked him as she threw his weight so he rolled to the bed, and she straddled him, rocking her hips in the way he'd taught her how.

"You're all mine. You can't be with anyone else. Just me. For the rest of your life. You can have every single part of me. Any time you want me, but you can't look at or touch another woman."

Ugly Beast ran his hands up her body, cupping

her tits. "Deal."

He grabbed her hips, drawing her down onto his length, making her cry out for more. He gripped the back of her neck, and she stared down into his eyes as he held hers. Making love to him, she felt him so deep within her. This was what she hungered for all of her life. This connection, this love. Ugly Beast shut down all of his walls, showing her how he truly felt. She saw it in his gaze, felt it in the way he held her, and she marveled at him.

When he spilled his cum inside her, flooding her core, he rocked her beneath him. "I'll never give you up, and any man who thinks he can take you away is going to deal with me. I'm not a good man. I'll never be a good man, but for you, Abriana, only you will know goodness from me."

She believed him.

Epilogue

Nine months later

"It hurts."

"I know, baby, I know. I'm here."

Ugly Beast glared at everyone around them. Abriana should be in the hospital, but instead, her water had broken, and now, in the clubhouse parking lot, with the ambulance crew, she was pushing. He held her hands, and she rested against him, screaming. He wanted to grab his gun and shoot the incompetent bastards for not bringing her something for the pain. Shouldn't they be prepared for this kind of thing?

Angry.

Pissed off.

Afraid, because like a pussy, he'd read the pregnancy books and knew there was a risk he could lose them both. His wife and his daughter. They had found out the sex, and he'd spent six months preparing the nursery at their home.

"You got this," Raven said.

Abriana whimpered. "I want to claw your face off right now."

"That's good. You'll love me when all the pain is gone. Come on, honey."

She squeezed his hands, and he took the pain as she screamed.

"That's it, come on, Mrs. Dickson. You've got this. Keep pushing."

Abriana screamed, and as she collapsed against him, Ugly Beast heard it. The unmistakable cry of his newborn daughter.

The ambulance driver was given a blanket and doing something between her legs. Having another man see her pussy bothered him, but after watching a couple of home birthing videos, given to him by her midwife, he'd decided he couldn't bring his daughter into this world.

His daughter gave another scream.

"You have a beautiful baby girl," the man said, handing them a swaddled baby.

Abriana let his hands go, and he held her against him as she took their baby. Staring over her shoulder, Ugly Beast knew he was fucked. His little girl was so fucking beautiful. Her eyes were so bright as she stared up at him.

"We made something so beautiful," Abriana said.

Ugly Beast looked up as someone gripped his shoulder. Smokey was there, nodding at him. The whole club surrounded them. They'd been here for the birth, and he knew this girl was going to be protected for the rest of her life, just as his wife would be.

Wrapping his arms around his woman, he pressed his face against her neck.

"Thank you, Eric," she said.

He smiled. Abriana rarely called him by the name he'd given himself. "I love you, baby. So much."

Abriana tilted her head back, smiling at him. "We did good."

Pressing his lips to hers, happiness flooded him. He never thought he wanted a family, but lying in the parking lot of the Hell's Bastards compound, he knew he wouldn't change it for the world.

She was his entire world, they both were, and he would protect them with his life. Like the club, his wife and baby girl had his loyalty, his devotion, and his very fucking being.

The End

www.samcrescent.com

CPSIA information can be obtained
at www.ICGtesting.com
Printed in the USA
LVHW040055190419
614781LV00001B/27